Too Early For A Glass Of Wine?

Joseph 'Tom' Riach was born in the Scottish city of Aberdeen. He is the author of four previous books of the personal motivation, business and financial achievement genre and he is the co-writer of one biographical novel.

Too Early For A Glass Of Wine? is his first novel to be published.

Cover by SelfPubCovers.com/DarkDesert/Joseph T.Riach

Joseph T. Riach

SUCCESSFUL LIVING BY JOSEPH T.RIACH

Mastering The Art Of Making Money

Self-Improvement Should Be Fun!

Winning Big In Life And Business

The Simplest Sales Strategy

NOVELS BY JOSEPH T.RIACH

Too Early For A Glass Of Wine?

RE-WRITE AND EDIT

The Cardboard Suitcase

All available in Paperback and Ebook formats at Amazon (.com and .co.uk), Barnes and Noble and other leading book stores.

Contact Tom at www.tomriach.com

Joseph T. Riach

Too Early For A Glass Of Wine?

Joseph T.Riach

ISBN : 978-1698966922

© Joseph T.Riach 2019 all rights reserved

All proprietory rights and interest in this publication shall be vested in Joseph T.Riach and all other rights including, but without limitation, patent, registered design, copyright, trademark and service mark, connected with recording this publication shall also be vested in Joseph T.Riach. See also back of book.

Joseph T.Riach

'Too Early For A Glass Of Wine?' is entirely a work of fiction. The names, characters and incidents portrayed in it are the work of the author's imagination. Any resemblance to actual persons, living or dead, events or entities is entirely coincidental. Some reference is made however to authors and their works, to actual wines and to some real locations.

THE CHAPTERS

Prologue	1
The Boy In The Corner	3
A Young Man Comes Calling	21
Home Alone	41
A Taste Of Honey	59
The Bad And The Ugly	77
The Man Who Painted A Train	109
Alive And Kicking	135
The Magician's Bistro	157
Down In The Docks	181
Love Came In Darkness	203
Deceit Doesn't Die	223
The Master Rose At Dawn	241
Four Villains And A Funeral	253
Back To The Future	267
Epilogue	271
The Literature And The Wines	275
Copyright and Disclaimer	289

Joseph T.Riach

PROLOGUE

"Is it too early for a glass of wine?" miaowed the lady of my life invitingly a little after four in the afternoon – and soon a bottle of Bandol rosé nestled in an ice bucket on the wrought iron garden table. This was shortly joined by a meticulous presentation of tiny triangles of superbly fresh carpaccio of veal and salmon, oozing colour and drizzled with light, patterned sauces so as to create the impression of nibbling a stained glass object d'art.

With those sublime flavours settling on my palate, I looked around me at the greens of nature, the changing blues of the sky and the taupes and ochres of man and land and wondered anew at my existence. What chance had brought me into the bosom of such love and tranquility?

Of course I knew that the answer to my musing was that chance had little to do with it. The life that I enjoyed was born from my own desire and design. Partly design in the exact sense, as in an architect or draughtsman at their drawing board producing a precise blueprint, and partly of a design not at all like that. Quite different in fact.

The second, and arguably more significant, element of my design, was one of choosing to live my life in a particular way, a way of caring and sharing. A way largely devoid of material ambition. My desire was to live in that manner and in the present moment, knowing that my tomorrows would be catered for in whatever way destiny saw fit to reward me.

"Well," I thought, "I must have done something right."

The carpaccio was divine, so too the wine. I wafted a kiss to my beloved lounging near me and raised my glass. We savoured another sip of Bandol.

Then I took up my pen and pad and started to write …

THE BOY IN THE CORNER

Tommy stood steadfastly staring at the wall in the corner of the cellar. He had been there motionless for four hours. His tears had long since dried. So too had his own excrement which his mother had smeared over his mop of blond hair and his face as punishment for having soiled his underpants. Tommy was six years old and indiscipline of that sort was not expected of him. He had to learn his lesson. Learn it he did.

One week later he lit a 'camp fire' with newspapers underneath the curtains in the sitting room of the family home and watched delightedly as his dad failed to beat out the flames. The fire brigade was called. Tommy almost wet his pants with excitement at the sight of the shiny fire tender arriving with bells ringing and disgorging a possé of impressively uniformed firefighters. The intrepid men unrolled their hoses, mounted ladders and proceeded to get the blaze, now threatening the whole house, under control. In the meantime, all the occupants – Tommy, his two brothers and sister (each much older than he), mum, uncle Charlie and bed-ridden grandad - were evacuated to the home of a neighbour. Dad stayed behind to help fight the flames.

Some days after the fire was extinguished and the resultant *"Kid Burns Down Family Home!"* screamer was no longer front page news, Tommy and the rest of the family, including dad with burned and heavily bandaged hands, returned to the house to clean up the mess, commence repairs and resume 'normal' life. This included Tommy being dragged aside by his dad to be told, "You'll pay for this." And pay he did.

As soon as his dad's burns healed Tommy was belatedly invited to an appointment with 'the tawse', a family member which appeared only on the special occasions of Tommy's beatings. The tawse, a heavy leather strap some two feet long and half an inch thick, was kept it seemed for Tommy's exclusive benefit as he never saw his father use it on either of his brothers or his sister.

In his sister's case, this in spite of the fact that some months prior to the fire fiasco, she cut material from her mum's one and only party frock to make a dress for her doll. In doing so she left a large hole in the frock, rendering it unwearable. But she denied being the culprit. Tommy received the blame, and the beating, instead.

So here he was once more listening to his dad's oft-repeated line (which Tommy didn't nearly believe) of, "This will hurt me more than you," as the blows rained down on his bared back and buttocks. The more that Tommy gritted his teeth and resolved not to cry or show pain, the more they came, ceasing only when his dad reached exhaustion point. The assault invariably ended with, "Let that be a lesson to you!" gasped by his sweating dad.

A lesson to Tommy it surely was. Several in fact.

The most notable of these was that Tommy learned how to cope with pain. First physical pain and then suffering of the emotional kind. Of course he was initially quite unaware of what he was doing. The strategy of how to endure the agony just came to him and evolved naturally. But, by his teen years and in later life, he was fully aware of the tactic and consciously developed, fine tuned and practiced it. He called it his art of detach and dream.

It worked on the basis that, whenever he found himself on the receiving end of a beating, be it from angry parent or exasperated school teacher, he shut out the discomfort through sheer will power. This involved telling himself that he wasn't feeling any pain and repeating it continuously until he genuinely didn't feel it. He just numbed himself out completely. In due course he came to feel nothing at all.

This however, wasn't entirely satisfactory to the young Tommy. After all, what, he reasoned, was the fun in not feeling anything? His fertile subconscious mind soon came up with a better, altogether more complete way to satisfy the entertainment aspect. In fact his mark two version of detaching himself from unpleasantness proved to be quite a triumph.

In this version Tommy removed himself from the punishment altogether. He pretended that it was being inflicted, not on him, but on someone else, preferably someone he disliked; and that he was somewhere else entirely and enjoying a very nice time. This most often meant that he was playing football, scoring goals and winning matches for his team with brilliant solo efforts. That, or he was with his friends having fun, eating sweets or chasing girls. It didn't matter, just as long as he was not 'there' receiving the beating. Such was the success of his detach-and-dream strategy that he sometimes felt that it almost made being punished worthwhile. But only almost.

Later, in his teens, he employed the same strategy during his not infrequent visits to the dentist. His teeth were brittle, anaesthetics non-existent, drills painfully slow and the dentist a surly bully of a guy who clearly enjoyed inflicting the maximum pain possible on his hapless victims. Tommy was above all that. Unbeknown to the dentist, Tommy 'left' his surgery as soon as he arrived. He remained there in body only. The 'real' Tommy, his inner self, wasn't there at at all. He was anywhere rather than under the spotlight in the dentist's demonic chair subjected to the hellish agony which, happily for Tommy, was being inflicted on 'someone else'.

The second major lesson that Tommy learned from all this was self-discipline. After all, it took considerable resolve to enact his detach and dream strategy. As a result, and increasingly throughout his life, he was able to employ in all sorts of circumstances, the iron will instilled in him, and by him, from his experiences as a six year old.

In the meantime though, Tommy was still a beginner in employing his detach, dream and discipline strategies in the face of punishment inflicted on him. He would require much more practice in order to perfect the skill. That practice was soon forthcoming.

~

When the family moved back into the house following the fire, Tommy's invalid grandad was returned to the room which he occupied and which, arson attacks notwithstanding, he never left. Tommy in fact speculated that his grandad may have actually enjoyed the excitement of the blaze and the opportunity it afforded him to be taken from his place of confinement and see the outside world. That hypothesis of his young mind was never however confirmed.

What was confirmed to the young Tommy was that his grandad was becoming more and more unwell. This feeling was substantiated by the increasingly frequent visits to attend to grandad carried out by Doctor Blister, the family medic and general practitioner. A sombre, unsmiling man with a down-turned lower lip, he arrived several times each week, often at night.

On these occasions he entered grandad's bedroom with his mysterious black case and stayed there sometimes for hours. When he emerged it was to much head shaking and whispered conversations between him and Tommy's parents. Eventually, at the culmination of one such visit, Tommy's mum came to him and said,

"Grandad is leaving us. Go to say goodbye to him."

Tommy took this to mean that grandad was going to live somewhere else, was maybe going on holiday or, at least, was being taken to a hospital to continue his treatment for whatever it was that caused him to be unwell.

Tommy was guided in by his mother to his grandad's bedroom, a room he rarely entered. The room was in semi-darkness and smelled putrid. Tommy likened the odour to a cross between his own excrement, close contact with which he had so recently been forced to endure, stewed cabbage which he detested with a vengeance and a sort of antiseptic smell such as he encountered on his not infrequent visits to the local children's hospital casualty department.

These latter events resulted from the countless bumps, cuts and bruises Tommy incurred on an almost daily basis from his always boisterous behaviour. The casualty department visits were of course always followed by a beating – 'for having got himself injured and forcing his mother to waste people's time by taking him there'.

Tommy often thought, "Why didn't she beat me before she took me there, then the nurses could have treated me for that too!"

Tommy liked the nurses at the hospital. They wore crisp, clean uniforms, had pretty smiles and were kind to him.

For now though, the smell as he approached his grandad's bedside was distinctly unpleasant. Grandad was sitting motionless, half upright in the bed. Tommy saw that he wore a brown-striped, flannel pyjama jacket and a faded, high-necked vest below it. He appeared to be sleeping, his face was haggard and grey. His left arm hung limply to the side and it was to there Tommy's mum guided him.

Tommy took hold of his grandad's hand as instructed by his mum – it was very cold – and said, "Goodbye grandad."

Then Tommy was turned around and ushered out of the room. The door was closed. Doctor Blister and his mum stayed inside. "Probably whispering again," thought Tommy.

It did occur to Tommy at this point that perhaps his grandad was dead, although he didn't really understand what 'dead' was. "Never mind," his young mind said, "If he is dead, whatever it is, I'll get the blame for it."

So Tommy prepared himself mentally for the thrashing which was surely in the offing. In the event, his grandad had indeed died. But Tommy was not held responsible. The culprit turned out to be someone called Old Age. That however, didn't prevent Tommy from receiving a beating on his behalf!

~

In the aftermath of Tommy's grandad's death, the undertakers called to clean and dress the body, install it in the coffin and set it up to 'lie in state' in the parlour of the house for friends, relatives and other mourners to visit, view and pay their respects.

The beating came about partly through Tommy's natural childhood curiosity and partly through his equally natural compulsion to do anything that he was told not to do – in this instance the strict instruction to stay well away from the parlour!

The parlour was a room which was totally out of bounds to Tommy at all times anyway. It was in fact, thought Tommy, out of bounds to pretty well everybody because no-one ever went in to it. Other, that is, than on 'special occasions'. As these were few and far between, the room tended to sit unused for weeks, sometimes even months, on end. This forbidden territory aspect of the place only added to its mystique in young Tommy's mind. The allure was irresistable.

Tommy had been allowed in there before however. It was when aunts, uncles, cousins, nephews and nieces, and other exotic relatives from far flung places appeared on their annual or bi-annual pilgrimages to 'revisit home'. At these times Tommy's mum spent the morning cleaning the parlour, opening the curtains and letting the light in and had Tommy help her with the dusting.

Then she prepared scrambled egg and tomato sandwiches on huge slabs of white bread, cut the crusts off and quartered the remainder into delicate bite sized squares. Tommy considered this to be very 'posh' but he got to eat the crusts, so he rather enjoyed it.

When the guests arrived they were shown into the parlour, being steered away from the other far less pristine and, frankly, unkempt areas of the house. There they were served the sandwiches on the best crockery taken out for the occasion. They were offered drinks from a 'special' cupboard which sat locked in one corner of the room. Tommy was dressed in his best t-shirt and shorts on these occasions, put on a seat in another corner and told to 'keep quiet unless he was spoken to'.

After the introductions and other pleasantries, Tommy's dad went to a vase which sat on the mantelpiece above the fireplace, extracted a key hidden within it and then ceremoniously unlocked and opened the drinks cabinet to reveal its treasure. That treasure included a variety of bottles of all shapes and sizes and of many different colours. The lemonade bottles Tommy recognised but he had not a clue what the majority of the other bottles were or what was in them; other than that the aunts, uncles and whoever else became rather jolly and talked a lot after drinking from them.

So, apart from the fact that he was excluded and not even permitted his solitary seat in the corner, this was the process which Tommy now envisaged to be taking place around his grandad's body. Tommy did not however hear any joviality emanating from the room. He thought, "Perhaps they're only drinking the lemonade."

~

On the second day following his grandad's passing, and after the visitors for the day had all gone, Tommy ensured that his mum and dad were occupied elsewhere in the house, then tip-toed to the parlour. He reached up to his full height, made contact with the door handle and succeeded in opening the door. He slipped inside and immediately noticed the scent. It was almost overpowering and a completely different smell to that which he had experienced two days earlier in grandad's bedroom when he went to say goodbye. The smell was stronger, sweeter.

The room was in total darkness, so he reached again, this time for the light switch high on the wall, and switched on the room's central, electric roof lamp. He saw that the coffin, which he rightly presumed to contain his grandad's body, was laid across three trestles in the centre of the room. The coffin was open, it's top was propped upright against a wall, and it was bedecked with many bouquets of brightly coloured flowers. Tommy realised that it was their heavy scent which had assailed him when he entered.

Tommy wanted to get a look inside the coffin and this time say 'hello' to his grandad who he felt sure would be happy to see him. But it was too high up for him to see into. He decided to pull one of the upright chairs in the room over to the side of the coffin in order to climb on it and see if his dead grandad looked in any better shape than he had when he had said 'goodbye' to him. He moved a chair over easily enough but, when he started to climb on to it, the chair tipped over.

Tommy instinctively made a grab for the nearest object in order to prevent himself falling. The nearest object was the coffin. His small hand locked around the edge of the casket. As his weight and the sudden impetus of his fall took effect, the coffin started to rock slightly. It wobbled a bit more and then the first trestle gave way. Quickly afterwards the whole assembly collapsed. The coffin turned fully over and spilled Grandad's stiffened corpse out on the floor – or rather on top of Tommy – who was under it, and screaming.

In later life Tommy entertained friends with his tale of 'the day my dead grandad dropped in on me' and described the incident as having appeared to him to have happened in slow motion. He talked of experiencing a weird sensation of being both a participant in the catastrophe and a spectator. He recalled there being a quite distinct, if minisecond, delay between the component parts of the collapse triggering one another and then the final, fateful implosion. There was no delay however in Tommy's mum and dad rushing to find the cause of the commotion.

There was equally no delay in a second commotion being caused by the hauling off of Tommy upstairs by his dad to be given 'the thrashing of his life'. Perhaps it was the thrashing of his life – there was no 'this will hurt me more than it will hurt you' – and his dad certainly put a huge effort into it. But Tommy felt nothing. He decided to let grandad take the beating on his behalf.

His dad was flogging a dead corpse!

~

Not all of Tommy's parental interactions were unpleasant ones. Far from it. His dad took him to the seaside near their home and taught him to swim. The lessons were rudimentary to say the least. Tommy was plunged naked (he had no swim shorts) into the freezing surf and left pretty much to his own devices. It was very much a case of sink or swim. Tommy chose to swim. He loved it. By his seventh birthday he was already swimming confidently, alone in the sea. His skill would stand him in good stead on at least one occasion later on in his teens.

His mum and dad were avid hikers, hill walkers and climbers. His dad lean and strong, his mum a stocky powerhouse. Most weekends and all holidays, summer and winter, were spent in the mountains. By the time that Tommy's eighth birthday arrived he had already walked up his first real mountain. He found that to be an exhilarating experience and, from it, his lifelong passion for life in the open, camping and climbing was established. The challenging environment of the wild proved to be the perfect foil to his otherwise rebellious nature and thoroughly appropriate to further developing his self-discipline, resolve and determination. It provided an escape from the confusion of life at home and tranquility in which to nurture his imagination.

~

Tommy, indeed, possessed a vivid imagination. His ability to detach and dream arose from that. That in turn was fed by his other great love – the love of books. Books featured heavily in Tommy's life. They were all around him as he grew up. His mum and dad had an impressive home library. They were members of more than one book club and each month there was the excitement of two or three new books arriving through the post. Tommy was not yet up to the *'Complete Works of Winston Churchill'* which adorned one shelf in the living room of their house, but he browsed through a surprising number of his parents' collection of books and read many. Without being fully aware of it, he gleaned an impressive amount of knowledge from them. In later life he regularly amazed friends and colleagues – and himself too – with impromptu nuggets of wisdom picked up from his reading in general and from his parents' library.

His mother was a particular fan of Agatha Christie, the queen of murder mystery writers. She just loved the genre and the stories. Every single Christie novel was on the shelves – and Tommy read every one of them at a remarkably early age.

His very first theatre visit too was to see an Agatha Christie mystery enacted on stage. It was his mother who took him at the age of eight to see *'Murder On the Links'.* The experience kindled in Tommy a lifelong love of live theatre.

In later life Tommy penned his own humourous tribute to Christie, the 'grand dame' as she was known -

Who dunnit? -

Was it the butler?

Maybe the the maid?

Or might be the lover,

Deceived and dismayed?

The chauffeur looks shifty,

The gardener too,

Somebody dunnit,

The question is who?

The charge of inciting violence through writing a murder mystery was read and the judge, eyeing me with suspicion, asked,

"You are a private detective, are you the defendant in this case?" "No, m'lud," I replied, "I've got lawyers what do the defending. I'm the dick who dunnit."

A narrowed eye and questioning look from the judge, "Are you fit to plead?" "Well my doctor says I suffer from hypochondria ...

but I'm bearing well with all my other ailments!"

This time a slow stare, *"Are you sane?"* I stared straight back, *"As any person in this room."* That brought a titter from the gallery. Bailiffs immediately removed him.

"Who are your lawyers?", with mounting exasperation.

"Lunt, Hunt & Cunn-ingham m'lud." The judge looked over to where four men in black gowns and wigs were seated. *"I count four?"* he queried. *"Quite so m'lud,"* and fixing my gaze on the judge, *" There are two Cunn-inghams in court today."*

"So tell me what happened on the night in question?"

"Well m'lud, I was hired to investigate the demise of nearly every type of bird, a murder of most fowls you might say. It was late when I got to the manor house. A woman opened the door in her nightdress. I thought what a strange place to have a door. She identified herself only as a famous crime writer whose books are popular ... but why is a mystery to me!"

"So is this the woman that you claim what ... er ... who dunnit?"

"Yes m'lud ... That's - " ... *and here I turned and pointed with a dramatic flourish to the second Cunn-ingham brief who sprang to his feet and, throwing off his wig and gown, revealed himself to be a ..... a woman! ... gasps in the courtroom.*

"That's - The woman who dunnit,

A lady real smart,

Known as the queen of the creative art,

An author of merit,

A writer of note,

'Tis Agatha Christie ... and ...

Murder she wrote!"

– but for now Tommy simply enjoyed the escapism, and escape from the reality of punishment beatings, which the stories afforded him.

Apart from his parents mini library, books flooded into the household from all of Tommy's scholastic, sporting and recreational activities. Books were the staple prize awarded by school for educational excellence and sporting success and by the likes of Boy Scouts for various achievements in the field. Tommy, who excelled in all departments, amassed quite a collection of his own.

'Twenty Thousand Leagues Under the Sea' by Jules Verne and Herman Melville's *'Moby Dick'* were two of his early favourites. He immersed himself for hours on end and removed himself from real life in the not so improbable, make-believe worlds of the mysterious heroes who inhabited them.

~

At age eight Tommy took to pilfering money from his uncle Charlie. His uncle was a master baker who, in the usual way of his trade, worked all night and slept all day. After he arrived back from work with the morning rolls and bread for the day, and ate breakfast with the rest of the family, Uncle (as he was generally called) headed off to bed while everyone else headed in the opposite direction so to speak; out for the day, off to work, or in Tommy's case, school. When Tommy returned from school, Uncle was often still asleep; his clothes tossed carelessly over a chair by his bedside in the bedroom which he shared with Tommy and his brothers. He left his loose change in the pocket of his trousers. Tommy, who never received 'pocket money' as did his school mates, and therefore had no way to keep up with them in buying the odd assortment of 'necessary' schoolboy items such as cream buns and cheap toy cars, soon learned where his uncle's cash resided.

With the stealth of a real cat burglar, Tommy would creep to within a few inches of where his uncle's head lay in slumber, and try to silently remove a few coppers from the trouser pockets. He was often successful and never got caught. Therefore he was never punished for his regular thefts which were, quite definitely, the most despicable sin he perpetrated and most deserving of receiving a beating for! His uncle never reported the missing money. Only in adult life did Tommy realise that of course his uncle knew of his dishonesty. Yet he chose to never remonstrate with Tommy nor report the thefts to his parents. He was a kind man.

With his ill-gained wealth, which he concealed at home inside a book about the art of kirigami with a cut out centre, Tommy could match the spending power of his school friends. He bought doughnuts, sweets, glass marbles and ... books!

The books he chose to buy were different from most of those

given to him as gifts or prizes, of which there were many. He didn't buy fiction and adventure, but rather bought instructional books on his favourite subjects, particularly books pertaining to football and mountaineering. Right up to the time that he left school to become a professional footballer, Tommy was the only lad in his peer group, or who he knew of, who owned and read a football coaching manual. *'Soccer Coaching'* by the former England international team manager, Walter Winterbottom, taught him tactics and techniques well advanced for a lad of his age. Likewise, his various books on hiking, orienteering and climbing helped him to develop a knowledge of his subject far in excess of his contemporaries. He was able to put that knowledge to real practical use in the varied and increasingly demanding expeditions he indulged in as he grew.

Yet, in spite of his remarkably mature ability to confront nature and survive in the wild, Tommy was still childlike in keeping with his tender years. And there was one more 'infamous' beating still to be earned.

Joseph T.Riach

A YOUNG MAN COMES CALLING

The young man stood by the roadside looking up at the high, wrought iron gate which guarded entry to the vineyard on the other side. A weathered wooden sign, loosely tied to the gatepost, read *Château d'Argentonesse*, so he knew that he had come to the right place. As he had not known what to expect he felt neither pleased nor disappointed. After all, he had never set foot in France previous to this adventure, let alone visited a great wine estate, so had no expectation either way.

Despite his comparative youth however, he had already acquired a taste for the produce of such a place and prospected in his mind whether some sampling might be on the agenda. Then again he hadn't known that his destination was to be the residence of a wine producer and he hadn't made the journey from his Scottish home to drink the elixir. He was here for a quite different purpose. But what?

With the puzzling question which had constantly occupied the young man's thoughts in recent days again foremost in his mind, he looked anew at the gate and the gravel track (it barely merited the title of driveway) which ran from it. This track drove dead ahead for a good half mile through the soldierly ranks of vines, disappeared over a rise of hill and presumably continued on to the young man's destination somewhere beyond. But the gate was locked and the young man could see no way of gaining entry.

At that very moment, as if some mysterious force had read his mind, the gate creaked open. The young man was startled. He had not realised that there was an automatic entry system. There was certainly no evidence of it. There were no cameras, intercoms or electronic gadgetry to be seen. Yet here was the gate opening as if someone, somewhere knew he was there. How could that be? No-one could be expecting him because he hadn't informed anyone that he was coming. Not that he could have forewarned them anyway as he had not the slightest idea himself of who it was that he had come to see!

Not for the first time, the absurdity of his situation hit him. Here he was, two thousand miles from home, virtually penniless and having travelled all this way to see he knew not who about he knew not what. Well that last part wasn't quite so. What had compelled him to make the trip was the dubious belief that his host, whoever that might be, could somehow help him to find his purpose in life and direct him to 'success'. Success? That last part alone was a laugh. The young man barely had a clue what the word meant.

He knew that he wanted to be rich but he was at least smart enough, or was it cynical enough about his own ability? to realise that he had no idea where or how to start getting rich. He did love books, had a passion for writing and dreamed of becoming a famous author, writing novels which would earn him incredible wealth and renown. But he lacked the conviction, the self-belief in his own talent and ability. "Who would buy my deluded ramblings?" he reasoned. And so his rudderless life meandered on.

Yet, in spite of all his misgivings, he was 'here'. The gate before him was open. The mysterious place and personage within beckoned. The young man took one more look all around. There was no-one to be seen anywhere. He was totally alone. Nobody to witness his dilemma or comprehend the folly of his circumstance. If he was walking into a trap of some kind, perhaps one set by a crazed lunatic or manic murderer, no-one would know. Such a stretch of the imagination didn't seem entirely unreasonable to the young man at that moment and given his situation.

"But," he told himself, "I am made of sterner stuff. After all, didn't I make the decision, come what may, to subject myself to the rigours of my journey to be here? Am I going to stop now? What have I to lose?"

"Only my life," he answered, his humour returning, and smiled. "And where is my life headed? Nowhere!" He took a deep breath and walked through into the vineyard.

As he did so, the gates swung closed behind him.

~

With the physical obstacle of the gate and the psychological hurdle of crossing the threshold into the unknowns of the vineyard and its owner behind him, the young man advanced with greater confidence. Or was it bravado? He could not go back, the gate was firmly closed. His only option was to head onwards and upwards, through the lines of vines to the top of the rise and whatever lay beyond. His mood lightened and his pace lengthened.

Now he took time to look around him and he saw that he was not in fact alone. At various points he saw small groups of workers, men and women, busy between the rows. He was too distant from them in most instances to see exactly what they were doing but, given the late summer time of year and the large wicker baskets scattered around, he concluded that they were harvesting the fruit. The question occurred to him, "Will my host, who doesn't know I'm coming anyway, be able to see me at such a busy time!" He would soon have his answer.

As he crested the summit of the hill he saw that the track dipped downwards for a short distance before rising again to another summit on which sat, magnificently silhouetted in the morning sunshine, the château. The young man paused to take in the view and dab from his brow the perspiration of his efforts. He reckoned he had another quarter of a mile to go.

Nearby a lone worker was very deliberately clipping bunches of grapes from a vine and placing them, seemingly with great love, in a basket by his side. He looked up at the young man from under the wide brim of a tatty straw hat. His face was kindly, lightly bronzed by the sun and displayed a certain humour, or so thought the young man. At any rate there were deep smile lines around his sparkling eyes and at the corners of his lips..

The young man thought to ask the fellow if 'the master' was anywhere around, in the château or elsewhere, but hesitated, fearing that the older man would understand only French and certainly not his feeble attempts at the language. Before he could get his rudimentary, "Est-ce que le maître est au château aujourd'hui?" out, the worker spoke – and in perfect English.

"Laugh lines are a symbol of joy," he pronounced. "You can tell just how happy a person is through reading the laugh lines across their face. The lines are the result of a lifetime of laughter and smiling; they tell a story of the happy times and exciting experiences enjoyed." Then he added, almost as an afterthought, "And they permit those like me to age gracefully too!" With that he laughed, a warm, alluring chuckle.

The young man was amazed, speechless. Who was this guy? He was clearly a mind reader of some kind. The young man had heard stories of country folk, often uneducated and illiterate but with great mind powers, second sight and so-called sixth sense. He could only think that this friendly peasant was one such psychic. Yet he spoke fine English?

Now he spoke again.

"Yes the master is in the house," almost mockingly, "But take note as you walk up there. Look around you and take in the beauty of this place. Riches are more to be found in the journey than at the destination you know. Opportunity is missed by most people because it is dressed in overalls and looks like work."

With those last words, delivered with a knowing grin, he returned to his labour.

Totally confounded, the young man tried a "Merci beaucoup", failed miserably and mumbled a befuddled, "Thank you," instead. Then he set off up to the château once more. If he had been confused about his presence here before, he was now doubly in doubt. Who were these people? What had he let himself in for?

As he stepped out towards the 'house' he did indeed look around him as the peasant grape picker had suggested. The views stretching down the slopes in every direction were of rows of healthy vines speckled green and tan in the sunshine before merging with the blue of the sky on the horizon. It was breathtakingly beautiful, or so thought the young man, and an idyllic place to live and work. He imagined himself writing in this environment, calm and unhurried, with time and space for his thoughts to take shape in his texts unhindered by distractions. Plus, of course, occasionally sipping a fine wine! Then he turned his attention back to the château.

Now he could see why the workman had referred to it as the 'house'. It was not a château in the classical sense of 'castle'. No battlements or turrets; it was rather more of a stately home. Yes it was grand, three stories in height and long. The main entrance was classically positioned in the centre of the ground floor and the windows which stretched to either side of it, and those on the first floor, were slender and high. The house had a steeply pointed, slated roof with similarly featured square towers at either end. The overall appearance was that of an elegant country manor. The young man would later learn that it was of eighteenth century design and built during the reign of Louis XV who had reputedly visited and spent a night within its walls.

The door now facing the young man was massive, ten feet high and solid oak. He pulled on the chain of the iron door bell which dangled to one side of it. The bell clanged loudly. Some chickens which had been pecking unseen in long grass to the side of the doorway clucked and scattered. The young man clanged the bell again ... and waited.

After some time and, with no-one having answered his call, he started to think anew that perhaps his journey here was a waste of time; an overly optimistic but futile attempt to find a hope that didn't exist. He felt quite stupid. After all, who in his right mind would drop everything he was doing, abandon his (admittedly dreary) routine, leave his (totally unsatisfying) work and travel all this way in the unlikely hope of finding a way to a new and exciting future?

"Mind you," he thought almost immediately, "When you put it that way it doesn't sound entirely stupid at all!" On that more upbeat note, the door opened.

~

Now the fun began. The middle-aged and not unattractive brunette who answered his ringing of the bell, faced the young man, looked at him quizzically and said nothing. What could the young man say? He had arrived unannounced to see someone whose name he didn't even know. He fumbled for words. Then he remembered the envelope!

The envelope was the key to his being here, his raison d'etre as the French would say. On it was written no name, just the address of the château in France, on the doorstep of which he now stood. The instructions he had received when given the envelope were very precise. He had been told to personally deliver it straight away to the address given. On no account was he to open the envelope nor look inside it. It was the young man's failure to adhere to this last requirement which now caused him to hesitate in reaching into his pocket, retrieving the envelope and giving it to the woman waiting silently before him. She eyed him again as he weighed up his options. In reality he had few.

The fact was that when he accepted the envelope and saw the address on it he quickly realised that his financial position was so dire that travelling to the destination named was impossible. He was broke. He decided to look in the envelope anyway just to satisfy his curiosity as to what might be inside before returning it to its donor with a 'thanks but no thanks' apology. But when he opened it he had been astounded to find that it contained five hundred pounds in crisp ten pound notes! Embarrassed by his discovery he immediately replaced the money in the envelope and resealed it with the intention of making the return the next day. By the following morning though, a new plan had taken seed in his mind.

Why not use some of the money to fund his trip to France? He could reseal what remained in the envelope and give that to the recipient at the destination. As that person didn't know that he was coming, surely he or she would be none the wiser as to what was in the envelope and, if they were, then he could offer to repay what he had 'borrowed'. The young man had decided to follow through on that latter course of action.

He took the resealed, and one hundred pounds lighter envelope, from his pocket and handed it to the woman. Without a word she took the envelope and closed the door. The young man was once more alone on the doorstep. Not for long. The door soon reopened, the woman gestured him to enter and then indicated that he follow her. He realised for the first time that his heart was racing and his palms were sweating. If this was the lunatic murderer's lair then he was in and trapped. No way out now!

After what seemed like a very long walk with the sound of their footsteps clacking on the pristine wood flooring, she stopped at an open doorway and ushered the young man into the room beyond. As he entered, an involuntary ripple of energy passed through his body; a not unnerving kind of chill, a vague feeling of homecoming, impossible to later describe. She pointed to a settee. The young man sat down. She spoke her first words of the morning,

"Josmas will see you shortly," in perfect English. Then she left, closing the door behind her.

~

The young man was somewhat dazed. Things were happening quickly. "At least," he thought, "I now know my host's name." Josmas was an unusual name, one that he was not familiar with. Male, female, first name or surname, he didn't know. It didn't matter.

He took his first look around the room and was enthralled to find that he was seated in a magnificent library. Bookshelves as high as the ceiling surrounded him on three sides. They were packed full with what he soon discovered, as he rose and started to browse, were volumes of every kind of work imaginable. Classics, contemporary, fact, fiction and every genre in between, they were all there. A formidable, and presumably, rare and expensive collection. His gaze settled on a leather bound set of the complete works of Charles Dickens. He fingered the copy of *'Great Expectations'* and mused as to how the story mirrored aspects of his own life and his presence here in the château. Then he drew *'A Tale Of Two Cities'* from the shelf and started to leaf through the pages.

"An admirable and, dare I say, somewhat appropriate choice in the circumstance," intruded the calm yet assertive voice from behind him.

The young man jumped almost out of his skin, nearly dropping the valuable volume in the process. He wheeled round to find facing him – the worker he had spoken with on his way through the vineyards! He still wore the same scruffy jeans and ragged top as when they first met. Only his work boots had been removed, replaced by threadbare carpet slippers. Their eyes met. The older man's kindly but piercing smile both unsettled the young man yet quelled his automatic, defensive adrenalin rush at the same time.

Josmas, for surely this was he, neither introduced himself nor asked for an introduction from the young man but carried on as if nothing untoward had occurred; as if they were old buddies in the midst of an ongoing conversation.

"I say that your choice of book is appropriate in that here we are, you and I, each of the same Scottish origin yet seeking our respective truths in a far off land. It is an admirable tale is it not? Degenerate Sydney Carton seeing the error of his ways and making the ultimate sacrifice of giving his life for the woman he loves."

The young man barely nodded. Josmas continued.

"But he got it wrong you know, poor old Sydney. He should have saved himself as well as the life of the other guy. It's a major mistake to assign a lesser value to yourself, to your own life than you do to the lives and wellbeing of others. There is no reward in heaven, only here on earth. Tell me, what is it in life that you feel most passionate about? What is the one thing that you most love doing?"

The young man was more than a little taken aback. Not just by the surprisingly unkempt appearance and unannounced arrival of his host, but also by his easy launch into meaningful dialogue and his quite sudden change in conversational direction to a personal question.

However, there was a charisma about the man. The young man neither felt threatened nor overawed. He found Josmas to be gently irresistible, he felt compelled to answer his question. Not just answer it but to answer it with honesty and open-ness. He found himself talking from his heart for the first time in a long time, perhaps for the first time ever, as he replied,

"Well sir, I truly love books. I love to read them and would like some day to write books of my own."

"All very well young man … but what are you doing about it?"

This time the young man was knocked back, almost physically. Not just by the directness of the question but by the fact that it hit him in the heart. Instinctively he knew that that was the intention. He realised already from his brief interaction with Josmas and his ability to preguess his thoughts that his host knew full well that he was doing nothing at all to turn his dream into reality. He was just kind of drifting from day to day hoping that something, he knew not what, would come along to magically change his life.

Then, quite unexpectedly, it came to him, he did have an answer. He shouted, almost triumphantly,

"I'm here aren't I!"

Josmas smiled. A satisfied smile.

"Well done young man. You have just proved the old adage that wisdom can flourish unknown to its bearer. You may be a long way from satisfying your dream of becoming a writer but yes, you have been prepared to take the risk of succeeding. You made the journey here in blind hope. Such courage is the hallmark of successful people. You took the leap of faith that here might you find the key to unlock your true potential, release the real and exuberant you imprisoned within yourself. It is you yourself of course who is the jailer. It is you who must turn the key to set yourself free. I can but show you the key and teach you how to use it. How would your proposed work as a writer help other people?"

Again the young man found himself magnetically drawn to Josmas's words. He was unbalanced by the directness of the unexpected question thrown in at the end of his statement but again, to his own surprise, the young man rose easily enough to the occasion. Josmas seemed to bring out the best in him.

"Books," he said, "Inevitably educate or entertain. The best of them do both. A skilled writer feeds his readers knowledge or ignites their imagination with his words. Either way, the reader benefits and their life is enhanced in some way or another. As a writer I can reach literally millions of people all around the world, spur their enlightenment and light up their leisure. Isn't it a source of the greatest satisfaction possible to be able to help so many people and in such ways?

"Indeed it is young man," came Josmas's reply. The young man detected a hint of smugness in his voice as if he had received just the answer he wanted to hear. Again there was another, and unexpected question to follow.

"Would you like a glass of wine?"

~

Had the young man been drinking at that moment, wine or anything else, he would have choked on it. What was going on? After all the confusion of what had unfolded in the last hour, here he was being offered a drink of wine when it was still only mid morning. Perhaps imbibing at an early hour was customary in the world of wine or maybe his host was in reality a befuddled drunkard and all that had preceded this moment was but the psychotic ramblings of an inebriated idiot? That however wouldn't account for his remarkable insights into the young man's thoughts, his lucid explanations and the pointed clarity of his questions. In order to be neutral to the possibilities pervading his mind, the young man answered with his own question,

"Isn't it too early for a glass of wine?"

"You may well be right," replied Josmas with a dismissive smile, but took a bottle from a nearby winerack anyway and proceeded to open it. He expertly peeled off the foil seal and produced from his pocket a dainty corkscrew such as the young man had not seen before. With a twirl of his fingers and a theatrical flourish, Josmas popped the cork with ease. The young man watched in fascination. He was impressed and said so.

"I've never seen that done before. My efforts at opening bottles of wine usually involve much heaving and sweating with the bottle between my knees. I inevitably end off splashing wine everywhere and with shards of cork floating in my glass. How did you do that?"

"Oh, that's *Smarty*," replied Josmas nonchalantly, pointing out the gold embossed name of the same on the side of the screw and held out the device for the young man to examine. He took it from Josmas and turned it over in his hands again and again, looking for its secret mechanism and admiring its chic beauty. He could easily envisage himself opening bottles of wine back home without the destructive drama of his previous efforts and to the wonderment and admiration of his assembled friends. Not for the first time, Josmas seemed to read his mind.

"I see that you like it. I'll sell you it for fifty pounds."

"Fifty pounds!" exclaimed the young man, "For a corkscrew. You must be mad."

Josmas ignored that and continued,

"It's a one off, the only *Smarty* in the world. You've seen how smoothly it works. It will save you time and effort, don't you agree?" ... the young man nodded his agreement ...

"Just imagine how you'll feel when you show it off in front of your mates?"

The young man could indeed feel his ego, and head, swelling up as he pictured in his mind the envious "Oohs" and "Aahs" of his pals. Again he was amazed at the other's ability to see inside his mind and tap into his emotion.

"Tell you what," went on Josmas, "As we have just met and you clearly can't be sure that I'm not deceiving you in some way, I'll let you have it for half the price. That's just twenty-five pounds. It's a quality piece which will last you for ever. Over fifty years that's just fifty pence per year; the cost of a morning roll. You won't get this chance again. Do you want it in its box or will I just pop it in your pocket?"

The young man was sorely tempted but still hesitated. Josmas said nothing. He waited, looking soft eyed yet steadily at the young man.

The young man, despite the comparative inexperience of his years, realised that he was being sold to. At the same time however, he was pretty sure that Josmas knew exactly what he was doing and was testing his reaction to it. As the young man saw it, Josmas had, within minutes of meeting him, identified a want of his, pressed his emotional 'buy button' and had proposed a unique solution. The young man appreciated that. He knew that the art of selling took insight and skill. The sort of skill that leads to success and the young man wanted in on his secret. He also wanted the corkscrew. There was just one obstacle ... eventually he blurted out the ultimate objection to any sale,

"Look I'd love to have it but the truth is I'm flat broke. I don't have the money anyway!"

Josmas looked at him reproachfully, eyebrows raised, "But oh my young friend, you do have money."

At that he turned his gaze to a nearby coffee table. On it, beside the recently opened bottle of wine, sat the envelope which the young man had delivered as his calling card. It was open. The cash from within spilled across the table.

The young man felt his heart skip a beat and the colour suddenly rush to his cheeks. The realisation that his breach of trust had been discovered caused him to take an involuntary step back. He had been exposed as the deceitful intruder he clearly was, an untrustworthy interloper and fraud. He tried to stammer an explanation, an apology, but his throat dried up and the words wouldn't come. It was a moment of the most excruciating embarrassment such as he had never previously experienced. For the first time in his life he wished that the ground would open up and swallow him. What to do?

He thought to flee the scene but the woman who had let him into the château had mysteriously reappeared. She stood between him and the door, blocking his potential flight. In his panic-stricken state the young man thought her appearance seemed darker than before and rather threatening. As he hesitated, unsure of what to do next, she brought her right hand slowly from where it had been concealed behind her back.

"Oh no!" thought the young man, "I have walked into an assassins' den after all. She has a gun. She is going to kill me!" He backed off, fully expecting to find a pistol pointing at him. He croaked a desperate, "No, no!" and held up an open hand in a futile 'stop' gesture. He waited for the crack of the gun and the bullet which would kill him. Neither arrived.

Instead he heard her gentle, "This is for you," and, when he opened his eyes, which he had screwed tight closed in anticipation of his ghastly demise, he found her before him, bright eyed and holding out to him ... a slip of paper.

"It's the certificate of authenticity for *Smarty*," interjected Josmas, who stood smiling nearby, "You'll want to have that." Then, turning to the woman, said, "Put it in the box with the corkscrew Jocelyn. Our guest can take it with him when he leaves."

The young man took those words as his dismissal and, truth be told, he just wanted to slink out of there and be free of the shame engulfing him. But his thoughts of departure from Josmas and the château were premature.

"Do you know," continued Josmas, once again displaying his disconcerting ability to carry on as if nothing had happened, "That the man who conceived the idea for that corkscrew did so at the age of twenty? By his thirtieth year he had become a multi-millionaire. It didn't come easy of course. The inventor first took his fully patented design to several manufacturers. All turned him down.

Yet three of those major companies subsequently started to sell corkscrews based on his design. It took the inventor ten years and multiple law suits, representing himself in court as he could not afford lawyers, to bring the corporate thieves of his intellectual property to book. During that time he was bankrupted, lost his home and all his possessions, his wife left him because of the stress, he suffered a mental breakdown and took to sleeping in the streets.

Yet, in spite of all that and in the face of seemingly insurmountable odds, he persevered, fought on and eventually won his cases against the big companies. That, young man, is the true face of success.

And you? You are going to walk out on me at the first hint of difficulty and for doing exactly what was expected of you?"

"What was that?" thought the young man, "Am I hearing right?" He turned to Josmas and speared, "What do you mean? I don't understand."

Too Early For A Glass Of Wine?

Josmas motioned to him to sit down.

"The man who gave you that envelope knew that you had no money, no way to get yourself here to this address. He believed that you would be curious and look in the envelope. He expected that you would use your initiative and take the risk of 'borrowing' some money to get yourself here. You have done exactly what he, and I, hoped for. You have put your neck on the line. The majority of people would not do that. Most folks choose to stay in their moribund comfort zone. So, I am pleased. You have shown commendable determination. Not quite on the scale of the corkscrew inventor, but it's a start.

Now, I have a proposal for you. Do you play golf?"

The young man was still taking all this in. He had 'borrowed' money entrusted to him but was being hailed as a success for doing so? This represented a dramatic change in how life and behaviour were viewed from the traditional way of thinking that he was used to and had been brought up to.

Nonetheless he could see a logic to it. Maybe he had been seeing and doing things in the wrong way altogether up to now?

He resolved at that moment to listen even more closely than before to whatever Josmas had to say.

And, "Yes," he did play golf.

HOME ALONE

Much as he tried, Tommy's dad was spectacularly unsuccessful in bringing his son to tears with his punishment beatings. Tommy resolutely refused to cry. Why should he? He was 'not there' receiving the beating. He was somewhere else, playing with his chums, having fun. Tommy's worst enemy or someone else who had caused him recent displeasure was the one suffering the agony. Even his grandad took a thrashing for him ... good old grandad!

But what Tommy's dad was unable to achieve through beatings, his mum could accomplish with consumate ease by ... cooking! Her efforts in that department were so dire in Tommy's mind as to be capable of making even grown men weep. And Tommy, at nine years of age, was a long way from being a grown man.

There was nothing in his young life that Tommy detested with greater intensity than his mother's cooking; particularly so her stewed vegetables. Both the sight and the smell of any vegetable stew or casserole of her creation absolutely repulsed him. That was before it came to the taste.

Tommy had the natural 'sweet tooth' of many kids. He enjoyed sweets, desserts and particularly relished both fresh and canned fruits. But, while many of his friends could equally find pleasure in consuming vegetables, Tommy could not. Not only could not – but would not! He absolutely refused to eat any of 'the dreadful stuff'.

His mum's most disgusting culinary effort in Tommy's eyes was her cabbage, cauliflower and onion stew. These vegetables she boiled to a point close to extinction, thus draining them of any crispness, flavour or (possibly unknown to her) nutritional value. What survived was a grey, soggy slime which resembled an alien infestation of earth in a horror movie. It tasted – as Tommy would define it in adulthood – like cat pee pickled hedgehog droppings. Try as he might, and he did try mighty hard for reasons of pure hunger, Tommy could rarely bring himself to put any of the foul concoctions into his mouth.

Tommy's family were not well off. His dad was a talented engineer but bypassed for promotion at work. He was not a political animal; 'far too straight for his own good' as mum often said. So the family food budget was tight. On top of that the culture of the time and place demanded that people appreciate what food was available and be grateful for it. Therefore Tommy's reluctance to eat what was put in front of him did not go down at all well with his parents.

"Rather the same as the vegetables not going down well with me," thought Tommy!

His refusal to eat the 'perfectly good food' (as his mother called it) always led to the same conclusion.

So it was that Tommy once again stood motionless staring at the wall of the cellar. The soggy mess of his stewed vegetable meal dripped from his head. On this occasion he was victim to the 'three strikes and out' policy of his mum regarding uneaten food.

This decreed that, when Tommy refused to eat a meal, he was sent to bed early and hungry. The food was reheated and served to him the following day. When he again refused to eat it, the same scenario as the previous day was repeated. Tommy was sent to bed hungry. On the third day the food was once more reheated and presented for eating.

By now it was worse than ever as far as Tommy was concerned. It looked and smelled just like vomit and that's what Tommy wanted to do when it was placed in front of him. Although desperately hungry by now, he again refused to eat.

In keeping with his mum's policy, the stew was tipped over his head and Tommy was sent to stand in the corner of the cellar for four hours. His mother then went out for the afternoon.

Before she left, she 'dared' Tommy to move from his place of punishment before her return. If he did move, she warned him that the consequences would be grave. In the event, it wasn't the possible dire repercussions which were foremost in Tommy's mind as she left. He was more excited by the realisation that he was in the house all alone for the afternoon. Everyone else was out. This had never happened before and he was determined to make the most of the opportunity!

Not un-naturally he quickly resolved to take full advantage of his 'liberty' to explore the family home. Especially those mysterious secret parts of it from which he was excluded. As these parts made up the majority of the house, he had a lot of exploring to do!

As soon as his mother left the house, Tommy was out of the cellar like a shot. Although he didn't know it at that moment, this was the circumstance in which his lifelong love affair with wine was to commence. It was not however a case of 'love at first sight'. Quite the opposite in fact. Tommy was just nine years old and about to get 'pissed'! As there was no way that any alcoholic beverage would be served to him in any shape or form by a family member, or indeed any adult, Tommy's imbibing of it had to be self-administered. He unwittingly did just that when left home alone that fateful afternoon.

~

From the cellar, Tommy's first port of call was to ... the parlour!

The parlour was, as Tommy well knew, strictly out of bounds. Especially so since his escapade involving grandad deceased and his coffin capsized. Tommy's invasion of the room had already landed him in considerable trouble. Nonetheless, undeterred by his prior experience, he was determined to examine, and perhaps sample, the contents of the mysterious drinks' cupboard. He knew there to be lemonade there and, having not eaten for three days and with the foul stench of dead cabbage to rid himself of, the sweet liquid was just what he felt he needed. He was, almost literally, dieing of thirst. In that state, any misgivings he might have felt with regard to revisiting the scene of his earlier crime were pretty well non-existent. Tommy's young memory was short and his 'need' for lemonade overpowering. He went to the parlour.

The vase on the mantelpiece, in which the key to the drinks' cupboard resided, was even more out of reach to Tommy than had been the coffin. This despite the fact that Tommy had stretched in height by a full twelve inches in the intervening years. Nonetheless he was sure that he could reach it by standing on a chair. Once again he pulled an upright chair from a corner of the room to a position in front of the fireplace. He climbed on to the chair very carefully. This time there was no loss of balance on his part. He stood tall on the chair, reached up and found that he could get to the vase with relative ease. He stretched to pick it up by its base. It was more weighty than he expected and top heavy. It wobbled insecurely in his hands for a few decidedly dodgy seconds. But he succeeded in lifting it down and placed it on the chair. Then he descended from the chair, took hold of the vase once more and tipped it upside down. Out fell the key!

Tommy took the key, crossed to the drinks' cupboard and opened it. One by one he took out the bottles, all the same ones that he had seen his dad remove from the cupboard on the isolated occasions that he had been permitted into the parlour when those 'special relatives' visited. As he delved further and further into the cupboard and withdrew bottle after bottle, there was no sign of any lemonade. Eventually every bottle from the cupboard lay scattered around him on the floor. There was not one single bottle of lemonade. Tommy was dismayed. He felt that he had to have a drink and was becoming more desperate for one by the second. That is when his gaze fell on the bottle of Barsac.

~

Besides enjoying 'plain' lemonade, as he thought of it in comparison to flavoured varieties, Tommy was partial to all the different coloured and fruit flavoured versions too. He very much liked orangeade and raspberryade, but his particular favourite was limeade. The bottle with the Barsac name looked like limeade to him. It was certainly the right yellowish colour. He couldn't make sense of the label however. It was quite different from any he had ever seen but he was quite sure that the bottle must be limeade or lemonade of some kind or why, he reasoned, was it there in the first place?

Fortunately for Tommy, the almost full bottle had recently been opened. With the aid of a knife, he easily enough prised out the cork with which it was re-plugged - although he did cut his finger while doing so. Blood dripped on to the carpet. Tommy stemmed the flow with a white lace tablecloth which adorned the coffee table which sat nearby. In the process he managed to knock the vase off the chair. It hit the stone hearth of the fire and shattered.

Aghast at what he had done, Tommy thought to clean up the mess he had made - but only briefly. First he had to have a drink; a drink of the 'limeade' which had caused him to create the disaster in the first place. Without even sniffing beforehand for a clue as to what the contents might be, Tommy tipped the bottle up to his lips and downed several large gulps, just as he always did with lemonade, limeade or any kind of 'ade'. Glugged in that way the liquid barely touched the sides of his throat, especially so given Tommy's state of aching thirst.

With the kind of delayed reaction thus created, Tommy had already greedily quaffed more than half of the bottle before he realised that he was not drinking limeade. He didn't know what he was drinking, that it was a fine Bordeaux wine, but it tasted ghastly; as much like poison as his immature mind imagined poison of some kind might taste. He found it to be worse by far than the awful cough mixture dispensed by the grim Doctor Blister on the occasions of his winter colds – and only marginally more palatable than his mum's repugnant stews.

He dropped the bottle. Like the vase before, it fell on the hearth and shattered, spilling the remainder of it's contents there, on the lace cloth and on the carpet. Tommy managed to cough up some of the foul potion he had consumed (also on to the carpet) but most of it stayed down inside him.

He rushed from the parlour and upstairs to the bathroom, leaving a trail of blood and semi 'sick' en route, intending to spew up there some more of whatever it was that he had drunk. But, at the top of the stairs, he started to feel dizzy.

He collapsed on to the top step of the stairs, doubled over and held his throbbing head in his bloody hands. He sat like that for several minutes.

Then he started to giggle. It was just a little giggle to begin with, a bit like a frog hiccupping. He wasn't sure that it was himself that had done it but then he did it again. He giggled some more but in a stupid kind of way. At first it seemed strange to him but then increasingly felt like quite good fun.

The door to his parents' bedroom was just beside where he sat. He decided to go in there to lie down for a bit until his giggling fit passed.

~

His parents' bedroom was indeed a place of mystery. Tommy had only seen the inside of the room on a few isolated occasions. Once, several years previously, during a midnight thunderstorm, he had been taken there to snuggle up in bed with his mother. He remembered the occasion well as he was genuinely terrified of the rumbling thunder and bolts of lightening. Also because it was the only time that he could recall being treated in that 'special' way; hugs and cuddles did not feature prominently, if at all, in Tommy's young life. It was dark at the time and he had seen precious little of the room or its contents. Before daylight came and the wind and rain had eased off, he had long since been packed off back to his own bed with no chance to discover any of the 'secrets' of his parents' room.

One other time he had tip-toed through to the forbidden territory of their room in the middle of the night to report to them that he had been sick. He had vomited his mother's fried porridge and cauliflower hotchpotch all over his bedsheets. Creeping in, in the pitch darkness, he heard a lot of movement in the bed, groaning and suppressed moans. He assumed that his parents were fighting;

not an un-natural reaction given that they did shout and scream at each other 'in there' on a semi-regular basis. Therefore, not wanting to get involved in the fight, or be a victim of it, he slunk back to his stinking bed. He needn't have worried about the 'victim' bit, he became that soon enough. There was a thrashing for him in the morning for the mess he had made in his bed, a second beating for not having reported it and the further punishment of having to sleep in his own puke for the next week.

So this room represented fearful past moments to Tommy and he felt himself to be embarking on a great adventure, and displaying considerable courage, by venturing there. But venture there he did.

~

Once inside his thoughts of lieing down evaporated. The excitement of being there overtook him. In the semi gloom created by the drawn curtains, Tommy's eyes first alighted on the chest of drawers nearest to the door which he had slid in through. He gingerly pulled open the top drawer. It contained his mother's underclothes. He knew the various garments to be that but had very little idea of how or why they were worn. The silk and nylon stockings he recognised alright, after all they were just like his socks. But why were they so long he wondered and how could they possibly keep her legs warm when they were not thick, wool knits?

Her panties too puzzled him. They varied greatly in size. There were large, baggy ones like shorts worn by boxers he had seen and then there were skimpy ones, mostly in black or red lace and satin, which wouldn't even cover her bottom. He concluded that these last mentioned must be ones she had saved from when she was a schoolgirl.

The bras, he had heard them called brassieres, he knew about. He had seen his mother wear one around the house in warm summer weather. She strapped it around her boobs to stop dad from tickling them. At least that is what the older and more knowledgeable boys at school had told him. Tommy saw no reason to disbelieve that but, for now, contented himself with putting one over his head to wear like a war helmet with each of the cups protecting his ears. He tied the strap under his chin.

Next his eyes alighted on something he had not seen before. He had no idea what it might be. It was a long, black, elastic belt of some kind. He removed it very carefully from the drawer, held between his finger and thumb as he had done when he picked up his first worm in the garden. He raised it high and let it dangle down in front of his eyes. He turned it round and round, puzzling as to its possible use. The belt had four shorter strands which stretched from it along its length. There were clips and buttons too. At last, Tommy got it ... it was a catapault! Now he had a helmet and a weapon, all he needed was a cape to complete his warrior outfit. The last named was easily sourced.

He crossed to one of the two free-standing wardrobes in the room, opened it and found it to be full of women's clothes, dresses, skirts, coats and jackets. He surveyed the collection and eventually withdrew his mother's fur coat. Tommy had only seen her wear it once or twice on so-called special occasions when she and dad went out for the night and didn't come back until late. Tommy knew that the coat must be warm to wear as his mum didn't wear knickers – boxers or skimpies – when she wore the coat. Or so he believed. He had heard his dad speak about ladies 'with fur coats and no knickers', so assumed that applied to his mum.

Tommy slung the garment over his shoulders and fastened just the top button at the neck. Now he was ready for battle! He had a catapault, a helmet and a cape. What next?

The second wardrobe beckoned. It surely had to be the one where his dad's clothes were kept. What might he find in there? He carefully opened the door and peered inside. His dad's various shirts, jackets, trousers, suits, coats and ties hung above him but it was what he saw coiled up in a corner of the cabinet, not unlike a deadly serpent waiting to strike, that sent a shiver down Tommy's spine. It was his 'old friend' – the tawse!

Tommy hesitated before reaching in to the cupboard and slowly withdrawing it into the daylight. He had never held it before. It was heavy and the leather stiff. It was a fearsome weapon. But it wasn't one that Tommy wanted anything to do with. On a sudden impulse, he decided to hide it. That way, he thought, his dad would never be able to use it on him again. He slid it lengthwise into the narrow space behind the wardrobe and pushed it further in out of sight.

With that accomplished, and Tommy felt quite pleased about it, his attention returned to finding what other treasures his dad's wardrobe concealed. His rummage around it and the various drawers built into it revealed little of interest until he caught sight of an old biscuit box. It was below and behind all the clothes, concealed in a bottom corner right at the back. Tommy liked biscuits and immediately assumed that his dad did too. Hence, reasoned Tommy, the fact that he had a secret supply hidden away in his wardrobe, probably to feast on when mum was asleep. Tommy took the box, laid it on the bed and opened it.

To his great disappointment there were no biscuits, not one. What was there totally confounded him. He had never seen any of the contents before and had absolutely no idea what they were or what his dad used them for. Carefully he took them out and examined them.

There was a small jar labelled *'Vaseline'.* Tommy opened the jar and found the contents to be an oily, opaque substance of some kind. He stuck his fingers into it, withdrew them and sniffed. He didn't care for either the feel nor the smell of the goo but rubbed some on his face as warpaint anyway. Then he cleaned it off his hands by wiping them on his mum's fur coat which was around his shoulders.

What mostly caught his attention and intrigued him however were several oblong foil wrappers. His first thought was that these must contain biscuits or chocolates but when he picked up the first packet the feel was all wrong. It was soft and pliable. He decided to risk tearing one open; his dad surely wouldn't miss just one of whatever it was? So open one he did.

What he found confused him even more. It was a sausage shaped rubber balloon of some kind but unlike any he had ever encountered before. It was not a bright colour like most balloons. It was the same colour as the Vaseline goo, and it felt similarly kind of greasy. When he tried to blow it up he found it difficult because the opening was much larger than normal. The taste was pretty awful too.

With the effort of blowing into the 'balloon' combined with its nasty taste, Tommy suddenly felt light headed and queasy again. Sweating and in need of fresh air he stumbled from the room, lurched down the stairs and rushed out of the front door of the house, thinking to spew up some more of whatever it was that he had drunk. Once outside, as the fresh air hit him, the nausea passed and he started to giggle again in the same stupid way as before. He felt strange, in an out of body sort of way; as if he was experiencing all that was happening but as in a dream. He was both disorientated and yet very merry.

A part of him suggested that it might be a good idea to go back inside the house to clean up the mess he had made before his parents returned home. But another part of him insisted that there was no mess to clean and, even if there was, he didn't give a toss. Either way, any plans he had in that direction were soon dashed.

As he staggered drunkenly outside the house, a gust of wind caught the front door and it slammed shut. Tommy was locked out of the house. The strange thing though was that by now Tommy didn't care. He had his battle helmet, cape and sling. He also had an unusual sausage shaped balloon.

Tommy galloped around in front of his house on an imaginary

horse, whooping nonsensical battle cries and laughing hysterically. A small group of bemused neighbours gathered to stare in disbelief at the spectacle of the lad covered in slime with a bra on his head, swinging a black suspender belt in one hand and an inflated contraceptive in the other.

Tommy's mum and dad, when they arrived home, did not share in the general amusement.

~

Tommy was unceremoniously dragged inside by his dad and that was when the full extent of the carnage he had inflicted on the house became apparent to his parents. Tommy was in no fit state to be confronted with the enormity of his misdeeds, so was spared the application of instant justice and packed off to bed. First thing the next day though, he was summoned by his dad to answer for his crimes.

His dad sat Tommy down in front of him in the sitting room. Similar to when a criminal suspect is charged by the police he read out a list of the offences committed. It included – ignoring the rules of the house and previous warnings as to his behaviour, defying his parents, breaking in and entering forbidden areas, raiding private property, stealing property, wanton destruction and vandalism of goods and property including an expensive fur coat, carpet, lace cloth, vase and bottle of wine, creating a public nuisance, bringing the family into disrepute, under age drinking, being drunk and disorderly – the list went on. Even Tommy was taken aback, and not a little impressed, by the extent of his own bad behaviour. He had, after all, been totally inebriated by the end of the afternoon and could remember nothing.

Having read the charge sheet, Tommy's dad did not ask if he had anything to say in his own defence as Tommy had seen enacted by judges in courtroom scenes in films, but instead spoke himself.

"The punishment required to make you pay for what you have done is far more than even I can administer; or at least more than I can dish out today. Rather than give you the two hundred strokes of the tawse you have earned right now, I am going to give you only the first instalment of twenty. You will receive a further twenty lashes on this day each week for the next nine weeks."

Tommy was genuinely taken aback at the severity of the punishment announced, but perked up when he remembered that he had hidden his dad's dreaded tawse. His optimism was quickly squashed however when his dad cut in,

"By the way I found the tawse," then added, "In addition you are grounded, not one week or one month but indefinitely. You don't go outside the area of the house or garden ever, except to go to school. And I mean ever!"

Being confined in any way did not sit at all well with Tommy. He was a free spirit and needed space to express himself. It was this last part of his punishment which hurt Tommy most, much more so than the twenty lashes to his bared buttocks which followed. Anyway, he didn't feel those. He was in the local hospital children's casualty department receiving attention for his hangover from a bevy of sympathetic nurses. The guy getting the beating was the

'Barsac fellow' – for making the worst limeade Tommy had ever tasted!

~

Thus it was that Tommy came to pass the next years of his childhood predominantly alone in his own house or garden. He was not allowed to play with the other local lads who lived close by. They came to consider Tommy to be snobbish and aloof. They grew up with this view of him unaware of the fact that his solitary demeanour was imposed on him and nurtured by his severe parenting.

Devoid of company, Tommy took to creating his own entertainment. He invented games to play by himself. As fresh air and the outdoors were his favoured environment, he took to spending all his time at home, fair weather or foul, in the garden. It kept him well away from his parents and from everyone else. It gave him his own space, the freedom he craved. His parents didn't object to him doing that, just as long as he didn't leave the premises. It kept Tommy out of their way too.

From an early age, Tommy was football daft. He did not however own a football. He wished for one and hoped every birthday or Christmas that one might arrive. As time passed and it became clear that that would not happen, he gave up on the idea. He did however acquire an old tennis ball from a classmate at school. It was better than nothing and would, in due course, prove to be a blessing in disguise, one worth its weight in ... well, real footballs. Tommy didn't realise at the time but, by perfecting his skill with the tennis ball, he would in later years find working with a full size football easy by comparison.

He practiced endlessly, literally hours at a time, juggling the tennis ball, keeping it up in the air with his head, thighs, left foot and right foot. He taught himself to control the ball equally well with either foot by compelling himself to use each foot alternately. The rough hewn granite wall which formed one side of Tommy's home was a big help too. It was perfect for knocking the ball against and receiving the unpredictable rebounds. Tommy made full use of the facility to work on and improve his reactions and ball control to an extraordinary level.

With his incessant practice Tommy learned to keep his tattered tennis ball constantly in play against the wall and off the ground for ninety minutes, the equivalent of the duration of an entire football match. The self imposed 'rules' of his game demanded that he went back to the start of his 'match time' whenever he lost control of the ball, missed a touch or let the ball hit the ground. Thus, even when he had reached eighty-nine minutes of successful 'keepie-up' in this way, but then lost control of the ball, he made himself restart again - and did so continuously - until he completed a full ninety minutes successfully.

With this ruthless self-discipline and dedication to the task he set himself, Tommy's exile in his own back garden did have a positive spin off for him in terms of footballing ability. It was a skill learned which he would use to good effect in later years.

Joseph T.Riach

A TASTE OF HONEY

Having told Josmas that he did indeed enjoy golf, his host wasted no time in leading the young man through the château and out to the back. There the young man was thrilled to find a fine nine hole, par three golf course laid out and winding its way through the woodland on that side of the hill. Jocelyn, as the young man now knew the master's assistant to be, brought him a half set of clubs and soon he and Josmas were teeing up and ready to play.

"Tell you what," said Josmas before hitting his first shot, "Lowest scratch score wins. You win you get *Smarty* for free. I win, you pay the full fifty pounds. Deal?"

The young man felt that he could hardly refuse. In the light of what transpired over the next two hours he wished that he had.

Long before they walked off the last green he was well beaten. Josmas parred every hole with ease while the young man, who played regularly at home and considered himself to be a handy player, struggled just to keep his ball in play. As they made their way back into the château he remarked to his host,

"I didn't know you could play like that."

"You never asked," was the Josmas reply, who then added, "Practice and preparation makes for perfection. I only took the bet because I knew I would win. Don't forget that."

The young man vowed not to.

Walking on through the hallway Josmas came out with the apparently disconnected question of,

"Do you know what the very first word I remember being taught in French class at school was?" No response was required of the young man as Josmas continued, "Of course you don't," and then supplied the answer.

"It was the word élève. In English it means pupil, as in 'a school pupil'. The word was rather appropriate in that context but that is not the sole reason that we were introduced to it early on. No, the greater purpose of our learning it was to introduce us to the accents common in the French language. In this case the acute, which tops the first letter é, and the grave which tops the second è.

More so than just an introduction to the accents, it was taught as a way of remembering them. Remember the word and you remember the accents, their names and which is which. Acute comes before grave alphabetically, phonetically (the way they sound) and visually, they point in towards each other. Remembering the word élève triggers your memory in these respects. It is planted in your mind as a trigger. Good, isn't it?"

"Yes, it is," the young man had to agree, but could not for the life of him see what that had to do with the golf match which he had just lost so easily, or to anything else. He quickly found out.

"Triggers are used as preludes not just to memory recall of that kind but to all kinds of actions," he continued. "Most professional golfers for instance, use a trigger movement to initiate their swing. They give no conscious thought to the swing and its various elements once in play on the course; these have been ingrained in their subconscious through constant practice. In competition they concentrate just on the trigger then the rest follows naturally. I didn't notice you use one by the way."

With that last remark, Josmas patted the young man on the shoulder, turned up his bottom lip slightly and gave a knowing nod.

"You had too much going on in your head to play well." At that he tapped his temple with his forefinger.

"In my suit and tie wearing days in business I also used a trigger to get me going with meetings and the like. I planned, prepared and practiced my presentations meticulously then, when the time to 'perform' arrived, I straightened my tie and said an inward 'It's showtime!' as I entered the meeting. That was my trigger – straightening my tie and repeating my simple line. With that done I made no conscious effort to recall what I had to say or do. I just relaxed and enjoyed the moment. It worked like clockwork."

The young man listened more attentively. His curiosity was aroused. There was so much depth, yet simple reason in his host's words. Everything he said demanded attention.

"A trigger movement, thought or words," went on Josmas, "Removes anxiety from your action and allows you to give every situation your best shot. Be sure that your preparation is thorough and complete then, when you 'pull' your chosen trigger, it will initiate a smooth 'swing' to whatever endeavour or performance you are undertaking. A well oiled trigger will serve you well – be it in golf, business or life generally."

~

By now they had arrived back in the library. The young man went to the envelope and the cash still sitting on the coffee table. He withdrew fifty pounds from the bundle of notes, left the rest there and handed Josmas his winnings. Josmas accepted the money with boyish joy and the gleeful whoop of someone who had scooped the jackpot in a lottery. He proceeded to take a massive wad of banknotes, there must have been a couple of thousand pounds there, from his pocket and added the fifty to it He really was over the moon with his win and his winnings.

"Would I," wondered the young man, "Still feel such exuberance in winning a small bet if I possessed wealth such as Josmas clearly does? It's loose change to him, but a small fortune to me. I came here hoping for guidance as to how to improve myself, succeed in life, get wealthy. Yet here I am, just a few hours after arrival, exposed as a petty thief, thrashed at golf and dishing out fifty pounds of cash I don't have for a trifling corkscrew to uncork bottles of wine I can never afford. Whatever next?"

"Next," chimed in Josmas, "Is dinner. Jocelyn will show you to the room prepared for you. You are staying? There is a change of clothes there for you and toiletries too." The young man shook his head in disbelief, hesitated, then followed Jocelyn from the library.

She led him to a stylish, well appointed bedroom suite on the first floor of the château. Following the mind scrambling events of his arrival at Château d'Argentonesse and the cash, corkscrew and golf fiascos, he welcomed the solitude of his new quarters and the chance to compose himself and gather his thoughts.

He lay out on the bed, stared at the ceiling and tried to figure out just what was going on. He failed miserably in that respect so opted for a short nap instead. But soon Jocelyn's knock on the door told him that it was time to accompany her to dinner.

He called for her to give him ten minutes to ready himself. When he emerged to her welcoming smile he wore the casual but smart clothes, exactly his size and taste, which he had found hanging in the closet and which he had slipped into after an invigourating shower. The nap had not really been quite that. He had tried to sleep but his mind was in turmoil.

"Why had he come here? What was expected of him? Who was the mysterious Josmas who seemed to read his every thought?"

The rinse down in cool water however, calmed and refreshed him somewhat.

He remembered that he was here in order to somehow improve his barren, uninspired existence. He remembered too that he had not eaten since his arrival at the château earlier in the day. He was ravenously hungry. Jocelyn must have known that too as she quickened her pace along the corridors and down the stairs to the dining room. The young man followed her eagerly.

~

When he entered the dining room he found Josmas already seated at the head of an elegantly set dining table of classical design. A centrepiece of a silver candelabra cast the only light. The room was otherwise in darkness. Only one other place had been laid at the table, next to Josmas at his side. It was to there that Jocelyn led the young man and seated him. She reappeared from time to time throughout the next two hours, serving the various courses and clearing away the dirty crockery and general debris of the meal.

The young man looked at his host. The glow of the candlelight cast shadows on Josmas's face which added to both the mystique and the quiet authority of the man.

"His is truly a most imposing presence," thought the young man. Not for the first time he felt inextricably drawn to him.

His host reached out to a bottle of wine which the young man now saw was open on the table.

"This is a 1989 Petrus," said Josmas, and paused for the significance of that fact to register with his guest. "It's the bottle I opened this morning. I hope it's to your liking?"

The young man knew what the wine was alright, and was already excited by the prospect of sampling the renowned vintage.

Too Early For A Glass Of Wine?

"It is one of the most expensive wines in the world," continued Josmas, "I bought it at auction some years ago. It cost me over three thousand pounds. That of course means nothing at all unless it's damned nice to drink. Shall we find out?"

Both men realised that remark almost qualified as the proverbial 'stupid question', and each smiled. Only a nod was required from the young man before Josmas dutifully poured out two glassfuls into the cut crystal wine goblets waiting to receive the treasure. A chink of glasses, a "Santé" from Josmas and a "Cheers" from the young man and then they were sipping and savouring the divine nectar.

"You may think that I drink this all the time," said Josmas, as the initial euphoria of the moment passed and he rested his glass on the table, "You would be wrong. The measure of any food, drink or any commodity in life is only that it serves its purpose, you like it and enjoy it. Believe me, I like very many and very cheap wines as much as I like the Petrus. However, my wealth gives me the choice. Were I poor I could drink only the cheaper wines, but I wouldn't be any less happy. Do you get that?"

The young man nodded, yes he did get it.

He also got it that he was hooked on every word his host uttered. He felt like a drowning man who had been dragged ashore and brought back to life. He was determined to take in every gulp of air, every breath of knowledge which his rescuer, who had just treated him to easily the finest wine experience of his young life, could deliver.

"I opened this Petrus because today is a special occasion," said Josmas, "A special occasion on two counts. Firstly, I shall be moving on from here in the next few days. This chapter of my life is closing and a new place awaits me where I must continue my work. You will be the last to benefit from my guidance here."

The young man didn't know what to make of the announcement, so said nothing. Did he detect a hint of sadness in the older man's voice?

"Secondly, this day marks the start of your journey into a new and bright future. I congratulate you on having had the courage to seek me out and take on the challenge."

Again he raised his glass and the two crystals clinked together once more as their eyes met and each man bowed his head slightly in deference to the other.

"When you said this morning," went on Josmas, "That it was too early for a glass of wine, you were only partly correct. Of course I was relieved that you declined the drink. I would not have been at all impressed with a young man drinking alcohol so early in the day. To succeed in life you must keep a clear head. In two other respects you were however, mistaken.

Firstly, the Petrus which you are now drinking must be opened well in advance to let it breathe. I find that a full twenty-four hours is best but it still tastes pretty okay at the moment, n'est-ce pas?"

The young man nodded in agreement, said, "It's a wee bit better than just okay," and took another sip. Josmas acknowledged with a smile, a sip of his own and continued.

"So in that sense it was not too early. Secondly, in the broader analogy of life, it is never too early to 'drink of the wine'. There is no point in putting off enjoying the good life until tomorrow. That may be too late. The time to act and to succeed is always now. We can learn a lot of life lessons from wine you know."

At that moment Jocelyn entered, carrying the first of the food and laid it before them.

"First let's eat," cried Josmas, "I am famished."

The young man said, "Amen to that."

~

The three course meal which followed was wholesome and delicious. Nothing fancy, but hugely satisfying peasant dishes prepared (apparently by Jocelyn) from fresh local meats and vegetables. It really was a hugely enjoyable and hearty event during which both men exchanged stories of mis-spent youth, laughed a lot and finished off the wine. The young man suddenly felt quite relaxed and at home. This kind of guy and this kind of place suited him perfectly he concluded. "This is where I want to be."

As coffee and an excellent Armagnac were served, both men moved to easy chairs in front of a vast, open, oak burning fire which Jocelyn had prepared (was there no end to this woman's industry and talent)? and Josmas resumed his discourse. The young man listened intently.

"I believe that you find the kind of life I lead here to be

agreeable?" Josmas once more pre-empted the young man's thoughts.

"It's better than that," agreed the young man, perplexed as ever as to how his host continually read his mind.

"But," went on Josmas, "It takes time, work and patience to get to this stage. Just like growing vines through to making wine is a long, slow process. Great wine, you know, has been likened to 'poetry in a bottle'. I like that description because, just like any creative art, winemaking requires knowledge, commitment and time. You must view your life development in the same way. Once you find something good, you need to take care of it. You must let it grow.

Think of your life and how you wish to shape it as first planting the seeds, your imagination, in the right soil, your mind. Then tending the plants lovingly, which is the nurturing of your young self. The watering of the plants judiciously and feeding them appropriately represents your growing and learning phases. Once ripe, harvesting the grapes and commencing the wine making process is the putting of your knowledge to work and establishing an enterprise; then bottling and waiting for the wine to mature is the building up of your business.

Lastly, the marketing and distribution of the wine for the whole world to savour is the enjoyment of the fruits of your labour. It's a staged process

You will see all these stages actually practiced on this estate; and you will see them as relating to life displayed by myself and by all the others who lovingly spend their days on the land with me here.

Too Early For A Glass Of Wine?

By studying us, and following my guidance, you will learn how to build towards your goals and get there in a constant state of contentment and joy. Is that clear to you?"

"I think so," said the young man hesitatingly, "But I'm still uncertain of where to start, what exactly I must do next."

"That's easy," said Josmas, "Start by being good to yourself."

"I think that I am good to myself," retorted the young man quickly, "I eat as well as I can, buy clothes and things which I like, socialise, meet with friends and generally have a good time ... or as good a time as I can afford to have. I think that I enjoy my life, well mostly, but not the dismal earnings which greatly restrict my ability to enjoy myself!" He laughed lightly at his own satire, and added, "Of course my work is no fun nor the feeling I have of being adrift in life and headed nowhere."

That sparked Josmas to exclaim with a slap of his chair armrest,

"Exactly! You have described precisely why you are failing. You relate being good to yourself with physical pleasures and material gain. Like so many in the world you do not understand the true meaning of being good to yourself. So," and here he leaned forward in his chair as if to share some profound secret with the young man, "I'll tell you the real meaning of being good to yourself."

~

The young man found himself listening intently. In a lowered tone Josmas very carefully said,

"Forget being good to yourself ... Rather think being *true* to yourself."

He emphasised the word *true,* drawing it out loud and slow. Then he sat back and waited for the significance of what he had said to sink in to the young man's conscious. The response of his guest came by way of a quizzical tilt of the head and a puzzled grimace, so Josmas continued.

"Deep within you, far beyond the realm of your conscious mind, lives the real you. It's the part commonly referred to as your inner being or your spirit. It knows who you are and what it expects of you. Just like fine wine, your true self is incapable of lying to you. Each sip of wine whispers to your taste buds with unconditional honesty. So it is with your inmost soul.

The way that it reveals itself to you is through your passion. You have already told me today that you possess a real passion for books and hope to become a writer of note. That passion is your inner being talking to you. It is telling you exactly what it expects of you. When you ignore what it is saying then you are not being true to yourself. Can you understand that?"

This time the young man was able to respond positively and brightly.

"So what you are saying is that I must follow my passion and become a writer, whatever it takes?"

"Precisely," said Josmas, "When you follow the guidance of your spirit and act out in life the same feeling that resides within you, then you are being true to yourself. You have a purpose in life. And it gets better." He paused before continuing.

"When a man recognises his passion and makes it his purpose to pursue his passion then he will inevitably help others while doing so. Don't ask why. It's an absolute law of life. Doing what you most enjoy and doing it with vigour always rubs off on other people. There's more."

He sat back for a moment for what would be his final sip of Armagnac that night, before applying his 'coup de grâce'.

"When you help other people, material gain and financial wealth will find you." A pause. "Note my words, 'Wealth will find you', you need not, must not, seek it.

What you must do is be good to yourself by being true to yourself. Honour your inner spirit by enacting in life the passion that burns within you. Be who you are. Act and say what you do. Do what you say. You'll become known as a man of passion and integrity and – dare I repeat myself? - wealth will find you." And then, almost as an afterthought,

"Oh, and share your passion and purpose only with the brightest and best people, there are still a few to be found," here he smiled at his own gentle irony. "Rather no-one in your life than the mediocre." With that Josmas rose, quite abruptly, from his chair.

"Goodnight young man," he concluded, "I'll expect you at breakfast," and ambled from the room.

The young man sat before the fire, staring into the flickering embers, for a long time. This had been the most remarkable day of his young life. His mind was in a swirl; so much had happened, all of it unexpected. He barely knew where to begin in working out or analysing the day's events. He decided not to try.

Instead he drained his glass of its remaining Armagnac and got, slightly unsteadily, to his feet. Was it the Petrus, the Armagnac, the emotion of the day or a combination of all three that caused his light headedness? He cared not. He knew only that his life had been turned upside down, already changed irreversibly and that tomorrow was a day that he was already anticipating with relish. What further treasures would it hold? With a contented smile on his face, he dragged himself off to bed.

But his day was not yet finished.

~

When he got to his room, he found that a copy of D.H.Lawrence's erotic novel, *'Lady Chatterley's Lover'*, had been placed on the bedside table. He knew the book well but had never read it right through. It was open at a passage which read -

"And when he came into her, with an intensification of relief and consummation that was pure peace to him, she lay still, feeling his motion within her, his deep-sunk intentness, the sudden quiver of him at the springing of his seed, then the slow-subsiding thrust."

"What is Josmas telling me now?" wondered the young man; for surely it was his host who had placed, or ordered to have placed, the book in his room. It certainly had not been there when he first was shown to the room by Jocelyn nor when he had dressed and left for dinner.

Just then there was a timid knock on the door, immediately following which, it slowly opened. Jocelyn slipped quietly into the room. She was barefoot, her auburn hair loose and flowing. She wore only a semi-transparent, full length, lace negligée and clearly nothing else. Her nipples pushed aggressively forward and the young man saw from her form and the blood glowing warmly from behind her perfumed skin that she was indeed a fit and shapely woman. She carried a small, silver tray on which sat a single crystal dish (the young man could not yet see what it contained) and a silver spoon. Jocelyn spoke, "You forgot your dessert."

She moved to the edge of the bed and sat beside the young man. He could now see that in the bowl was golden honey. Jocelyn carefully scooped up a spoonful and held it to the young man's lips. She moved it around teasingly, tempting him to reach out his tongue to taste it. The young man reacted to this with total obedience. It was as if he were hypnotised, compelled to do just what Jocelyn led him to. Eventually the spoon touched his lips and he tongued his first taste of the nectar. Jocelyn held the spoon in his mouth for several seconds, then withdrew it slowly. Then she placed the spoon in her own mouth and slowly sucked on it while eyeing the young man through flirtatious lashes.

She replaced the spoon on the tray and put the tray aside on the bed. Turning more fully to the young man, her gleaming eyes fixed on his, Jocelyn slid the shoulder straps of her gown off and down, one at a time. First the left side strap with her right hand and then the right side strap with her left hand. The gown fell away, holding tantalisingly for a few seconds on the swell of her breasts before falling to her waist and revealing their firm beauty. The young man watched spellbound, lost for words and unsure what to do. He need not have concerned himself. The older woman was in full control.

She turned back to the honey pot, dipped her fingers in the honey and transferred the honey seductively to her own nipples. These still stood erect, a dark crimson against the white of her skin. Very slowly and provocatively, she massaged the honey around first one nipple and then the other, clearly relishing the experience. All the while Jocelyn looked directly into the eyes of the young man, sometimes lowering her gaze slightly and licking her own half parted lips.

She slowly raised one arm and put her hand around the back of the young man's neck, first caressing the nape and letting him feel the slightest scratch of her fingernails. Then she gently pulled his head forward and down to her breasts. With her free hand Jocelyn raised her left breast and presented the nipple to his waiting lips. The young man's mouth was already watering as with a starving man in anticipation of long denied nourishment.

Soon the nipple was between his teeth. He nibbled and sucked, savouring the combined flavour of her womanhood and the sweetness of the honey. He devoured one nipple, one breast and then the next nipple, the next breast. He alternated his attention between them as Jocelyn rubbed more of the honey on to them and moaned at each touch. With head thrown back and crying ever louder, she arched her back and pushed her chest ever more upwards to receive his lips, his tongue.

All at once she gave a great shudder, screamed lightly, lunged forward and clung on to the young man. She stayed like that, sobbing lightly for several minutes. The young man simply held her, enjoying the intimacy of her embrace while stroking her hair and her back.

Eventually Jocelyn eased back from his arms. The young man was unsure of what to next expect or what he should do. He wanted to proceed with the encounter to its next natural stage but something, the power of the woman, held him back. His dilemma was soon resolved. As she withdrew from his hold, she casually pulled her negligée up and around her shoulders. Standing up, visibly shakily, she rearranged her hair and picked up the tray. Then, without a word, Jocelyn crossed to the door and left.

For a long time the young man sat on the edge of the bed and didn't move. He was completely befuddled. The most incredible day of his short life had just become even more bizarre. What was he to make of it? He didn't know. He was delighted, confused, happy – yes he was smiling – and the sweet deliciousness of his 'Jocelyn and honey dessert' lingered on his lips. But mostly he was tired.

Quite without warning, the day caught up with him. He felt his head swirl and he fell straight back on the bed from where he sat on the edge. He passed out like a light. And that is exactly where the young man was found the following morning when his concerned host came looking for him.

Joseph T. Riach

THE BAD AND THE UGLY

Tommy pulled back his foreskin and started to 'jiggle his cock', as he called it. Masturbation had recently become a daily fascination for the twelve year old and he did it whenever the urge took him. On this occasion he was in the deserted gents' toilet of the equally deserted Rannoch Moor railway station, a remote place in the Scottish highlands. Lost in pleasuring himself thus, he was unaware of another human presence until he felt the hand placed on his shoulder and the words,

"I didn't know you did that?" Followed by, "Come on, the train is here."

Tommy abruptly ceased his 'jiggling', dropped the kilt he was wearing over his instantly flaccid penis and ashamedly followed his adult carer and travelling companion to the platform.

The companion was Hamish McIntosh. He was the secretary of the local climbing and hiking club of which Tommy's mum and dad, both avid mountain hikers, were members. An outgoing and popular bachelor among the hiking and climbing fraternity,

McIntosh had volunteered to take Tommy with him on a two week trek around the Scottish highlands during the school summer holidays. Tommy's parents readily agreed. They liked and trusted Hamish, a frequent visitor to their home, and welcomed the dual opportunity of having Tommy's mountain experience and knowledge of Scotland enhanced by the trip and of being free of him for a couple of weeks. Tommy was delighted with the opportunity too.

The route that McIntosh had planned for himself and Tommy to follow comprised of an extensive circular tour taking in a lot of wild territory and several climbs. There were flat stretches too and rest days when they didn't do too much or travelled by bus or train. This was one of the latter.

They got on to the train and Tommy settled back to watch the gorgeous scenery of mountains and rivers roll by. McIntosh read a book, 'The True Story Of The First Ascent Of Everest' by Sir Edmund Hilary. Little was said and no mention was made by either party to the earlier incident in the toilet. Tommy felt that he had been caught doing something naughty, something he was not supposed to do. He was grateful that there was no beating involved as he was sure would have been the case had it been either of his parents who had chanced upon him. Tommy resolved to forget the matter and just hoped that McIntosh would do likewise.

Besides, reckoned Tommy, the worst that could happen now would be that McIntosh would report him to his parents when he got home at the end of the holiday. As returning home was still almost the full two weeks in the future, that was far enough off in Tommy's young mind to seem very remote.

The overnight stays during their trip were split between camping out and staying in climbers' huts and hostels. Tommy's preference was camping out. He simply adored 'the great outdoors', sleeping rough, cooking on camp fires and washing down in freezing mountain streams. But the evening of the train journey was spent in a busy hostel in a small highland town and the next nights after that they shared with other climbers in cramped mountain bothies. It was some nights later before they camped out again.

By that time they were on the Isle of Skye and had hiked along the Trotternish peninsula, a massive highland ridge, to almost the northernmost point of the island. They set up camp in the shadow of an isolated rocky pinnacle. It was an awesome site with sunset views tinged indigo and violet stretching before them over the Atlantic Ocean to the west. Tommy collected twigs and some dry peat and lit the camp fire. McIntosh cooked fresh pigeon he caught in a trap. Tommy watched him do that and took careful note of the technique and skill involved. They feasted together then sat back against a boulder to finish off their meal; Tommy with lemonade and McIntosh with beer.

It was then that McIntosh reached into his sporran, the leather pouch he wore at the front of his kilt and a general depositary for cash, documents, pens and stuff, all the paraphernalia which most people carry in their pockets or handbags. Tommy thought that he was reaching for his compass as they had just prior to the moment been discussing their location and the route planned for the next day. Instead McIntosh produced a crumpled piece of paper and handed it to Tommy.

"You might like to see this," he said.

Tommy opened out the paper. There was a scribbled text written on it with the heading *'Doctor Mole'*. Tommy knew what this was. He had seen it before. It was an immature, erotic poem of the kind that pubescent boys share with school mates over giggles and lewd remarks; but such material also kindles a sexual reaction in young lads. Tommy was very surprised to have been handed this to read by an adult but wanted to enjoy the content. He started to read.

As he did so, his young penis immediately stiffened and gave him the warm throb which he experienced while masturbating. McIntosh, sitting close beside him, put his hand on Tommy's knee as if to lean in closer and share the read. Soon however, he moved his hand up Tommy's thigh below his kilt and found his erection.

"Not bad, not bad at all," he said rather hoarsely.

He held the immature member for a time and then started the rhythmic up and down motion which Tommy knew as cock jiggling. He did it quite slowly at first but soon increased the pace. The combined effect of the erotic material he was reading and having his cock pulled, and by someone other than himself, soon brought Tommy to a climax. McIntosh sensed the moment arising and, just before the gush of semen came, he pushed Tommy roughly on to his back, lifted his kilt up to fully expose his genitals and wrapped his mouth around his cock. As Tommy ejaculated, McIntosh sucked.

Tommy could do nothing. The physical pleasure in itself was undeniable yet, at the same time, he instinctively knew that something terribly wrong was going on. He wanted no further part in it. He needn't have worried. As quickly as the whole thing had started, it was over. McIntosh sat up quite abruptly, licked his lips and said, "Not bad," once again, then added, "Let's get some sleep."

With no further ado, he retired to inside their small mountain tent.

Tommy sat shell-shocked for some time. His erect penis had subsided as quickly as it had risen and, in place of the excitement he had felt while reading the 'dirty poem', he felt confused and then angry. He screwed the *'Doctor Mole'* paper into a ball and threw it on to the embers of the camp fire. As he watched it burn, he vowed to himself that there would never be a repeat of what had just happened. As would become the case in all his endeavours throughout his life, Tommy would be as good as his word.

Tommy did not go into the tent that night. Fortunately, the weather was mild and dry and would remain so for most of the rest of the trip. He snuggled into his mountain bag and slept in the open; except he didn't sleep much. His mind was racing, going over again and again what had occurred.

"Should I tell someone?" he thought, but then, "Who to tell?" He was in really wild territory, miles from anywhere. "Anyway, who would believe me?"

He was a kid, his travelling companion and carer a respected adult. Lastly, and what seemed to be of greatest importance to Tommy, was the undeniable fact that he had enjoyed the physical pleasure he had felt. Because of that, he felt guilty, ashamed and kind of responsible for what had happened. The fact that he did not appreciate McIntosh's behaviour and already despised the man for what he had done to him, cut no ice. He felt that he could not expose himself to the shame or ridicule of confessing to what he had been involved in. He decided to say nothing to anyone.

The experience left Tommy – bemused – is the only word. It was the first time that he'd shared an intimate sexual act with another person, albeit that he had neither asked for it nor would he have. Although in those years there was less publicity and less general knowledge regarding homosexuals, rape and abuse in the public domain and among younger people, Tommy and his peers knew that homosexuals existed. The lads called the ones who preyed on young boys 'poofs'.

As regards Tommy and his friends knowing about queer men who might take advantage of them, it was common knowledge to them that the leader of their local Boy Scout group was 'like that'. But had he tried anything with any of his boys the fathers would simply have got hold of him and given him a good kicking in down a dark alley. So nothing ever happened and, if it had, it was dealt with.

There was no such thing as being traumatised by such events. The term and publicity surrounding it didn't exist. Therefore no-one got traumatised. Tommy certainly didn't. He, although only twelve years old, dealt with the situation. It was over and done, certainly would never be repeated, and he got on with life and growing up. A valuable lesson learned and an experience not to be repeated.

The morning following the assault, McIntosh emerged from the tent at first light and readied himself for the day. He behaved perfectly normally, as if nothing out of the usual or untoward had occurred. For Tommy it was different, he felt hurt and vulnerable. He decided however to get on with the trip and make the most of it. Although Tommy became sullen and resentful with McIntosh and refused to speak to him most of the time or allow any physical contact between them, he set about continuing to enjoy the hiking, climbing and the country life in general.

He reasoned that the weather was good for sleeping outside, so that is what he would do and leave the tent to his abuser. Anyway, there were only a couple of nights in their remaining schedule in which they would be camping out. Most other nights they would be sleeping with other people around them in a mountain hut or hostel. The last night of their trip was one.

~

In the late afternoon Tommy and McIntosh arrived at a popular climbers' hostel which McIntosh used a lot. He was well known there. The hostel was large enough to justify having a full time, on site warden. A chubby, jolly farmer's wife, her name was Betty McGee.

Betty prepared mugs of steaming tea for Tommy and McIntosh when they arrived and chatted to them for a long time in the kitchen. She was particularly interested to know all about their trip, where they had been, what they had seen and what they had done. Eventually McIntosh left to go through to the communal dormitory to unpack his rucksack, leaving Tommy alone with Betty.

As soon as he left, Betty moved closer to Tommy and, in a conspiratorial whisper, asked him, "Did he try anything with you?"

Tommy didn't need to answer. He immediately turned a bright red. He tried to stammer a belated, "No," but the word wouldn't come. She moved closer again and put a motherly arm around his shoulder.

"Never you mind. He won't try anything here. But," she added, "If he does, use some of this."

She went to a drawer in the kitchen table, took out a small, brown paper bag and took it over to Tommy. Handing it to him she said, "It's dried, ground chilli peppers."

Tommy was none the wiser. At that age he hadn't a clue what they were. Sensing his ignorance, Betty went on, "Just throw some in his face if he comes near you. He won't come back a second time."

Still Tommy did not really comprehend. He had no idea as to what effect the chilli powder would have when thrown at someone. He was soon to find out.

Many years later, Tommy wondered at the fact that there clearly were people who knew McIntosh, saw through him and realised what he was capable of. That they never reported him nor did anything about it remained a mystery of the times.

For now though, Tommy took the bag and mumbled a, "Thank you," to Betty. He felt more drawn to her as a caring mother figure at that instant than he ever did to his own mum.

He left the kitchen to go through to the dormitory. On his way there he stopped off at the gents' toilet, in need of relieving himself after the large cups of builders' tea Betty had welcomed him with. McIntosh was already standing at the urinal. When he saw Tommy enter, he turned to face him and said, "What do think of that?"

His penis was exposed and erect. The member seemed huge to Tommy's junior eye. But, in a blink of that eye, he plunged one hand into the bag of chillis which he held in his other hand, drew out a handful of the powder and chucked it straight into McIntosh's face. Then, for good measure, he tipped the remainder of the bag's contents over McIntosh's cock. He ran from the toilets with McIntosh screaming behind him. As he headed for the kitchen, McIntosh gave up the chase.

Betty McGee had heard the commotion and came running to meet Tommy at the kitchen door as he arrived. He blurted out to her what had happened. She immediately pulled Tommy over to the kitchen sink and started to run his hands under the cold water tap.

"Did you get any in your eyes? Let me see," she said. She examined his face and asked if he felt any burning sensation.

"No," said Tommy, "Only on my hands. They are red hot."

"Well," replied Betty, "Just imagine what our friend is feeling!" then laughed out loud and couldn't stop.

Soon Tommy joined in too and, when other climbers arrived to see what was going on and learned the reason for Betty and Tommy's hilarity, they joined in also. Soon everyone was doubled over in laughter. The story went round the hostel like wildfire. Tommy became the hero of the hour and McIntosh an object of derision.

Some climbers went in search of him, intent on 'sorting him out'. But he slunk away from the hostel via a back door soon after the initial chaos. Those who saw McIntosh leave described him as crimson faced, unable to see and walking in obvious discomfort with a peculiar, almost comical, shuffle.

~

The next day Betty McGee drove Tommy home. She explained to his parents why it was she and not McIntosh who had brought him back. Neither Tommy's mum nor dad asked Tommy if he was alright. But his dad, on hearing the news, exploded into a rage such as Tommy had never seen; not even when Tommy had torched the family home or when he had flipped grandad from his coffin.

His dad went straight on the telephone to his friend Gordon Diack, a thickset ex-army man. Between them they quickly rounded up a possé of other fathers and then, armed with an assorted arsenal of wrenches, pick-axe handles and crowbars, they went out to find McIntosh and 'fix him for good'. When they got to McIntosh's apartment, they were too late. The police had beaten them to it. They had picked up McIntosh just minutes before.

It later transpired that McIntosh had turned up at the casualty department of the local hospital in the early hours of that morning. The serious condition of the burns to his eyes and to his genitals had led the medical staff to alert the police as they suspected that he had been involved in something untoward. When the law officers arrived at the hospital, McIntosh told them that he had been fooling around on his own with the chilli powder and that his injuries were an accident of his own making. The police had little alternative but to believe him, and left.

When they got back to the police headquarters however, they learned that a Betty McGee, a warden at an out of town climbers' hostel, had been in to tell of an unsavoury incident at the hostel the previous evening. Several climbers had also visited to report the same occurrence. The policemen put two and two together and raced back to the hospital to apprehend McIntosh. He had already left. They missed him by just a couple of minutes.

After the visit of the police to the hospital, Mcintosh guessed that he was in trouble. He rushed home from the hospital in order to pack his bag and flee town. He was descending the stairs from his apartment when he met the police on their way up.

Unknown to McIntosh, the police officers' arrival saved him from a terrible beating. He had no sooner been bundled into their squad car and driven off when Tommy's dad and his friends arrived.

News of McIntosh's arrest appeared in the media that same evening. In little time, the families of several other young victims came forward to report incidents similar to Tommy's experience. Any doubt about his guilt as a serial molester of boys was eradicated when the police searched his apartment. They found general paedophilic pornography and, more tellingly, the names and addresses of a host of boys whom McIntosh had taken on camping, hiking and climbing expeditions. Most damning however, were photographs of McIntosh in the act of assaulting many of his victims. He had preserved these as mementos of his sickening regime and in the arrogant belief that his perversions would never come to light. Now they became confirmations of his guilt.

When news of Tommy's chilli powder defence came out, McIntosh's public humiliation was complete. Many thought the considerable pain inflicted on him by one of his victims to be a most fitting punishment. He was in due course tried for his crimes, convicted and sentenced to four years imprisonment.

Tommy, along with his parents, the police and all of decent society, hoped never to set eyes on the miscreant again.

~

The events of that summer changed Tommy dramatically. Previous to the hiking holiday with McIntosh, he had been a mischievous boy attending primary school. Afterwards he became a delinquent teenager attending secondary school.

Shaking off the shackles of his 'permanent grounding' years and parental beatings, he became fiercely independent and a law unto himself. The only discipline in his life became that discipline which he imposed on himself; particularly with regard to physical fitness and football training. Other than that he did what he wanted, when he wanted.

Strangely perhaps, in light of his open hostility to authority in any shape or form, he enjoyed his new senior school. The one misdemeanour he was not guilty of was playing truant. Tommy never skipped school because he found it just so much fun to be there and creating mayhem. Every day, from the moment he arrived at school in the morning to the time that he left it in the late afternoon, was just one continuous riot of laughter for Tommy and his friends.

Gone was the regimental discipline of primary school, now his school day was split into several periods and Tommy moved freely around the school between them. He studied a variety of subjects in different classrooms and with different teachers. In truth Tommy did little studying, at least not of the formal kind, but he found the teachers to be fascinating. They were an odd assortment and that's where the fun began.

Most of the teachers approached their work with the objective of treating Tommy, and all their pupils, as young adults. The difficulty for them was that Tommy didn't behave like one. He was more intent on taking the mickey and he was quick-witted enough to be rather good at it. He gave every one of his masters a nickname appropriate to their general demeanour, the clothes they wore, their mannerisms, their speech or their favourite sayings. These provided a source of endless hilarity for Tommy and his classmates.

There was Cocky Hunter, a scruffy little maths teacher who resembled a rag and bone man. He cycled to and from school on a wreck of a bike with a rusty chain which clanked. He could be heard rattling along the road long before he could be seen. Tommy regularly sought to 'help him out' by squirting lubricating oil on the handle grips and saddle of his bike while it was parked in the school yard. By the time that Cocky finished lessons for the day and went to collect his bike, there was a throng of schoolboys hiding behind the bicycle shed waiting to see him get covered in grease – again!

Hairy Mary taught geography. She had the movement and grace of a young fashion model but the face of the 'incredible bearded lady' at a funfair sideshow. Waiting for the class to settle down at the start of a lesson, she would call, "I'm waiting!" Then, when the hubbub and chatter continued, would call again, "I'm still waiting!" Needless to say, Tommy and his chums did everything to ensure that she was still waiting come time for the class to end.

Query Will was Tommy's art teacher. He was not queer, well not in the vulgar sense of the word popular at the time, but he was strange. His name derived from his propensity to query everything that his pupils did and also to his remarkable physical shape. Viewed from the side he resembled a giant, walking question mark. From his feet to his midriff was a vertical line but then, at his waist, his body bent backwards almost at a right angle. From there it slowly turned upwards to his massive, rounded shoulders before his head hung out and forward on his downward slanting neck. Whenever Query asked Tommy, "Why?" Tommy's favourite reply was, "Take a look at yourself sir!" This caused hysterical laughter in the class, to which Query would turn, look and say, "Why?" Cue for entire class to fall about uncontrollably.

Mr.Snowflake Tate, of the English department, was another 'why' man. What became his catch phrase was, "Why was there civil war?" except that he mispronounced 'civil war' as 'seevee woh'. The objective of the class every lesson was to get him to say 'civil war' in his own, remarkable way. On the occasions when, despite their best efforts and the use of every contrivance they could think of, the class could not get him to say the magic words, Tommy simply approached him at the end of the lesson and asked,

"Please sir, would you say civil war for me?"

Snowflake (so called because of his chronic dandruff which regularly blanketed the shoulders of his dark jacket) inevitably replied,

"Why do you want me to say seevee woh?" - at which everyone collapsed in laughter yet again.

Snowflake though was a 'good guy'. He frequented a pub close to the school and went there every night after lessons. Tommy and his crew were already visiting such places and, despite their age, getting served. On the occasions that they bumped into Snowflake in his favourite watering hole, they shared beers and jokes with him. Snowflake never reported any of the lads to the school as he was required to do.

Hatchet Hemmingway was quite the opposite. He had made it his mission in life to catch and report for misbehaviour every errant schoolboy he possibly could. Hatchet wore a raincoat and a tweed hat just like those of Inspector Clouseau of comedy film fame and behaved in exactly the same clumsy, pseudo spy-like manner.

He knew that many of the boys went to a local snooker hall after school. The hall was strictly out of bounds for the pupils as such places were, in the eyes of the school hierarchy, dens of iniquity where 'criminals hung out'; that reputation of course being exactly what attracted the youths to them in the first place.

Hatchett lurked outside the hall every day after school hours, his hat pulled down to conceal his eyes and the collar of his raincoat turned up. His strategy was to note the names of all the boys he saw entering or exiting and then report them to the headmaster at the school for punishment the next day. His disguise was so ineffective and his presence so well known to every schoolboy 'within a fifty mile radius' that Tommy would come out of the snooker hall, cross the road immediately to where Hatchet thought himself to be concealed and introduce himself with,

"Hi there sir. Almost didn't see you. It's Tommy. That's two 'm's and a capital T."

Mister Lockie was a physics master with an extremely broad, highland accent. At times it was almost impossible for Tommy, or anyone, to make sense of what he was saying – even for those pupils who hailed from the same part of the world as he did!

On one occasion Tommy completed an exam paper with his answers written entirely in the phonetic sound of Lockie's accent. Of course the paper was returned to Tommy with a nil mark and Tommy was called on to explain the gibberish of his answers. He replied,

"I have answered exactly as you have instructed. I have repeated all your teachings, just as you said them. If you can't understand my work, then who can?"

Tommy was duly cuffed round the ear and hauled off to see the headmaster of the school. To him, Tommy repeated his explanation of events. After listening, with what started as a suppressed grin on his face and ended with a broad smile, the headmaster said,

"Yes, I see, you do have a point. But you'll have to apologise." Tommy returned to his class and did apologise to Mr.Lockie as instructed – in broad highland dialect of course!

Fun as these daily escapades were, they did not come close to satisfying Tommy's grander aspirations in the field of getting up to no good. His education and upbringing in general, and the school in particular, encouraged pupils to think for themselves above all else. Academic success for its own sake was considered important but less so than showing initiative and learning to work things out independently. Tommy felt it to be his duty to demonstrate to all and sundry that he could put that principle into practice.

His imagination and ambition extended to the realisation of

events of disruption far in excess of what had been attempted before. Where better to exhibit his ingenuity and free thinking spirit than in the school itself? And he had two major initiatives in mind.

~

A swimming pool had been under construction at the school Tommy attended for two years prior to his arrival there. Shortly after Tommy came to the school the pool opened for use. Work on the pool building however was still ongoing and it was this that created Tommy's opportunity. He noted while attending his swimming sessions and life-saving lessons that, with workmen still coming and going, access to the pool was not one hundred percent secure. In particular the pool could be accessed through ventilation hatches on the roof. Tommy's first idea was to go 'midnight swimming'.

Tommy's good friend, Haggis, so called because his mother was a prize winning cook of the famous Scottish dish, lived directly across from the school. Tommy and the other members of their group gathered there of an evening to enjoy a few beers, listen to pop music and generally misbehave. When midnight came on the appointed evening of the first midnight swim, they crossed the road from Haggis's home to the school.

Earlier in the day they had moved one of the workmen's ladders which were lieing around the grounds and concealed it by the perimeter wall. Using the ladder, they climbed up and easily got over the wall. Then they ran to the side of the swimming pool building and, using another of the workmen's ladders, similarly 'borrowed' and concealed earlier, they scaled the thirty feet to the flat roof. On the roof, they detached the bolts holding one of the ventilation hatches in place and then, using a rope ladder, in this case 'borrowed' from the school's army cadet corp, they shimmied down and into the pool. Thus did Tommy and his pals enjoy midnight swimming sessions in the school pool on a semi-regular basis.

Towards the end of the school term, Tommy realised that the nocturnal visits of he and his friends to the pool would have to end. The building works were almost completed and the contractors were already removing equipment from the site. Concluding checks would result in the roof hatches being secured from the inside. So Tommy 'hatched' his final daring plan.

He and his friends would surreptitiously pay a midnight visit to the pool one last time – but not to go swimming!

~

William Williams, nicknamed Bill Squared by Tommy, was Tommy's chemistry teacher. It was he who first introduced Tommy to potassium permanganate. Tommy learned that the chemical compound dissolved in water to create an intensely pink or purple solution. Only a few crystals were needed to discolour a large quantity of water. That knowledge gave Tommy a 'brilliant idea' for some serious fun. He duly 'borrowed' a whole fifty centilitre jar from the science laboratory. His dastardly plan was to dye the school swimming pool purple!

On the appointed night Tommy and friends met in Haggis's house across the road as before. At midnight, and armed with the jar of potassium permanganate crystals, they crossed the road to the school and scaled the fence as before. They went to the swimming pool building, raised the ladder and climbed up to the roof as before. They went to open the ventilation hatch as before – but it wouldn't budge. It had already been sealed from the inside.

Disappointed, Tommy climbed back down. His friends followed, all ready to make their way back to their base on the other side of the road, drink more beer and debrief on the failure of their mission.

On an impulse, Tommy decided to take a last look around the building. He had seen workmen in the process of replacing a door at the back earlier in the day. When he went to examine it he found that they had not completed installation of the new door. They had temporarily boarded up the opening instead, presumably with the intention of returning to complete the job the next day. Tommy quickly summoned his mates who had already started to make their way back across the yard to the wall.

Between them, and with the help of some builders' tools left lieing nearby, Tommy and his friends easily removed the boarding. From there it was simple enough to find their way to the pool, tip the potassium permanganate crystals into it and make their getaway. They stopped to replace the boarding on the temporary door and, in no time at all, they were back in the safety of Haggis's house across the road. Their combined adrenalin rush and quite a few beers kept them bubbling excitedly about the success of their venture through the night.

Eventually, in the early hours of the morning, Tommy and the others drifted off to their respective homes. They had only a couple of hours to rest and to recover their composure before turning up 'all innocent' at school in the morning to find out the success or otherwise of their vandalism and the extent of the disruption caused.

When Tommy arrived at the school gates the first thing he saw were the policemen. Two stood outside the gates as if guarding them and two police cars were parked inside in the school grounds. Several police officers were gathered around them. Tommy made his way past them and to the great hall for morning assembly. The headmaster's mood was severe as he rose to speak.

"There was a break in at the school last night," he commenced, "Nothing is stolen but a substance has been put into the swimming pool. As a result all swimming activities for today and until further notice are cancelled."

At this time there were audible groans from those pupils who had been due time in the pool that day and had been looking forward to it. Tommy felt sorry for them. There were also giggles from some elements in the hall too. These were the pupils who had already got wind of what had happened.

"The pool," continued the headmaster, "Must be drained. It and all the equipment will have to be inspected and cleaned, repairs made if necessary. This is not funny."

At this point he stopped and stared around the hall. Some lads who were tittering felt his gaze fall on them but Tommy sat stony faced. The headmaster continued,

"There is considerable expense involved in all of this Apart from the money there is the cost of disruption to school life and activities. The police have been called in and they may wish to question certain individuals. If that is you," and again he paused and his gaze swept around the room causing some with guilty consciences to cringe, "Then you will be summoned during the day. That is all."

In the event neither Tommy, nor any of his friends, were called upon. The police did talk to some senior form pupils. It seemed that any suspicions they had were focussed on older boys. Nothing came of their investigations of course. The crime remained unsolved.

With access to the pool barred, all pupils including Tommy were denied the opportunity to see the result of his handiwork. Days later however, Tommy was told on good authority by a builder who had been at the pool on the morning of the dyeing, that the result was spectacular. He confirmed that the whole pool had been transformed into a bright, brilliant purple!

"Whoever pulled that stunt had quite some nerve," cooed the brickie.

Tommy smiled and said nothing. He was pleased to know that someone recognised talent when they saw it.

~

After the hiatus of the purple pool escapade, Tommy found that he felt rather deflated. Life in the school did gradually return more to normal, or at least as close to normal as Tommy and friends permitted. He and his mates still enjoyed their daily fun. The incessant winding up of their hapless teachers continued unabated along with daily pranks aimed at all and sundry.

A favourite, and particularly disgusting stunt, was to cover the top of the toilet bowls in the staff toilets with clingfilm. With the transparent covering in place, the seat of the toilet was lowered over it and unsuspecting victims would not know until way too late that the clingfilm was there. By then their 'human waste' had spilled out everywhere except in the bowl!

Those toilets exclusively for the use of masters and administrative staff were out of bounds to pupils of course and permanently locked. The key hung in the school's general office in the administration department. Pupils were not permitted, and rarely required, to go there. The trick for those pupils determined, for whatever reason, to access the office was to have a valid reason for the visit. That was most easily acquired, as Tommy discovered through frequent experience, by misbehaving in class to such an extent that the master in question sent him to 'administration' to make a punishment appointment with the headmaster.

The wait to see the headmaster invariably involved a long delay in the reception area of the general office. From there it was a simple task for Tommy to reach over the public counter and nick the staff toilet key from the hook on which it hung. Then he made the excuse of needing to go to the toilet himself. He went to the staff toilet of course, set up his 'ambush', locked up behind him, returned to the office, replaced the key on the hook and waited for the headmaster.

When, some time later, all hell broke loose as an incensed master stormed from the toilets soaked in their own mess and demanding that the culprit be found and all but guillotined, Tommy had the perfect alibi. He had been with the headmaster receiving punishment at the time!

~

Tommy was never a smoker of cigarettes, nor of anything else. His dedication to sport and physical fitness saw to that. But many of his friends did smoke cigarettes. They, and the countless other smokers of all ages in the school, were generally referred to as the 'smokers' union'. The union met each day at mid-morning break in the pupils' toilet at the far end of the school, the one furthest from the general office, administration and masters' rooms. There was no actual 'meeting'. The occasion was just a case of all the smokers going there for a desperately needed puff between classes.

Smoking was frowned on by the school. Smoking while in school uniform and on the school premises was considered to be a particularly heinous offence.

So, when the headmaster got wind of what was going on right under his nose so to speak, he vowed to put a stop to it. He wanted to catch the culprits red-handed and make an example of them. Unfortunately for the headmaster, just as he had 'gotten wind' of the smokers' union and their exploits, so too did Tommy 'get wind of' his intention to launch a raid on the mid-morning smokefest. Tommy's informant not only told Tommy of the intended raid but also disclosed the exact day and time. Tommy soon warned all of his smoker friends regarding the headmaster's intended coup. He also shared with them a 'wizard' plan he had in mind to frustrate it.

So it was that on the appointed morning of the headmaster's raid, the headmaster marched into the pupils' toilet at the head of an impressive possé of other masters and prefects (pupils appointed to liase with staff and provide a positive role model). Among the 'role models' was Tommy's 'mole', himself an avid smoker! The sight that greeted the headmaster as he entered the latrines totally confounded him.

He found the facility absolutely crammed full of pupils, more than two hundred of them. There was literally no room to move, barely room to breath in fact. There were boys of all ages there, from every form, and every one of them, so thought the headmaster, caught in the act of smoking. He believed in that moment that the smoking problem in the school, of which he had previously heard only vague rumours, was in fact a full blown epidemic. Now though, he had the opportunity to 'wipe out the plague' in one dramatic swoop. The vermin were all here, trapped like rats and about to meet their fate. And, right at the head of the pack was ... Tommy!

He, along with every other boy there, surreptitiously hid his hands behind his back and assumed an exaggeratedly guilty demeanour. If the headmaster picked up on the act or suspected for a moment that all was not quite as it appeared to be, then he didn't show it.

"You boy," demanded the headmaster of Tommy, "What is in your hand! Show me!"

Tommy slowly moved his left hand from behind his back and held it palm open to the headmaster. It was empty.

"The other hand too," demanded the headmaster.

Tommy replaced his left hand behind his back and, slowly as before, presented his empty right hand for the headmaster to inspect.

"Both hands boy, I want to see both hands. Now!" shouted the increasingly angered head of the school.

This was the moment that Tommy, every boy crushed into the toilets and practically every pupil of the school, most of whom now formed an unruly mob of spectators outside the toilets, was waiting for. Very deliberately he brought both hands from behind his back to reveal that he was holding … a cream bun!

"What is that?" spluttered the headmaster, totally caught off guard by the surprise exposure.

"It's a cream bun, sir," said Tommy in mock innocence.

"I can see that," roared the headmaster, "But what is it doing in here?"

"Being eaten, sir."

That brought the house down. By now everyone, including some of the masters, was laughing. A few teachers though did manage to keep their composure and the serious demeanour demanded of the occasion.

"Why are you eating that in here?" pressed on the headmaster, determined not to be defeated but by now starting to sense that his anticipated triumphant purge of the smokers' union was in danger of descending into farce. "Don't you know it's unhygienic to consume food in a toilet?"

"There's less smoke pollution here than on the street sir ... and it's cold outside," answered Tommy, to the barely suppressed glee of the smokers.

"Get out ... and report to my study at close of classes," was the headmaster's frosty response.

Then he turned to the rest of the crowd, all still with their hands hidden behind their backs. He was still hopeful that they were concealing cigarettes. As there was no way that he and his enforcers could get into the toilets to confront each pupil, he instead ordered everyone out. As they filed past him at the entrance, the masters and prefects stopped each boy and had them show what was in their hands. Every single boy repeated a version of Tommy's 'reluctant guilt act'; and every single boy eventually revealed ... a cream bun!

A subsequent search of the toilets by the masters and prefects revealed no concealed cigarettes nor discarded butts. No evidence of any kind in fact to incriminate anyone. As the headmaster could not facilitate all of the 'toilet and cream bun' participants in his study after classes, Tommy's scheduled appearance there was cancelled. Apart from insubordination there was no 'crime' to charge him or any other pupil with.

The following day the headmaster addressed the entire school at morning assembly as was his daily custom. He recounted the event of the previous day and expressed to the gathering how surprised and disgusted he had been to find that eating of snacks in the toilets was common place. He treated his audience to a lengthy discourse on food hygiene and the dangers of disease; at the end of which he stated that eating in the school toilets was henceforth forbidden. Notices to that effect were subsequently posted in every toilet. No mention was ever made of smoking!

~

About this time Tommy was taking an increasing interest in girls. But his hopelessly naive attempts at chatting up prospective dates were pathetic in the extreme and doomed to failure.

His, "Haven't I seen you some place before?" was met with a dry, "Yes, that's why I don't go there any more." And when he tried a, "Can I buy you a drink?" to a girl who caught his eye in the local soda fountain café, she disparagingly replied, "I'd rather have the money!"

These, and other notable failed forays in the amorous encounter department, persuaded Tommy that, for the timebeing at least, his talent and future still lay in the world of causing mayhem and sticking a middle digit up at authority. With the achievement of the purple swimming pool adventure behind him, Tommy turned his imaginative mind to his next 'grand project'. But what could possibly match the audacity of that outstanding plot?

He concluded that, whatever it was, it had to be more visible to more people than the swimming pool episode. However impressive the success of the purple pool project, the fact remained that, widespread as knowledge of the escapade was, (and yes it had even reached the local newspaper), very few people actually ever saw the purple pool. That included himself. He felt that he had to come up with something more visible, an event that would be directly witnessed by many. But what?

As with anyone who has a mind open to finding an opportunity and actively seeks it, the answer to his dilemma soon arrived. It was as unexpected as it was pure genius – or so thought Tommy.

One day, while browsing in the window of the local joke factory – a shop which sold an endless variety of novelty items and juvenile pranks such as farting cushions, itching powder and stink bombs – his eyes alighted on Chinese fire crackers and, right beside them, electrically ignited smoke bombs. The solution to Tommy's next project conundrum came to him in a flash ... He would blow up the headmaster of the school!

When, later that same evening, he excitedly put his proposal to his friends, they were at first sceptical.

"You can't blow up the headmaster!" they exclaimed, "We're not bloody terrorists."

They calmed down somewhat when Tommy explained,

"I don't mean it literally guys. I just mean it to look like it."

He then outlined to them what he had in mind.

"As with the swim pool stunt," he went on, "It will need a team like before and it must be planned and executed with military precision. Are you in?" There was no question but that the answer would be a resounding – "Yes!"

~

Thus it came to pass that, on the last day of the school term, Tommy and his friends took up their positions in the school hall for morning assembly. Tommy sat at the back of the hall. In his pocket he had a small electric torch battery. At the designated moment he touched the battery point with the open end of a light electric cable. This wire ran along the floor from where he was seated, the full length of the hall, up on to the stage at the front and into the two smoke bombs and fire crackers concealed below the lectern at which the headmaster made his morning address.

The 'bombs' and the cabling were placed there the previous evening at the end of the school choral and dramatic society's end of term presentation. Installing them proved easy for Haggis who was a cast member of the show and Tommy's collaborator assigned the task. In the general melee of the audience leaving and the hall being tidied for the next morning, he nipped on and off the stage unseen in seconds. The lectern was always covered with a full length, velvet cloth which concealed the apparatus perfectly. The cables too were well hidden. They ran from the lectern through the extensive flower arrangements which surrounded the stage and were thus invisible to the casual eye.

As Tommy took his seat at the back of the hall, another two members of the gang seated themselves at the very front over where the cables ran from the stage and back through the hall. Their task was, as soon as the smoke bombs went off, to cut the ignition wires and kick the short ends away from where they sat and towards the stage. This ensured that no-one could find the source of the ignition of the bombs. At the same moment, Tommy reeled in the trailing wires from his position at the back of the hall. As soon as he did that he passed the battery and wires to another accomplice who, in the general panic and hilarity of the moment, left the hall. Thus there was no evidence to be had of who had planted the bombs and crackers, ignited them or was otherwise involved in the dastardly deed.

Once all of the school's pupils, the masters and assorted staff had assembled in the hall they remained standing for the headmaster to make his customary grand entrance and mount the stage. This he did and took up his place at the lectern. He motioned for the assembly to be seated. He signaled for quiet and started to speak.

"Good morn ... " is as far as he got. At that moment Tommy touched the wires. The bombs fizzed off, the crackers banged and the headmaster disappeared in a flash of light and a cloud of smoke.

In a touch which turned out to be a master stroke, one of the gang who was a leading light in the school photographic society, was primed with his SLR camera ready for the moment. He jumped to his feet, also unobserved in the general bedlam of the moment, and ran off a series of shots of the headmaster standing speechless and bemused in a cloud of smoke. The resulting photos showed him surrounded by his fellow masters in various comic poses, jumping to their feet, falling over each other and generally bumbling about in Charlie Chaplin-like confusion. Two days later the images, anonymously donated of course, were the front page feature of the local newspaper. For Tommy – fame at last!

On this occasion, there was no police involvement. Only a thorough 'internal investigation' into the incident which went on all day. In this instance Tommy's name did feature heavily among the prime suspects but, with no evidence to link him, or anyone else, directly to the crime, and no-one prepared to 'turn Queen's evidence', there was little the headmaster or any part of the school hierarchy could do. It was the last day of term. They reluctantly adopted a 'tomorrow the horrors will be gone' attitude.

But, courtesy of the hilarious photographs which preserved the moment for posterity, the infamous 'blowing up of the headmaster' caper lived on in the collective memory. Tommy's reputation as a hellraiser par excellence was assured.

THE MAN WHO PAINTED A TRAIN

It was ten o'clock and the young man had still not shown up for breakfast. Josmas himself went to look for him. He knocked on the young man's bedroom door and, when there was no reply, let himself in.

The young man lay across the bed, legs dangling loosely over the side, and still fully dressed as he had been at dinner the previous night. It proved impossible to arouse him and he didn't seem to be breathing. Josmas had Jocelyn, who appeared less concerned about the young man than he, summon the paramedics. By the time they arrived, the young man was already stirring. A checkover of heart, blood pressure and other vital functions revealed nothing untoward. It was concluded that the young man had simply fallen exhausted into the deepest of deep sleeps; this being a not uncommon condition, particularly with young people subjected to excessive effort, excitement and lack of rest over a long period as had been the case with the young man.

As the young man himself pointed out later, he made a 'drop of the hat' decision to travel to France. He set off on the arduous journey with scant preparation and little prior sleep or food. He rested and ate even less en route and arrived to a succession of surprises and exhausting experiences. There was also the heat and humidity of the region, intense at the time of the year, and quite foreign to a fair haired, light skinned, young man hailing from cooler, northern climes. As is the case with young people, he recovered quickly.

Nonetheless it was agreed that the young man should have a quiet day. After a very light salad lunch consumed on a terrace overlooking the magnificent rose garden which Josmas had himself planted and which he lovingly tended morning and evening each day, he was treated to a tour of the vineyards. The winemaker enthusiastically regaled the young man with the story of wine and how it is made; with particular reference, of course, to his own particular vines and wines and the estate in which they were strolling.

"When I acquired this property," Josmas confided, "It was run down and derelict. The château had been abandoned for many years, the land was but a barren wilderness."

"Wow, kind of like my life," thought the young man, but said nothing.

"Yet," continued Josmas, "When I looked at it I didn't see a ruin, I saw an opportunity. I recognised that here lay the chance to create something fabulous, a place of wonder in which I and countless others could find joy and fulfillment. So I asked the owners to give me the property."

"Surely you mean 'sell' you the property," interjected the young man, confident that Josmas had made a slip of the tongue.

"No," shot back Josmas, "I asked them to give me the property ... as in give it to me for nothing, free, no payment."

"You what!" spluttered the young man, "You just came straight out and said 'give me the property for free', just like that?"

"Exactly," said Josmas, "Just like that."

"That took a bit of nerve," came back the young man, "Surely it was rather cheeky. Didn't they just laugh at you?"

"Yes young man, as a matter of fact that is exactly what they did. They did laugh at me."

"How did you react to that?" asked the young man, "Did you get angry?"

"Far from it," said Josmas, "I let them laugh. I gave them time to get over their enjoyment of what they saw as an audacious piece of nonsense, a joke. Once they quietened down, I said nothing. I waited calmly and I stared at them pointedly. Then I cleared my throat and repeated to them slowly and very deliberately what I had said before. I restated that I wanted them to give me the estate, the château, the entire property and everything in it for absolutely nothing, zero. Then I stayed silent in order to allow the seriousness of my proposition to sink in."

At this point the young man too was silent, waiting fascinated to learn what happened next.

Josmas went on, "After a short time I continued by pointing out to them that the property had been derelict these many years and painted a bleak picture of the further decay that would occur in future. I reminded them of the not insubstantial regular costs they were incurring on an ongoing basis. I knew the precise figures involved from my research into the business, my due diligence.

Again I paused to give time for that to sink in with them. I could see they were rattled.

Next I followed up by 'painting' an entirely different, optimistic and inspiring picture of how the estate would flourish under my custodianship. I 'showed' them the valley full of healthy vines, surrounding villages in full employment with workers feeding happy families, a magnificently restored château and a cellar of vintage wines selling for thousands at auction.

Lastly, I asked them how many bottles of my high quality wine they would like to receive free from the estate every year in perpetuity once I had it up, running and producing. I suggested two figures, both of which pleasantly surprised the owners. They chose the higher quantity of course. It was lower than I would have gone to. With that the deal was concluded. I moved in one month later."

"That is amazing!" cooed the young man, "Unbelieveable."

"Not really," said Josmas casually, "You see, I simply asked for what I wanted. I wanted them to give me the property for free, so I asked for just that. In life you must ask for what you want. However improbable your request, you have no chance at all of realising it unless you state it. Often you will be rejected. As in the case of these vineyards, sometimes you won't. Of course there's a second reason that the sellers agreed to my request."

"And that was ... ?" queried the young man dutifully.

"I delivered on what I promised," replied Josmas, "Or rather, I impressed on them with my self-confident assertiveness that I was a man to be relied on, that I would deliver on what I promised. They had to believe that in order to agree to the deal. I demonstrated to them with my research and knowledge of their business that I was a man of vision and a man of substance, a man who would deliver on what he promised. And yes, I have delivered on what I promised, I always do. Would you?"

Again the young man found himself temporarily lost for words by Josmas's rapid change of tack; the quick fire question placing him on the spot. He didn't know what to say. Josmas helped him out.

"Put it this way young man. Were you to meet the young lady of your dreams, the girl with whom you wanted to spend the rest of your life, would you not do all in your power to persuade her to be with you? Would you not wish to show her that she would be safe for life in your hands? Would she say 'yes' to your proposal if she doubted either your sincerity or your ability to provide the life you promised her? When she said 'yes' to your proposal, would she not be accepting that she believed that you would deliver on your promise of 'bliss together for eternity'?"

"Yes," agreed the young man, "I can see all that, it does make sense. I have yet to find that particular girl ... ", - here he curled his lip and shrugged a little – "But I do know the enthusiasm and hope that the prospect of such a relationship creates in any man, myself included! What you are saying is that I must bring that same passion and belief to bear in all areas of my life? ... just as you said that I must follow my passion and become a writer, whatever it takes?"

"Yes young man!" exclaimed Josmas, and then further mystified him by adding, "The young lady you seek may be closer than you think." He continued with,

"Show that you genuinely care for people and their situations. When you do, they will then entrust you with providing the solutions they seek but which they themselves are incapable of finding. Ask for what you want and deliver on what you promise. Then everyone is satisfied.

The estate owners wanted to see the vineyards, château and surrounds returned to their former glory, they longed for a healthy vibrant community in the valley. Their desire to achieve that objective far outweighed any financial considerations. I realised that and proposed a solution in which they could believe. You, in your life young man, must aim to do likewise."

~

Here Josmas hesitated for several seconds in his dialogue, as if weighing up whether or not to divulge to the young man what he wanted to say next. Then, having decided, he continued.

"There's one other thing about my acquisition of the wine estate which I want to share with you. It's very important."

"Go on," said the young man. He was by now fully attentive to anything Josmas had to say and wanted to hear more.

"When I researched the history of the area and talked to local people, I found that reference was made on several occasions to a large cache of wines, a secret cellar if you like, hidden somewhere in the grounds. It was reputedly those wines stolen by the Nazis during the war and squirreled away to be reclaimed by them later. Of course the robbers never got to return for their ill-gotten gains. They either fled the allied armies' advance or were killed. No actual record of the wines ever existed and various searches over the years failed to find them, or indeed any evidence that the horde had ever existed. The story of the wines became no more than a legend and even that eventually faded into obscurity.

However, the idea that a stash of valuable wines may be buried somewhere in the grounds fascinated me. I do like a good mystery. Unknown to the owners, I initiated my own search. Past attempts to find the treasure had centred on finding where it was hidden. I approached the task from the opposite view point. I looked for where the wine might be in full view.

Working on that basis I soon found the wine. I uncovered the 'secret cellar' within the walls of the château itself, in the library in fact. It was where no-one thought to look previously - behind the shelves of the wines, wine-making and oenology books section. In the secret chamber I found concealed tens of thousands of pounds worth of antique wines! There were Lafites, Latours, Haute-Brions,

Moutons, Yquems and Cheval Blancs. A veritable Alladin's cave."

"W-o-w!" exclaimed the young man, letting it out slowly and with emphasis, "Ama-a-zing! You didn't tell the owners?"

"Of course not. I went ahead and arranged the transfer of the property to me and stipulated that the contract show that I owned the estate and everything on and in it, in its entirety. It was legally sound." Here Josmas paused again,

"So you see, I knew just what I was doing. There was no risk involved in the deal. More so, I was sure to gain from it. There was one other thing ... I contracted to sell all the wines to interested buyers before I signed for the château."

"What?" said the young man, puzzled, "You sold the wines before you actually owned them?"

"Yes of course," replied Josmas, "You must always sell before you acquire. Never forget that. Doing so means that you always ensure a profit and that you eliminate risk."

The young man did not need to say anything in order to assure Josmas that he was listening intently and waiting to hear more. His body language, leaning in towards his host and his dropped jaw, quizzical expression said it all. Josmas continued.

"People believe that entrepreneurs are risk-takers. They are right. Many entrepreneurs take huge risks. They possess the attitude that, if you are going to fail, fail big! Most will tell you that they would not have achieved their success without having taken the risks which they did. The fact is that most 'ordinary' people don't have enough ambition, they don't risk success. This is all true. I believe in it wholeheartedly.

However," and here Josmas paused and wagged a raised finger, "I also believe in working smart and eliminating risk."

The young man's attentive expression asked the 'How?' It also expressed a degree of doubt.

"Don't believe me?" continued Josmas, picking up on the young man's hesitation. "With the wines I worked smart, n'est-ce pas? I took away all risk associated with acquiring the château and ensured that I would come out ahead in the deal whatever happened. It's a form of insurance if you like."

"The thing is," confessed the young man, "I've never been a great believer in insurance. At least not up until now," he added thoughtfully, "Perhaps I'll have to rethink that one."

~

"Yes you will," said Josmas, "I first learned the principle of insuring risk in a most unusual way. It was from a man who was neither educated nor literate, but he was smart.

I attended a football cup final to follow my home town team. In a pub before the match I got speaking to an opposition fan. His team were hot favourites to win, my team rank outsiders. Over a pint together he asked me, 'Have you put any money on your team to win?' I wasn't much of a betting man anyway and replied, 'No.' He quickly said, 'I have!'

'What?' I replied, thinking that I had misheard him, 'You mean you have a bet on your team?' 'No,' he replied more slowly, 'I said I have a bet on *your* team'. 'But surely,' I pressed on in my naive ignorance, 'You want your team to win?'

'Of course I do lad, and I'll be very happy when they do win. But, if they don't, if they don't,' he emphasised, 'Then I'll have the profit from my bet on your lot winning with which to drown my sorrows! You see lad, it's win-win. I'll either be happy or quids in. Either way I'll have a great day!'

When I thought of this later, I realised just how sound a strategy this fellow's way of doing things was. I realised it was smart and that it could be employed in many different ways in life and business. I realised that it was a variation of insurance. So is selling before you buy. When you do that you insure against loss. You can employ the same principle when acquiring or setting up any business."

"How do you do that?" asked the young man, fully engrossed and keen to know.

"One way," answered Josmas, "Is, before you acquire or set up your business, to place adverts in the appropriate places for the goods or services you hope to supply. If you get no response then you know that your business proposal, or your advertising, is off track and you need to go back to the drawing board and rethink your plan. But, when you receive a positive response to your publicity, then you know that you are on to a winner. You approach all the prospects with your proposal, sell your product to them and have them pay for it up front. Then, and only then, do you establish the business, create and provide the goods or services."

"So," queried the young man, "You promote and sell something which doesn't yet exist?"

"Precisely," said Josmas. "Once you know that there is a market and that you have customers waiting, then you use their cash to provide what it is they have asked for. You use the clients' money to finance your business. You establish a business at zero cost and zero risk. Just as I have done here." Josmas swept an outstretched arm at the vineyards around them. Then he sat back to allow time for the enormity of his revelation to sink in to the young man's comprehension. It took a while.

Eventually the young man leaned forward and, stroking his chin, said,

"Okay, let's say then that I wanted to write a book of some kind, let's say a book about wine making," here he nodded to Josmas for his approval.

"Yes," said Josmas, "Go on."

"Okay, a book about wine making. I place my advertisement for my book, which I have not yet written, in appropriate places, places where I know people interested in wine making will see it?" He waited for Josmas's further approval. It was readily given with another nod of encouragement,

"Yes ... ", and opened palms urging him to go on.

"Then, when people inquire about it in sufficient numbers to justify me taking the time and effort to write it, then, and only then, do I write it. Is that right?"

"Spot on," replied Josmas, "Don't forget to have them pay you beforehand too. That is important. It will be easy enough. In the case of a book you will most likely be selling it by mail order anyway, so customers will expect to pay up front. Simple isn't it?"

"Yes it is," agreed the young man, "I had never thought of that."

"Few people do," said Josmas, "That gives you an advantage. Remember too, you can apply this approach to any project, any business at all. Any enterprise, large or small. Look at my vineyards and château!"

Here he smiled broadly with both warmth and humour but more so, thought the young man, with wile and wisdom.

The young man was utterly impressed but, before he could respond or express his thanks for what he had just learned, Josmas suddenly changed course again.

~

"Did I tell you my favourite insurance sales joke?" Then answered his own question, "No, of course I didn't." He proceeded –

"This guy sits down in front of the telly to watch the football match. He has his cold beers and cheese sandwiches beside him and is all ready for the kick off. Just then there's a knock on his door. Reluctantly he gets up, goes to the door and finds it is an insurance salesman. Quickly he tells the salesman that he is not interested in buying any insurance and anyway, he is watching the football. The salesman persists and says, 'I have a very special offer for you. I can cover everything in your life from the cradle to the grave!' 'Hmm,' says the guy, 'Cradle to grave? You had better come on in.'

Half an hour later, the salesman leaves. The man settles back to watch the last hour of the match happy with the cradle to grave insurance solution he has just bought. He reaches for his less cold than before beer but before he can sip it there is a knock at the door. He thinks not to answer it but eventually, slightly irritated, does just that. At the door is another insurance salesman. Quickly, the man tells him that he doesn't need insurance. He assures him that he is well covered with everything from the cradle to the grave catered for. 'Really,' says the salesman, 'I can give you protection for everything from the womb to the tomb!' The man hesitates, thinks and goes, 'Hmm, womb to the tomb? You'd better come on in.

Half an hour later the man sits back to catch the last half hour of the football match, content that he is now fully insured, with every eventuality from cradle to grave and womb to tomb catered for. He reaches to take a first bite of his now stale sandwich and a sip of his distinctly warm beer. Just as he does so there's a knock at the door. He storms angrily to open it and finds there yet another insurance salesman. 'Look,' he shouts, 'I am trying to watch the football. I do not want insurance, I am already covered completely. I have got full cradle to the grave and womb to the tomb protection. There is nothing you can do for me. Nothing at all. Go away!'

The salesman held his ground, smiled with quiet self-assurance, raised his eyebrows and said – 'Erection to Resurrection?' "

The young man roared with laughter at the classic punchline. Josmas joined in too. As their laughter subsided, Josmas added,

"Every man knows that within him is his erection," that brought more chuckles from both men. Then, adopting a more reflective demeanour, Josmas came closer to the young man and said, "But few men know that within them is their ressurection."

The young man was genuinely puzzled. Josmas sought to enlighten him.

"Oh, I don't mean ressurection in the biblical sense, certainly not the rising from death nonsense. I mean ressurection as in learning from experience. In that context you should experience daily resurrection, you should strive for it in fact. Aim to renew yourself, to be a better, kinder, more caring version of yourself each day. It's about devotion and it's about commitment. Rise to the occasion young man," and here he first smiled and then broke into laughter again. The young man joined in.

~

The young man was totally in awe of all that he heard. Truth to tell he had never met anyone who came remotely close to expressing how to live life with the clarity and excitement which Josmas conveyed. Just being in his presence made the young man feel alive and ignited his desire. As if feeding off the young man's thoughts once again, Josmas continued,

"A man's life is akin to wine in a bottle. It waits there in the dark slowly maturing until it is ready to be opened and face the world. In those first moments following the cork being popped, the wine blinks in the sunlight, absorbing the new experience and slowly breathing, taking in its first lungfuls of comprehension of the new world 'out there'. After a period of such adjustment the wine is ready for drinking.

In terms of your life this is the point which you have reached. It is time for you to drink and enjoy the fruits of the wine. You, young man, are passing through the tasting phase of your life."

Here he stopped and looked all around at the beauty surrounding them, as if he were enjoying the same tasting phase of which he spoke. The young man remained silent, waiting intently for Josmas's next gems of wisdom which he felt certain were in transit. He wasn't to be disappointed.

"For now you are swilling the wine in the glass, studying the colour, the tinges round the edges. You are tipping the glass to see more so the shades and the light and sniffing to pick up the scents and fragrance to prepare the palate for the experience to come. Then the wine is on your tongue – fruits, spices, flowers, whatever – all are to be sampled. You can choose your favourite later but now all are to be enjoyed until, like life, you find your passion and concentrate on that. In life I call this 'trying this and that'."

Josmas sat back for a moment and drew in a large breath of the fresh, country air; once more as if he was sampling it to determine his preferred choice, then continued,

"People speak of multi-tasking as if it's a virtue. Yet you will only truly succeed when you concentrate on one passion, something you enjoy and go after it with all your might.

Even when in the learning, do a bit of everything phase, you should do them in series not concurrently. Don't mix your wines for example; drink one tonight and then another tomorrow ... and so on. That way you have the chance to fully absorb the features of a particular vintage before moving on to the next. After sampling several over a period of time, settle on your favourite – or favourites," here again he stopped to shrug and grin, "In life, do likewise. Try this and that, then select your favourite and pursue that enterprise or vocation with all your might. You, young man, are destined to write. Do you like trains?"

~

"Uuhh, uuhh," thought the young man, "Where are we off to this time?" But by now he was already becoming used to the abrupt changes of thought and subject which Josmas practiced and even looked forward to them. He almost expected them.

"Yes," he replied, "I am rather fond of them, I travel by train whenever I can." Then added, "I don't watch much television ... " – here Josmas interjected with a sharp, "Wise man," – as the young man continued,

"But I do like those 'around the world by rail' travelogues which takes viewers to weird and wonderful locations all over the globe in every kind of train imaginable and ones from every era."

"Well we share that in common young man," responded the host, "I too love trains and travel in them whenever possible. Let's go back to my study for afternoon tea and I'll show you something that will interest you."

By now the young man would have been more surprised if Josmas had said that he would show or tell him something not of interest. Everything about this man, his life and the place he inhabited was exceptional, anything but ordinary.

They walked slowly up the gravel track to the château in the mid afternoon sun. Josmas remained silent. The young man fell in with that mood, for now enjoying the stillness, calm and sense of freedom. He truly felt at ease with himself, more so than at any previous stage in his life. He also felt a gathering certainty within him that his life was changing as never before and that it would never be the same again.

Soon they were in Josmas's study. The ever attentive Jocelyn brought the tea and biscuits. She made no eye contact with the young man nor spoke to him. Josmas told the young man that it was here in the study, and in the library, that he did most of his 'inside' work but disclosed that his preference was for the outdoors, fresh air, exercise and his beloved vineyards.

"Me too," said the young man in reference to the outdoor life, "It's where I am most at home. Truth to tell I enjoy the solitude."

"Aahh," interrupted Josmas, "That is good. Successful people possess the ability to enjoy their own company, thrive on it even. They don't require constant noise and meaningless chatter."

The young man nodded in agreement with that and continued,

"But tell me, what is your 'inside' work?"

~

At that Josmas smiled and slowly pointed upwards to a large, gilt framed, oil painting which hung on the wall above the open, stone fireplace.

"You painted that?!" exclaimed the young man, "It's magnificent."

And it was. The work of art showed a 1960s era steam locomotive in stunning emerald green livery hauling a train of passenger carriages over an immense, red oxide painted, steel girders bridge.

"That painting took me a year to complete," said Josmas. "I enjoyed every second of the work. Of course it wasn't work, the endeavour was sheer pleasure. My painting shows the Flying Scotsman crossing the Forth Bridge. Doesn't it make your heart skip a beat?"

"It sure does," sighed the young man, who was running an admiring hand over the canvass to feel the texture and as if to more closely absorb both the fine artwork and the unique scene it represented.

Josmas carried on, his tone lowered and respectful as if he were in a hallowed place. It soon became clear to the young man that that was exactly the case as far as Josmas was concerned. In little time, he too, was irresistably drawn into the same reverent mood.

"The Forth Bridge is a massive cantilever railway bridge which stretches for over a mile and a half across the Firth of Forth just west of Edinburgh. It was the biggest of its kind when built and remains one of the two biggest such bridges in the world. It is easily the most impressive though and a wonder of Victorian era engineering. It's almost unbelievable to think that over fifty-five thousand tonnes of steel were used in its construction which took eight years before its opening in 1890. It's often referred to as Scotland's Eiffel Tower. It well merits the title. It is simply awesome."

Here Josmas took a long breathe. He also took a white tissue from a box on his desk. The young man thought he was going to wipe a tear from his eye but he merely dried his palms before turning his attention back to the painting and to the locomotive. Pointing to it specifically, he carried on,

"The Flying Scotsman is the name given to the high speed rail service between Edinburgh and London which was inaugurated in 1924. The first locomotive to carry the name eventually went out of service in 1963, being replaced by diesel ones. Then, in 2006, the restoration of the original steam locomotive was initiated. A long ten years and over five million pounds later, the magnificently restored loco rolled out on to the tracks to a euphoric welcome from railway enthusiasts and the general public alike; a generation of whom had never seen any steam locomotive in action, let alone the thunderingly beautiful Flying Scotsman.

Today the Flying Scotsman runs private tours all over Britain and attracts tens of thousands of spectators where-ever it goes. In fact, organisers have stopped publishing its schedule, such is the clamour of people crowding to see it and bringing life to a complete standstill in the cities, towns, villages and countryside on its route.

Never was this more apparent than when the legendary loco made the iconic crossing of the mighty Forth Bridge. Over a quarter of a million people reportedly turned out to witness the unforgettable spectacle! Don't you find that incredible young man?"

Here he waited for a reply but, when none was forthcoming (the young man was riveted to the story and could find no words), he continued,

"Well you shouldn't. You see, not only is there a heart wrenching nostalgia among many for such treasures of a bygone era, there is also an appreciation of the beauty and grandeur inherent in them and the fact that they are the physical embodiment of what started as mere seeds of imagination in the minds of their creators. The Forth Bridge and the Flying Scotsman are proof positive to all that a man's dreams can become mammoth achievements of inspirational magnificence. They show that anything is possible. People take both comfort from that and the encouragement to strive to realise their own ambitions. I certainly hope that you do?"

"Yes," coughed the young man, barely able to speak such was the emotional impact of Josmas's story.

"You know," said Josmas, "As a boy I watched in wide-eyed awe from a ferry boat on the firth as a steam-hauled passenger train crossed the bridge high above me. Did the event motivate me to build in adulthood my own Forth Bridge of life and ride the footplate of my own Flying Scotsman over it? I like to think so. I also like to think that it will have the same effect on you. The painting is here to remind you every day."

The young man let the last remark pass. It puzzled him but then so too did much of Josmas's comments. He didn't doubt that there was a point to it. Josmas was very careful with his words. Nothing was said without there being meaning to it.

~

As if to emphasise that aspect of his character, he changed subject quite suddenly once again.

"Did I tell you about my near neighbour, 'la grande dame' Marlena? She lives in le manoir (the manor house) just down the road from here. The locals christened her la grande dame after the famous Veuve Cliquot champagne of the same name. Like the champagne they consider her to be a silky classic, perfect for all occasions," here Josmas paused to chuckle reflectively at his own humourous turn of phrase, then continued with a more earnest, "She is indeed a sparkling and colourful individual. She lives life to the full."

"Wow," said the young man, "She sounds amazing. I would sure love to meet her."

"I dare say you will young man, you'll have plenty time to do so." Here again the young man picked up on Josmas's words but didn't understand at all what he meant. As far as he knew he was stopping for two or three days at most so was unlikely to have much spare time for socialising with the locals. On top of that Josmas had indicated that he himself was going somewhere soon. Nonetheless Josmas pressed on.

"Marlena's escapades and the stories of them, most often told by herself, are legend. A few months back, for example, she visited friends in Provence. She tells how she flew to the Côte d'Azur, collected her hire car at Nice Airport and drove out on to the Promenade des Anglais. At the first traffic control heading east from the airport she stopped for the red lights and, according to her own account, barely noticed the two motor scooters which pulled up beside her, one on each side. In a flash each of the riders opened an unlocked door of her car, grabbed her handbag and light luggage and sped off.

Marlena is not noted for her lack of emotion. Shortly afterwards a distraught Marlena sobbed her sad tale to two officers at the Commissariat Central de Police who turned out to be less than sympathetic to her plight. She told of how she blubbered out that such a thing as the daylight robbery she had experienced would never happen where she lived.

The response had been one of 'And where exactly do you live?' from one of les flicques who, she noted, was concentrating more on the not unimpressive smoke ring he was blowing from his last inhalation of Disque Bleu than on his own question. She had replied with some pride that her home was in Aucune-Mouches-sur-Nous in the Perigord Noir.

At that point the officer had exclaimed 'Haa-a!' had stuck out his lip, upturned his palms and raised his shoulders in the classic Gallic shrug, that pièce de résistance, as she put it, of French gestures which means anything and nothing. He had apparently accompanied his performance with another French staple, the 'Phooff,' blown out through his curled lip and a disparaging, 'Troisième monde,' (third world) as he grimaced to his colleague who had responded with a lazy, conspiratorial nod.

This disdainful performance and direct insult to Marlena ('if anyone insults my home and my people they insult me!') had turned Marlena livid and she instantly rediscovered the not inconsiderable tour de force of her normal being – a woman to be reckoned with.

'Oui Monsieur,' she had retorted, her statuesque figure thrust square in his face, 'Aucune-Mouches-sur-Nous is a beautiful and remote backwater and we do not lock our doors there. We do have break-ins ... but in our village people come not to rob us but to leave gifts for us. When I return home I find fresh fruit and vegetables, cheeses, milk and eggs, and flowers, on my kitchen table; and kind notes of friendship inquiring as to my well-being or inviting me to a local fête or soirée in someone's home.

And here – what do you do? Here you welcome the riff-raff from the four corners of the earth, tolerate their criminal behaviour and accept it as normal. Then you have the impertinence to refer to my paradise on earth and it's kind and caring people as le troisième monde. You monsieur are an imbécile!'

With that she had stormed from the building. She reported that her belongings were never recovered and she received no communiqué of any kind from the Police Nationale in Nice nor anywhere else. She did however confess, and here she laughed openly when telling her tale, to having kicked a police motor scooter parked outside le Prefecture de Police as she left and shouted back to anyone within earshot, 'Putains de la mère du diable!' I'll leave you to work out what that means," said Josmas in closing. But the young man was already laughing loudly,

"Oh I know okay sir. She seems like my kind of lady," and the two men laughed again together just as old friends do. After taking a moment to draw breath and wipe a tear from his always kindly and compassionate face, Josmas took hold of the young man's arm and, in a more candid tone, added,

"You can choose to see life as a series of misfortunes as so many people do or you can choose to see misfortunes as opportunities - as Marlena does."

At this he stopped and looked directly into the young man's eyes as if to check that he was listening and was ready to absorb the full substance of his next words.

"It's inevitable to make an error from time to time, as Marlena did in failing to lock the doors of her car. The trick is not to make a habit of it. You can choose whatever life you want you know. Why not choose to be outgoing, open and take risks like Marlena? She turned her misfortune into a self-effacing fun story for all to enjoy. Equally importantly she exposed the incompetence, cynical laziness and blinkered way of life of the inept city boys.

Too Early For A Glass Of Wine?

An open heart policy may well be taken advantage of at times but without it there is no real life. The rewards of an open door approach to life such as Marlena and her neighbours practice far outweighs any damage that may be caused by not employing it. Those who abuse your generosity are the real losers."

With that Josmas released the young man's arm which he had continued to hold as he spoke. He shook his head thoughtfully as if agreeing with his own words and acknowledging the truth of their profound wisdom.

He waited, apparently for the young man to respond but, for now, the the young man could only ponder on how easily he found himself engaged by Josmas's story telling. He noted how the telling of the tales appealed to all his senses – sight, colour, sound, taste, scent – and to his emotions, and was fascinated by that. He wondered to himself if perhaps this remarkable story-telling ability of his host was one of his secrets of success. He made a mental note to ask the great man just that.

He also determined to use story telling in the future himself, both in the written word (of course) and verbally, when working to impress others. He had already accumulated considerable experience in life and encountered many amusing and bizarre events and people, all of which would make great stories. What could be better to tell others than about his experiences here with Josmas? The young man could even retell the Josmas tales, they were after all, totally engrossing – as the young man was at that very moment experiencing!

"It definitely works," he thought. He felt warm, mesmerised by the stories and empathetic with Josmas. He was reminded of the comfort and safety he had felt as a child having bedtime stories read to him. He couldn't help but be drawn to Josmas and, even at moments when he felt insecure, threatened even, was amazed at how easily Josmas turned the situation around and brought him back to believing in him and hanging on his every word. Yes Josmas was a truly remarkable man!

With words defeating him and his head once more abuzz with thoughts and questions, questions and thoughts, the young man chose that moment to make his exit. He retired to his room for an afternoon nap which caught up with and embraced him with considerable ease.

When he awoke it was time for dinner. He showered, dressed and made his way towards the dining room. Josmas intercepted him in the hallway however. He announced that they would eat out at a local restaurant that night.

ALIVE AND KICKING

At fifteen years of age Tommy was already a strapping six foot plus in height, lean and well muscled. Long gone were the days when anyone would dare to physically abuse him. If his physique did not deter potential assailants then the testosteronic rage simmering within him and quickly apparent at the first hint of confrontation certainly would. He was a lad to be wary of.

He didn't tolerate seeing other smaller or weaker compatriots being abused either. He instinctively sided with the underdog and felt duty bound to defend those he felt were subjected to bullying of any kind. Much of the independent spirit and sense of self reliance he displayed in such situations stemmed from his outdoor pursuits, hiking and climbing in the mountains. So it was to the mountains that he decided to go to mark his fifteenth birthday with his first winter, solo climbing expedition.

He told no-one of his plan, particularly his parents. He simply informed them that he intended to cycle on the Friday evening after school to a climbers' hostel in the mountains which the family used on a semi-regular basis. Tommy arranged to meet up with them there to celebrate his birthday when they arrived over the weekend. He borrowed the sleek racing bike of a friend for the first part of his journey in preference to using his uncle Charlie's rusty, pre-war relic which he most often rode, made it to the hostel in fine weather and stayed there the night as planned.

The next morning he set off from the hostel to hike, in the far more wintry conditions at the higher altitude, to what would be his base camp at the foot of his favourite mountain, Lochnagar. Yes, it is a mountain, but named after the lochan (small loch) which sits in the basin of its massive, central corrie. The floor of the corrie, shielded by six hundred foot high cliffs on three sides, rarely catches the full light of the sun. It's a dark, foreboding place.

Lochnagar was the first mountain Tommy ever ascended, walking up with his parents when only eight. Ever since that time he found it to be an awesome place, wild and beckoning. He knew from his reading that the romanticist writer Lord Byron loved the mountain too. His famous words in praise of it read -

England, thy beauties are tame and domestic

To one who has roamed over mountains afar

I long for the crags that are rugged and sombre

The steep frowning glory of dark Lochnagar

- and were etched in Tommy's mind. Beautiful words to describe a haunting place, and totally apt. The mountain held a magical allure for Tommy.

Too Early For A Glass Of Wine?

It was cold, brisk and windless as he set off in the early morning mist from his base at the foot of Lochnagar. He knew to expect far less benign weather further on as he headed for 'the Black Spout', his chosen climb to the summit. He was well equipped with ice axes, crampons and full Arctic survival gear. He would need them. The mountain was particularly dangerous after heavy snow or when in thaw, and conditions on the summit could be subarctic.

Sure enough, the weather soon closed in. Long before Tommy crested the ridge at the top of the gully, a full blizzard was blowing. He made it to the summit however and snuggled down behind the boulders to hungrily devour his Kendal Cake energy bars and hot soup. Then it was time to get off the mountain. He had no intention of snow-holing overnight in those conditions.

He headed down towards the lower summit and its cairn which was the marker he needed to hit en route to a safe descent. In the nil visibility of the blizzard, he knew that precise navigation was necessary to reach it as the direct line took him close to the top of the six hundred foot cliffs and ice overhangs on his left. After an hour of struggling through the thigh high snow, Tommy had not sighted the cairn.

He realised that he had missed it, either to the left or to the right. There was only one safe choice. He made a ninety degree turn to his right. This because, if he had missed the marker to the right, then he was not in danger of going over the cliff edge. By turning right he would be walking further from the danger. He was familiar with the terrain there and knew that he could make it safely off the mountain that way.

But, had he missed the marker to the left, then he was perilously close to the cliffs, perhaps already on an ice overhang and in deadly danger. He made his right turn and slogged on. In just thirty minutes the marker appeared through the swirling snow. He had indeed missed it to the left and had therefore been absolutely on the cliff edge! Tommy escaped tragedy that day by just yards, maybe only inches.

Two hours later he emerged exhausted below the snow line ... into brilliant, late afternoon sunshine! He felt as if the heavens welcomed him back, assured him that he had not only survived but had passed the test asked of him. It had been quite a challenge for Tommy but one which he had willingly confronted. It stretched him to the limit, yet it rewarded him handsomely precisely because of that. The sense of self-reliance and achievement he experienced was immense.

It was matched by his sense of disappointment when, after the trek back to the hostel and hoping there to regale his parents with the story of his triumphant adventure, he found that they had been and gone. The warden of the hostel simply informed him that 'they were very angry that he had gone off into the mountains alone' and had left to return to town that afternoon.

"Clearly," thought Tommy, "They were not sufficiently concerned about my welfare as to come looking for me." There was no mention either of 'happy birthday' wishes to pass on to him. From that day onwards Tommy refused to acknowledge, or let others acknowledge, any of his birthdays. For him they ceased to exist. He resolved to go his own way in life, even more so than had been the case up to then.

He had no expectation that others would be like him and he never insisted that they should be. But, "Boy," he thought to himself, "My way is exhilarating!" He consciously decided to tackle life as an adventure every minute of every day and push himself to do more, be better. He felt with greater certainty than ever before that nothing was ever achieved through being timid, through avoiding risk.

"Life, real life," he concluded, "Is not for the faint hearted."

~

What Tommy saw as his parents indifference to his interests and exploits was not limited to his wilderness adventures. Tommy's even greater and over-riding passion was football. He dreamed of becoming a famous professional player. He told all and sundry of his yearning but received only mockery and derision in return; after all, every kid wanted to be a footballer. His determination however was not diminished by the naysayers. He practiced relentlessly, juggling a football for hours on end until he could keep it in the air for the duration of an entire football match.

In the beginning he chattered endlessly to his family of his great ambition but by the time his sixteenth birthday came around he had long since ceased to do so. It seemed to his young mind that he received only ridicule ('you'll never be a professional footballer', 'all the boys say that' and 'you are never good enough') in response to his open admission of what he wanted to do with his life. He received no encouragement; only an absolute insistance from his parents, his mother in particular, that he live out her ambition for him, rather than his own ambition for himself. This meant school, study and academic qualifications. His parents never went to watch him play, not once.

Had they done so they would have found that there was every possibility that Tommy could become a professional player and that he most certainly was good enough. For all the lack of encouragement regarding his dream which he received from home, he received the opposite and in full measure from the management, trainers and followers of the youth team he played for; and indeed from everyone associated with the game in the surrounding area. These people supported him unconditionally. They were his cheering section. To them Tommy was a 'hot' footballing property, a young lad going places. Yet to get to even where he was at that stage had not been easy. Tommy had had to do it alone Then again, making his own way in life was by now pretty much normal for the young lad.

His footballing prowess had first come to the fore at primary school. But Tommy attended a rugby playing school where 'footballers' were looked down on. Those choosing to play football were frowned on as 'disloyal' by the athletics staff and those like Tommy who made that choice were picked on and sidelined from many school activities. On top of that came the indifference of his parents. They had neither the will nor the interest to put themselves about and find the right outlet for Tommy's footballing aspirations. He did it himself.

He took to hanging around outside the ground of one of the local semi-professional clubs which ran a highly successful under eighteens youth squad. Tommy was only thirteen when he made his presence known to them. At first he just retrieved balls kicked over the wall into the street but, as he became a familiar presence to the players and those who organised the general affairs of the club, he got to play a small part in training and then even in kick-about practice matches.

It was in one such match that Tommy's breakthrough moment occurred. He performed a flick and turn with the ball before scoring a goal with a fierce shot with his 'wrong' foot. This brought instant applause and gasps from the club officials present and the players.

"How do you do that?" came the question and, "You can use both feet?"

Tommy's replies, made in perfect innocence, were the same to both queries - "Doesn't everybody?" He did, after all, consider the move he had performed to be completely normal; he'd been doing just that in his back garden since he was eight!

In little time he was playing in the reserve youth team and quite soon afterwards became a central fixture in the youth team itself. The fact that he was playing with young men, many years older than he and physically further developed, when he first broke through, did not faze him at all. Tommy took it all in his stride. He loved working with experienced players and real coaches. One coach in particular was a former international player of some renown. Tommy hung on his every word and frequently stayed behind at the end of evening coaching sessions to quiz him about every aspect of the game.

Tommy understood early on that it was often just small differences which separated the successful players from the also rans. He knew that being that bit fitter, stronger than other players (many who did not enjoy training and shirked doing it) gave him an advantage. He trained extra hard, doing stints on his own morning and evening throughout the week. It was during this spell that he took to practicing early morning fitness sessions on the beach near where he lived. He toughened himself up performing endless army style sprints up and down the giant sand dunes until he was exhausted. At the end of each session his shower was a naked splash in the freezing sea.

~

One morning he plunged into the sea and swam a little further out than he intended to. When he turned to swim back to shore he found that the tide was against him and sweeping him out to sea. Tommy was a strong swimmer, he had since age six been swimming almost daily and often in the sea. That counted for nothing in this type of circumstance. What did count however was his survival training. Just as with his mountaineering, which he had learned from both practical involvement with experienced climbers as well as theoretical study from books and classes, Tommy had learned how best to deal with the situation which faced him through his early sea swimming experience, membership of the school life-saving club and the grades he had achieved.

First, he knew not to panic and waste energy. Second, he knew to swim parallel to the shore rather than try to swim towards the shore against the current. The theory being that the rip tide pulling him out to sea would abate and reverse at other points along the shoreline. Of course, he had never up to this point been in a situation requiring that he test the theory in practice. Sure enough though, his training held good.

After ten minutes of swimming along the coast, with the small pile of his trainers, tracksuit, shorts and singlet on the sand rapidly disappearing from view, he struck out for the shore once again. His relief was immense when he realised that he was making headway towards the beach. Soon his toes touched sand beneath him and, from there, he half swam, half paddled back to the safety of the shore.

Once on sandy terra firma he doubled over semi-exhausted from his efforts. He stood like that drawing in huge gulps of air for some time. When he was ready, he straightened up and started his long, naked walk back to where his training gear lay. In the short time he had been in the water he had been washed almost a mile down the coast! He was feeling distinctly chilly by the time he got to his clothes.

Just as he approached them, and anticipating the warmth of their embrace, his attention was caught by a movement in the marram grass below the sand dunes ahead of him. Looking up, Tommy saw a figure crouched there and watching him. Realising that he had been spotted, the man got up and hurried off. He ran behind a dune and disappeared. Not however before Tommy had got a good look of the voyeur's face. It was a face Tommy knew and sight of it sent a chill through him far more biting than that of the freezing sea and cutting wind. The man watching him had been Hamish McIntosh!

Tommy had not set eyes on the man since the events of four years previously. Truth to tell he never gave his abuser a second thought. What had happened had happened and it was not something Tommy dwelled on. He had supposed McIntosh to still to be in prison, but clearly that was not the case. He wasn't in the least bit afraid of the man - Tommy was physically strong and frighteningly independant - yet the pervert's presence on the beach that day did concern Tommy ... but only briefly. Another bigger and life changingly significant event was just around the corner.

~

Tommy's 'near death' experience in the sea occurred towards the end of the football season. It had been a successful one for Tommy's team. They had become champions of their league and, on the last day of the season, won the national knock out cup competition too. The local newspapers featured the team, and Tommy in particular, prominently in their sports section. A photographer even came to Tommy's house – and a reporter too. Tommy was asked about his professional ambitions. A short article about him featured in the paper a couple of days later. His dad was disinterested and his mother displeased. Their ambivalence was soon further tested.

As Tommy left his house a few nights later, en route to enjoy some celebratory beers with his team-mates in a local pub (which, fortunately as far as he was concerned, didn't look too closely at their clientele or question ages), he was stopped in the street by a stranger. The man was oldish to Tommy's eyes, wore a crumpled grey suit but smart red tie and sported a healthy head of grey, curly hair. He simply said,

"You're Tommy aren't you?" and then, "I'm just on my way to see you."

He told Tommy that he was Billy Beattie, the local scout for the famous Manchester United football club. Tommy was speechless. Billy continued,

"I want you to come down to Manchester, two or three weeks to start with and see how you get on. I believe you'll do well. Can I speak to your mum and dad?"

Together, they retraced Tommy's footsteps the short distance to his home. Once there, Billy introduced himself to Tommy's parents and came straight to the point of his visit. He easily overcame the objections of Tommy's mum, assuring her that no cost was involved on her part, that her son would be in very good hands as regarded accommodation and discipline and that he would 'probably' be back home in a week or two. When he said those last words to her he surreptitiously flashed a wink to Tommy. Tommy thought, "I'm going to like this guy," – and he did.

Over the next week Tommy excitedly quizzed Billy all about his trip, the football club and Manchester. Billy in turn briefed him each day about what was going to happen and what was expected of him. On the day of Tommy's departure, just one week after their first meeting, Billy came to collect Tommy from his home in a taxi and they drove to the local airport. Tommy was treated to, and about to enjoy, the added thrill of his first flight in an aeroplane. He felt like a real V.I.P.

Billy wished him luck, expressed his confidence that Tommy would be a long term success in Manchester and waived him off to his new life. Tommy too was absolutely determined that he'd not be coming back. Returning was not an option.

~

Tommy's first weeks as a full time professional footballer fairly flew by. They were exciting times. From day one he was lodged with a kindly old couple, Mr. and Mrs.Wilde. Tommy always referred to them as Mr.Wilde and Mrs.Wilde. He never once heard their first names mentioned, so never knew what those names were. He felt that they expected to be treated with the respect of their full titles, so treat them with respect he did.

Tommy's fixed weekly wage was paid directly to his landlords. They retained the lion's share of the money as payment for Tommy's board and lodgings and gave him the small amount left over as his spending cash. In addition to that Tommy was paid a win bonus by the club. This was equal to a week's wages. There was no reward for drawing or losing a match. At Manchester United the players were expected to win. Anything less amounted to failure and failure was not rewarded.

The team played once per week and almost always won. Thus, in a normal week, Tommy would actually earn double his standard weekly wage. On the odd occasion that the team played twice in a week then Tommy's wage could be three times his basic.

Neither Tommy nor the Wildes ever saw any of the bonus money. That was payed in its entirety into a bank account held by the club in Tommy's name. As with all the players throughout the club, from the biggest stars to the most lowly groundstaff boys, this money was saved for them until the day they left the club or retired from playing football, however many years in the future that might be. Tommy never suspected for a moment that he would be collecting his bonus pot rather sooner than he would have wished.

In return for Tommy's board and lodging fee received from the club the Wilde's were charged with ensuring Tommy's welfare, particularly with regard to nourishment and sleep. The house rules were simple. Tommy could go out of an evening after his standard supper – which every evening without fail consisted of a very large beef steak, three eggs and a mountain of chipped fried potatoes – but he had to be back in the house by nine and in bed by ten o'clock.

He was wakened each morning at eight o'clock exactly. For breakfast he had to drink a pint of fresh milk into which was stirred three raw eggs and two heaped spoonfuls of sugar. He was supplied with ham sandwiches for lunch and sent off to walk the one mile to the training ground at nine-thirty. He had to be at the ground, stripped, kitted and ready for action at ten o'clock precisely.

After two and a half hours of training which included physical exercises such as running up and down the spectator terracing surrounding the main pitch with a team mate on his back, technical work, ball skills and match practice, he retired to the dressing room for massage, treatment to any sprains or bruises, a hot shower and an ice cold bath. Once dressed he was fed hot, sweet tea with the other lads and ate his sandwiches. An hour of classroom tactical training followed before he was released for the day.

At this time most of the lads headed off to local cafés, snooker salons or to meet girlfriends. Such was Tommy's determination to not only succeed in his new career but to be the best however, that he chose to strip off again and head back out to the training ground for extra practice. So too did Sammy MacEvoy.

~

Sammy was another of the youth squad players. He had already been with the club for a year and was doing well. He hailed from Northern Ireland and was a child of 'the Troubles' there, brought up to a life of mayhem and constant conflict. Not entirely un-naturally therefore he was an introspective and aggressive lad. He took an instant dislike to Tommy.

This was partly because he saw Tommy's presence in the squad as a threat to his place in the team and partly because Sammy and his family were devoutly catholic. In Tommy he saw a protestant Scot. Not that Tommy thought of himself as such. In fact the religious aspects of Tommy's upbringing had already convinced him that the whole religion thing was a 'con', a load of nonsense. He had nothing to do with it. He was entirely unaware of the fact that Northern Ireland's predominantly protestant population were mostly of Scottish origin and that many catholics, such as Sammy's family, literally hated them as a group for it. Tommy didn't nearly understand Sammy's hostility towards him. The whole Irish thing was news to him – but not for long.

Tommy did try to get on with Sammy, he was a team mate after all, but it seemed that, at any opportunity, Sammy would pick a fight with him. As Tommy was over six feet in height and strong with it, while Sammy was a 'shorty' only five foot six, Tommy didn't seriously see him as a physical threat. Sammy though was a 'terrier', the equivalent of a small, barking dog, always snapping around Tommy's ankles. Tommy was not averse to a punch up so he did retaliate and defend himself during the frequent, Sammy-inspired squabbles that arose between them in training. As time went by, increasingly the coaches had to intervene to pull them apart.

Eventually both lads were hauled up before the head coach and warned as to their conduct. They were left in no doubt that they would be out on their ears if they didn't start to behave. Tommy felt hard done by. He didn't see himself as the instigator of the confrontations but, true to form, he didn't blame Sammy or drop him in trouble. He took the dressing down 'like a man' and said nothing. If Tommy thought that his honourable behaviour would soften Sammy's attitude towards him, he was gravely mistaken.

Apart from the catholic/protestant side of things which, as far as Tommy was concerned, was an issue only in Sammy's mind, there was the additional difficulty that they were vying with each other for the one place in the team. Both Tommy and Sammy played in the same position, both were better than just good players and both were determined to win the place. As far as the coaches were concerned this rivalry was a good thing. They believed in healthy competition between the lads and encouraged it. After all, if the aspirants were to become successful senior players they had to display in training that extra bite and degree of ruthlessness which they would need to possess when they stepped up to senior football. As a result of that the practice matches were full blooded affairs, and particularly so when Tommy and Sammy were in opposition.

Tommy had been with the club for six months when his seventeenth birthday came around and, apart from the skirmishes with Sammy, happily revelling in his new career. These really were days of 'sunshine and roses' for him. He was released from the general apathy and confines of his family home. He was free at last to pursue his ambition and make a name and a place for himself in his new world. As he saw it, he was being paid for having fun! Things could not have been better for him ... until a full scale practice match was called for one Wednesday afternoon.

~

It started badly for Tommy. Firstly in the sense that he had to stand up a date he had made for that same afternoon with his recently acquired girlfriend. He met Pat at a local dance hall two months previously and had become rather infatuated with her. She was a few years older than Tommy and, as such, Tommy was finding his education in matters amorous and carnal advancing at an unprecedented rate.

Pat worked in a cotton factory and Wednesday was her half day off. Tommy had planned to spend the time in bed with her at her apartment – but the match put paid to that idea. As the game was announced to the players only at training that same morning, Tommy had no opportunity to contact his girlfriend.

Tommy took to the field with the thought of the broken date on his mind but very soon forgot about it as the match swung into action. He would soon have a 'break' of another kind – and an altogether more painful one – to consider.

The youth players, first team fringe players and reserves had been divided into two teams. Sammy MacEvoy was in direct opposition to Tommy. All went well for the first half hour. Tommy was in fine form and enjoying himself. He scored a spectacular goal and received warm applause from the assembled players and coaching staff taking in the game and there to assess who and what they saw – and they liked what they saw of Tommy. The one person not liking what he was seeing was Sammy. He scowled and seethed inside. He wanted to punish the 'protestant bastard'. A few moments later he saw his chance.

As Tommy shielded the ball and let it run slowly out of play for a throw-in, he eased back and, with no-one near him, prepared to pick up the ball. Unseen to Tommy however, Sammy was charging up at full speed on his blind side. There was no possibility of Sammy catching the ball before it rolled over the byline ... and he didn't try to. Arriving far too late to make any sort of legitimate challenge for the ball he launched himself feet first, full length and studs up into the back of Tommy's left leg. It was a vicious challenge. Tommy was thrown off the pitch and hit the ground hard.

Tommy played football, and indeed lived his life, in permanent 'tough' mode. He had been brought up not to feel pain and certainly never to show it. His immediate, subconsciously controlled reaction to the challenge was to get up and carry on as if nothing had happened. That's what he did. He lifted himself from the ground straight away and angrily turned to his aggressor.

"What the hell did you do that for!" were his only words before his knee gave way and he collapsed in agony. It was the worst pain he had ever felt. The club doctors took Tommy from the field and then to the hospital. Tommy was operated on that same night. When he awoke the next day it was to the news that he would never play football again!

"That can't be true!" blurted Tommy to the surgeon who had just informed him of the extent of his injury, "I've never had an injury in my life."

"Maybe not," replied the doctor, "But, apart from the gaping wound behind your knee, you have a fractured patella (knee cap), a split cartilage and ruptured cruciate ligaments. There's also vein damage and internal bleeding. You'll need a lot of rest. Recuperation will take several months. There should be no long term difficulty in walking or moving about normally. I doubt however if your knee will stand up to the turning, twisting and general rough treatment involved in playing football. We'll see."

~

Tommy was devastated. He fell into a deep depression. Being laid up in bed for weeks or maybe months did not sit well with him. Fortunately he had his books to escape into. He used his time of confinement to read many fine volumes. These included John Buchan's 'The Thirty-Nine Steps', Wilbur Smith's 'River God', 'The Ghost Runner' by Bill Jones and 'Tough Jews', Rich Cohen's remarkable insight into the New York gangsters of the early twentieth century, whose lives and times increasingly fascinated Tommy. He found 'The Man Who Mistook His Wife For A Hat' by Oliver Sacks to be a particularly engrossing read. Each of them inspired him in different ways. All made his solitary convalescence that bit more bearable. Each book, in its own way, aided his recovery.

His spirits were also lifted, albeit temporarily, when Pat came to visit him. She brought him a bottle of wine as a pick-me-up. Apart from the infamous Barsac incident of his childhood, Tommy had never drunk wine. Beer was his comforter of choice. In the event though, the wine worked very well. It turned out to be a deliciously refreshing Chablis. They shared a long and intimate conversation while consuming the whole bottle before Pat informed him that she would not be seeing him again – but she wished him well.

Tommy was taken aback. He had hoped to continue his relationship with Pat. He assumed that it was his injury and the ending of his football career which caused her to end their liaison so abruptly. "After all," he asked himself, "What other reason could there be?"

He put her surprise decision down to what some of his fellow players at the club called 'the pizza syndrome' principle. This stated that when a man could work out why a round pizza is put in a square box and is eaten in triangles, then, and only then, is he ready to understand women! Tommy barely knew why pizzas were round let alone the rest of it, and anyway, was in no condition to pursue the question further, so he let it drop. As she turned to go Tommy called after her,

"Thank you for everything Pat," and he meant it, "Particularly the crash course in shagging."

They both laughed. She faced him fully for a few seconds, shrugged her shoulders and smiled one last, almost poignant, smile. There was a tear in her eye. Tommy couldn't know why.

"And," Tommy called after her as she left, "I'll see that you get your wine back. Paid in full." In due course he would be true to his word.

~

Six months to the day and right at the end of what would have been his first year as a playing professional, Tommy stood on the training ground with a football at his feet again. The coach, standing twenty yards away instructed him to kick the ball to him with his right foot, but not too hard. Tommy duly obliged with no difficulty. The ball was rolled back to him.

"Okay, now the left foot." Tommy hesitated. "Come on lad, it's now or never."

Tommy hesitated once more, steeled himself, then made the strike. The pain shot through his left knee, sharp and sudden. The message it carried, stark and clear. Tommy would not be playing football again ... ever. In a corner of the training ground Sammy MacEvoy watched the event being played out on the pitch and allowed himself a satisfied smirk. It didn't go un-noticed by Tommy.

The following morning Tommy was summoned to the office of the 'big boss' himself at the main stadium. Tommy had rarely been there and had never met the man. Along with the other lads, apprentices and groundstaff boys, Tommy's visits to the stadium were limited to the occasions when they went to see the senior team play and to afternoons in the boot room, polishing their way slavishly through the hamper load of dirty players' footwear stored there.

When Tommy entered his office, 'the boss' was standing in front of his desk but immediately bounded forward, arm outstretched to shake Tommy's hand. He welcomed him by name,

"Hello Tommy," and continued with, "I've heard great things about you son. It's a pity no-one else will!"

With that he picked up two envelopes from his desk and explained,

"In this envelope is your flight ticket home. You leave this afternoon. In this second envelope is your bonus cash. I've included payment for all the wins you played in plus I've added in all the wins in the months since you were injured."

Tommy immediately appreciated the generous gesture and said so.

The boss continued, "You'll find there's a tidy sum. I hope it helps you to get over your disappointment and get set up in whatever life awaits you. Goodbye son."

With that he crossed to his office door and held it open for Tommy to leave. Tommy, almost in tears, straightened himself up and managed to croak, "Thank you sir."

Then he left the office, the stadium and Manchester behind him and flew back to the city of his upbringing.

He left a large chunk of his heart and most of his pride behind him too.

Too Early For A Glass Of Wine?

THE MAGICIAN'S BISTRO

Josmas and the young man set off by foot for the eatery of choice. It was only about a mile distant, not far from the estate gate where the young man had stood the previous day. It was a pleasant walking distance to develop a pre-dinner appetite and a not overly demanding staggering distance for returning to the château afterwards!

The restaurant did not turn out to be the smart establishment the young man had half expected it might be. Rather it was a rustic country bistro called *Chez Magicien*, chic, not pretentious, relaxed and reasonably priced. It was owned and run by an Italian chef, Monsieur Bertoli, and his Flemish wife who managed front of house. The cuisine though, as the young man would soon discover to his delight, was quintessentially French.

Once seated at their table, Josmas ordered a kir aperitif. The traditional kir was, as the young man knew, traditionally made with an Alsace Aligote dry white wine and a dash of crème de cassis blackcurrant liqueur from the Marseille area of France. Josmas however, asked for three kir royales, a mix of champagne and crème de pêche (peach), very light and refreshing. He explained that the third drink was for a good friend who would be joining them for dinner. Just afterwards Martin arrived.

Martin turned out to be a chirpy Englishman and a professional magician. He lived nearby but performed to audiences all around the world. No sooner had he settled beside Josmas and the young man and savoured a first sip of his kir royale, than he turned to the young man and asked,

"Have you ever paid to see a live magic show?"

"Good heavens," thought the young man, "Here we go again. Another guy like Josmas who goes straight for the jugular, into conversation and an apparently inconsequential topic without as much as an introduction. What would be the point this time?" he wondered. "Err .. yes," he replied.

"So," went on Martin, "You paid to be tricked?"

The young man thought for a few seconds, "When you put it that way, then yes," he agreed.

"Although you were tricked in the context of the content of the performance," went on Martin, "You didn't feel cheated in terms of the money you paid because the type of show you were entertained to was exactly what you paid for?"

The young man couldn't quite see where this was going. Not for the first time in the last couple of days, he felt bewildered. But he did want to be enlightened, so he simply replied, "Carry on."

Carry on Martin did.

"Let's say young man that you set up a business. You wouldn't stay in business very long if you cheated your customers. You'd quickly become very unpopular indeed if you took their money but then did not supply them with whatever goods or services you had promised they would receive?"

"Absolutely," agreed the young man.

"But," continued Martin, "Your customer would have no need to know exactly how you ran your business; how you made your profit would be entirely up to you – unless of course you were involved in drugs, gun running or some illegal activity of course – but we're not speaking of that. We're talking about a legitimate, respectable enterprise. So far, so good?"

"Yes," replied the young man, now with some confidence, and added, "As the businessman, I wouldn't really want others, especially my competitors, to know the secrets of how I made my profit, would I?"

Now Josmas cut in. "Precisely young man. There's a future for you yet," and smiled. "There's more." He nodded to Martin to continue.

"When you pay to see a magic show, you know that the lady who disappears from the trunk or closet on the stage hasn't disappeared, or the woman who is apparently sawed in half certainly hasn't been. You know that you've been tricked into seeing something that isn't there or not seeing something that is there. Either way, what you think that you do or don't see is an illusion. You leave the theatre after the show scratching your head and wondering 'How did the magician do that?' You might even feel that if you could figure out how the trick was done, the illusion created, then you too could perform the same trick and perhaps become a big star illusionist too. Am I right?"

It was easy for the young man to agree. Martin's reasoning made perfect sense.

"Okay," cut in Josmas, "Apply that same thinking to making money. The man who creates financial wealth is the equivalent of the stage magician. You young man are the budding entrepreneur. You know that the 'entrepreneur/magician' is doing something that you can't see and which he won't tell you about. If you could see what the successful businessman was doing then you could copy it. Now suppose for a moment that what the wealthy guy is doing is actually remarkably simple and the only reason you can't work out what he's doing is because it's so blindingly obvious, then shouldn't it be simple to work out what he's doing?"

"Well err, yes and no I guess," said the young man, "What I'd say is that if it's so simple, why can't I see what it is that he's doing?"

"Easy!" exclaimed Josmas, and slapped the table, "Because you're not asking the right question. The answer is always in the question."

"What's the right question then?" shot back the young man.

"Tell him," said Josmas and once again nodded to Martin. Martin wasted no time in enlightening him.

"The question is not 'How did he do that?' ... the question is in two parts; I'll use the instance of the lady 'disappearing' from the box. Part one, the question is – 'Which way did the lady leave the box'? Part two is that the question – which itself provides the answer remember – should be followed by simple logic. The young man looked blank, waiting for the fuller explanation. It wasn't long in coming.

"When the lady disappears from the box on the stage, how does she leave the box young man? You know that she's no longer in the box, or at least that's most often true, there are variations, but for our purpose she's no longer in the box. Don't ask where is she? Ask, how did she leave the box?"

"Very well," said the young man, rising to the bait, "How did she leave the box?"

"Simple," said Martin, the triumphant twinkle in his eye of one about to make an impressive revelation, "Up, down, front, back or sideways!" This was followed by silence all around. The young man looked at Martin, Martin looked at Josmas and Josmas eyed the young man. "The lady has to go up or down or out the side, front or back. There's no other way." Martin was enjoying himself.

Once more Josmas chimed in, "So you see young man, when you want to know how I or other entrepreneurs achieve the success that we do – ask the right question. The answer will be entirely logical.

"And", cut in Martin, "Don't forget that they'll try to keep their secrets of success from you by creating distractions. The big moves hide the small ones. That's what magicians do on stage to prevent you seeing the simple things that they are doing. In magic it's often referred to as 'smoke and mirrors'. The source of the expression is based on magicians' illusions, where they make objects appear or disappear by extending or retracting mirrors amid a distracting burst of smoke. The bigger the distraction the more complex the trick that can be accomplished."

The young man looked thoughtful again.

"Alright, I can see all that ... as far as it goes. But I still can't for the life of me see how what I've learned so far will make me wealthy or successful – or able to escape unseen from a box on a stage," he threw in slightly sarcastically, and immediately regretted it.

Josmas and Martin both stayed silent. They sipped their kir. So did the young man. Eventually Martin spoke.

~

"Alright young man, once, just this once, I'm going to break with the traditions of my profession and sworn secrecy and reveal to you how, exactly how, I accomplish an illusion."

Saying that, he produced three small, silver cups from his pocket and a coin. He placed the cups, bottom side up, on the table and then put the coin under one of them. He made an elaborate show of shuffling the cups around for a bit and then asked the young man to identify the cup under which the coin was to be found.

Not unexpectedly, the cup which the young man chose did not conceal the coin. Neither did the second cup he picked. Having failed at the second time of asking, Martin then said,

"So obviously it must be under this one," and turned over the third cup to reveal no coin there either. Then he added, "Of course, it was here all the time," and turned the first cup over again to reveal the coin.

Josmas and the young man both laughed and applauded.

"Well done," acknowledged the young man, I enjoyed that. So come on then, how did you do it?"

Martin looked at Josmas in mock disbelief, Josmas shook his head and rolled his eyes,

"Wrong question," he drawled. "Think man."

So the young man thought for a moment before exclaiming,

"Ah yes. Where did the coin go? Err, no, no ... how did the coin disappear!"

"Yes!" cried Martin, "And the answer?"

"I got it," said the young man, "Up, down, front, back or sideways!" A victorious smile to the other men, "But I still don't see how?"

"Never mind," commiserated Martin, "Rome wasn't built in a day. I'll show you how."

First he pointed to the table, knocked hard on it with his fist and ran his hand over it.

"Did the coin go down young man?"

The young man carefully examined the table, reasoned too that Martin couldn't have rigged it, so answered,

"No, not down."

"What about sideways?" quizzed Martin, and handed him the cups to inspect. They were crafted from stainless steel and, examine them though he might, the young man could see no way that the coin could have passed through the side of the cup. He also expressed his belief that Martin hadn't deftly slid the coin out from under the cup.

"Fair enough," said Martin, "That only leaves up," a barely discernable smile on his lips. Again the young man studied the cups, knocking and banging them on the table, turning them over time and time again in his hand before eventually giving up and stating with not a little exasperation,

"I can't see any way that the coin could have got out through the top."

Martin paused, looked at Josmas who smiled, and then deliberately queried,

"Who said anything about it getting *out* through the top?" He waited for the significance of his question to sink in. "I said up, not out!" Then he continued.

"Magicians sometimes invent their own tricks, sometimes they use variations of established routines. Either way they most often manufacture their own props. Whether it's the closet on the stage from which the lady disappears, the saw used to cut the woman in half or the cups that you are now looking at, our props are central to our ability to create illusions.

Too Early For A Glass Of Wine?

They must be perfectly crafted to the finest detail and operate flawlessly. How they work must be totally invisible to the human eye and undetectable under random inspection. On top of that the magician has to have the skill, speed, sleight of hand and ability to mislead audiences, create distractions and operate his equipment effortlessly and invisibly. It takes all of that combined expertise to effectively and entertainingly present an illusion.

The cups which you are holding," the young man was again turning them over in his hand, "Are precision engineered stainless steel, turned to one hundredth of a milimetre."

At that he took the cups from the young man and placed them top side down on the table again. Then he turned them over one by one revealing a coin under each one. He replaced the three cups over the three coins. When he lifted the cups from the table, all three coins had disappeared.

"Yes," he said, "Each cup contains a concealed coin. I can lift or drop the coin with the invisible mechanism built into the cup. That is the winning combination of having perfect preparation in every aspect of your performance. Inventing the 'trick', designing and building the equipment, practicing your art. All must be meticulous."

"And that," said Josmas, "Preparation, practice and performance is what I do with my vines and vineyards to produce the finest wine possible. It's the recipe that all successful people employ. And you young man, it's what you must do in order to achieve great things in life. Are you up to it?"

The young man was not yet quite sure about that but, as he turned the cups over in his hands once more, he felt a surge of confidence rising in him along with the belief that, with these extraordinary characters to guide and support him, he was at last well on his way.

~

Just then dinner arrived. The main course (le plât de résistance) was confit de canard, a speciality duck dish of the region which the young man absolutely adored. He enthused about it to Madame Bertoli to such an extent that she eventually brought him a second portion.

Josmas chose a local Pècharmant red wine to accompany it. Nothing grand like the Petrus they had enjoyed the night before but, just as Josmas had said, it was every bit as delicious and enjoyable. However, it was when Madame Bertoli brought the wine to be opened at the table that the young man gasped in surprise. He felt anger first, then doubt, well up within him.

Madame Bertoli held the bottle of wine in front of Josmas for his approval. He nodded that all was well and she proceeded to open it, producing from the pocket of her smock - a *Smarty* corkscrew! The exact same model that Josmas had sold the young man as a unique exclusive the previous day for fifty pounds. The young man went livid. Turning to Josmas he shouted,

"You tricked me. You told me that 'my' *Smarty* was the only one in the world. You lied!"

Josmas looked at him impassively and quickly took control of the situation with the calm authority which the young man had come to realise that he could assume in any situation. Very relaxed and quietly, Josmas said,

"I did not lie to you."

As he said that he took Madame Bertoli's corkscrew from her and indicated to the name embossed on its side. It read *'Corky'*.

"This is *Corky*," Josmas said, "You own the only *Smarty* in the world. Each corkscrew in the range is unique as is stated on the certificate of authenticity which I gave you. Did you read it?"

The young man hung his head a little and semi-shamefully mumbled, "No." But then, perking up a little, he repeated, "You still tricked me."

"Tell me," said Josmas, "Did Martin trick you just now when he explained about magicians, how they construct their acts and entertain audiences who pay to be fooled? No," Josmas answered his own question. "I am guilty only of showing you how to make situations and wealth work for you.

Failing to check documents, terms or any detail relevant to a deal will in most cases prove fatal to progressing in life. Were you really so foolish as to believe that the corkscrew I sold you was the only one of that design manufactured? Of course that could not be. Yet *Smarty* is unique, as is every single one in the series. Each has its own personal name and certificate to prove it. That is what I offered you and that is what you got."

The young man at this point felt somewhat humbled. How could he have been so misguided as to doubt his host's integrity. He already saw in Josmas a man to be trusted and someone that he could believe in. What was more he had demonstrated by his reaction that he had not taken in the lesson so recently given him by Martin; the lesson of working smart. In respect of how bad he felt at that moment about being foolish and unlistening, things were about to get even worse, as Josmas continued.

"Tell the young man Madame, where you get that line of corkscrews from. Tell him how much you buy them for and how much you sell them for." Madame Bertoli was only too eager to share the information with the young man.

"My wine dealer in Bordeaux sells them to me at five euros each, that's about four pounds sterling. I sell them to my customers here for three times that. Everyone wants to have one when they see me uncorking the bottles with it."

"Tell me about it ... " mused the young man self critically.

"On top of that," she continued, "I give one free to every table that spends over fifty euros on their meal. That's how you got your *Smarty*, isn't it Monsieur Josmas?"

"What?!" raged the young man at Josmas, "You sold *Smarty* to me for fifty pounds and you were given it free?"

"Absolutely," said Josmas, casual and smiling. "But I did offer it to you for twenty-five pounds." He seemed impressed with his own generosity. "You chose to gamble that away though on a bet you couldn't win."

"I don't quite agree with your last statement sir. I'm a handy golfer and play a lot," growled the young man.

"I'm a scratch golfer and playing my own course," was Josmas's slightly dry retort. "I only bet on sure things. So too should you. When you do you will never lose. Remember that a situation or event can only be 'sure' when you control it. Have you learned nothing?"

"Tell me something," he continued in his usual manner of moving easily between points and introducing new ones, "If you ate here every night of the year and spent fifty euros each night, Madame Bertoli would give you three hundred and sixty-five corkscrews. Is that right Madame?" He directed his question to the restaurateur who was still hovering nearby and religiously taking in every word.

"Oui monsieur," came the reply expected of her.

"Now," if you sold each one of those for the same twenty-five pounds that I offered you, you would take in ... let me see ... " he did a quick calculation, "Yes, that would be nine thousand one hundred and twenty-five pounds. Quite a return on zero outlay wouldn't you say? I've already demonstrated to you how to sell them and you know how easily they sell. How much did you say that you earned per year in your current employment?"

"I didn't," replied the young man stonily, but his mind was racing. Josmas's take on the affair was, he had to admit, totally viable.

Of course, reasoned the young man, he wouldn't eat at the restaurant, spend fifty euros and get a free corkscrew every night but, even if he bought them at wholesale price from Madame Bertoli's wine dealer in Bordeaux, he could make a tidy sum selling them on at twenty-five pounds each back in Britain. He felt more than confident that he could do that.

Time for Josmas to once again confound him by apparently reading his mind.

~

"Do you have an idea for a business?" he asked the young man.

"Could be," he replied secretively.

"Tell you what," said Josmas – (Josmas used that term a lot thought the young man. It was usually a prelude to a proposal of some kind) – "I'll buy your idea for one thousand pounds. I'll pay you cash now."

With that he drew the wad of notes, which seemed to go with him everywhere, from his pocket and counted out one thousand pounds worth of tenners on to the table. The young man hesitated, it was a lot of money. Josmas went on,

"Look, you arrived here with almost nothing. Okay, you've got three hundred and fifty pounds left from the money in the envelope. If you spend another hundred getting home that still leaves you two hundred and fifty pounds plus the thousand pounds I'm giving you for your idea. A twelve hundred and fifty pound return for a few days in France with riveting company," here he paused to smile, "Accommodation, free meals and fine wine seems a pretty good return to me. What do you say?"

"He was right," thought the young man, the money represented more than a month's wages in his dead end job back in Britain. What had he to lose?

"Alright," he said semi-reluctantly, "I'll sell you my business idea for your thousand pounds."

Josmas raised his head slowly and looked sternly at the young man. "Oh no you won't!" he emphasised, and started to scoop the money from the table. "I'll tell you why."

"What now," said the young man, completely perplexed, "Do you not think that my idea is worth your thousand pounds?"

"Oh I know it is not worth my thousand pounds," retorted Josmas with a decidedly satirical tone, "Remember, I know what you are thinking."

"Yes," said the young man, temporarily deflected from the subject in hand, "I've been meaning to ask you. How do you do that? Know what I'm thinking all the time; sometimes before even I know?!"

"We'll come back to that ... but yes, it's important. For now though let's stick to your business idea and my one thousand pounds. A thought for you to chew on − If, and only if, your business is worth a thousand pounds to me, then how much more must it be worth to you? Ask yourself the question, ask yourself the right question. I'll repeat – If your business is worth a thousand pounds to me, then how much more must it be worth to you? Think of that. Ask yourself that same question any time in the future should someone offer to buy something, anything, from you. So, in that respect, I am doing you a favour by withdrawing my offer.

However, there is reason from my own point of view as to why I will not pay you my thousand pounds. I know that your idea is not worth one thousand of my pounds because it would be stupid of me to pay for an idea which doesn't involve an original or patentable design of some kind. Ideas which do not have that are, in themselves, worthless. Everyone and his dog has ideas. They, the ideas, only assume a value once they become tangible. Don't believe me?"

Here Josmas stopped for a moment to take a sip of wine. He eyed the young man over the rim of his glass. Then he continued.

"Go down to your local patents or intellectual property register office without, at the very least, a detailed description of an original design, and you'll be laughed out of the place. Your idea, whatever it is, does not meet that minimum requirement ... does it?"

"No," said the young man sheepishly, "You are right."

"Look at it this way," continued Josmas. "The '*Smarty*' corkscrew business was born from a personal difficulty which the inventor experienced and wanted to improve on for his own convenience. He then realised that other people surely had the same difficulty opening their wine bottles as he did. He developed it into a commercial success on that basis. But first he had an original, unique design which he drafted and patented.

If your idea was to buy up corkscrews here in France and sell them for a profit back in Britain, not a bad little potential earner, there's no way you could patent that. If, on the other hand, you were the inventor of the corkscrew, then you could register your design. You could do so even if you had yet to actually manufacture one. Simply thinking of how a new type of corkscrew might work, a new way to market an existing product or provide a service of some kind, are just ideas. As such they have no value. Therefore it would indeed be foolish of me to pay good money to find out what's on your mind.

That's not to say," he continued, "That you should go around telling everyone about your ideas. Your competitors, anybody in fact, might have no interest in buying your idea but that's not to say that they wouldn't be happy to steal it and put it into operation on their own behalf. For that reason, always keep your cards close to your chest.

You don't want someone getting in ahead of you and opening the same French bistro, in the same area of town and with the same cuisine and features that you have in mind, before you do, do you?"

"What!" exclaimed the young man. "How could you possibly have known that was my business idea. I only just thought of it!"

"Simple," said Josmas and, smiling to Martin, said, "Tell him Martin." Martin duly obliged.

"In order to present a convincing stage performance I have to understand my audience. I must be sure that they will react in specific ways to certain situations; that they'll see what they are supposed to see and behave accordingly. For that to happen I must have good knowledge of basic psychology and how all humans instinctively behave in set circumstances plus, and from that, be able to direct their responses in situations created by me.

Asking an individual to pick a card from a deck is a simple example. I can 'push' a particular card to them. For that to work I must create the event and know how they will react to the event."

Here Josmas cut in again.

"To put what Martin has just revealed into the context of who you are, why you are here and what we have been doing this evening, consider this ... You are a young man looking for clarity in life and a way forward, a way to prosper. I have exposed you to numerous insights and tricks in the last forty-eight hours; your mind is buzzing. We visit a restaurant such as you have not previously experienced, enjoy cuisine and drink wines such as you cannot get in your home town. Then I have primed you with the 'making money from corkscrews' scenario and asked if you have a business idea. Who wouldn't think of the French bistro idea? And that's the whole point. It is the answer to your question of how do I know what you are thinking before you yourself know."

Once again Josmas had the young man's full attention. He carried on.

"Two things. Firstly you may be a unique individual with your own exclusive personality but all of us unique individuals originate from the same blueprint. In basic ways we all behave and we all think in the same manner. The message is, know yourself first, learn and recognise how you think and react in situations and then you'll have more than just a good idea of how others will think and react in the same situations.

Secondly, when you want to win in life and business, you should create your own winning circumstances, as I did in the golf play with you and also regarding *Smarty*. You must create situations which will influence people to think and act in just the way that you want them to.

Madame Bertoli wants her clients to buy her corkscrews. They are a tidy earner for her. She creates the circumstance in which people will buy the corkscrew by displaying it in action when she opens the clients' wines. She knows how her clientele will react. The same way that I knew how you would react when I opened the wine in front of you. You see? All people have basic, instinctive ways of thinking and reacting which are part of their core DNA. Smart operators who want to be on top of situations and control their interactions with others in their lives use that knowledge to create circumstances advantageous to them."

~

Eventually the three men bade their farewells to Monsieur and Madame Bertolie and took their leave of the bistro. Josmas had a new corkscrew, *Crafty,* to fill the void vacated by his sale of *Smarty* to the young man. Martin went his separate way and the young man and Josmas wandered back to the château in the still warmth of the late evening. For a long time both were silent. Then Josmas spoke.

"Are you happy young man?"

"Right at this moment?" asked the young man of himself, then replied, "Yes. At this moment I feel an awakening within me. You are responsible for that. As regards my life generally though, no, up to now I wouldn't say that I've been happy. At times I may have thought I was but, truth to tell, I've been mostly just kind of stumbling along."

Josmas nodded in acknowledgement of that.

"Most people harbour a desire to be happy," he stated, "But the vast majority have little idea of what constitutes real happiness. So they have no idea what it is that they are looking for. Therefore, inevitably, they never find it. Even if they did find it, since they don't know what they are looking for, how would they ever recognise it?"

"I guess they wouldn't," ventured the young man, "I'd sure like to be happy and I feel that financial wealth would be a big help, or at least I have up to now but now I'm not so sure?"

"Aahh," continued Josmas, "There are those who associate happiness only with financial wealth. Most such people truly want to be rich. Yet even those, if asked to define the exact amount of money and assets they wish to acquire and the time frame within which they intend to acquire it, will be incapable of answering. Their desire to be wealthy is just a vague, undefined idea. How can you get to where you hope to be when you don't know where you are going?"

Josmas allowed the young man to dwell on that thought for a few seconds. Then he picked up on his topic once more.

"There can be a link between happiness and material wealth, they can coexist in your life. You first must understand that true wealth, and therefore happiness, is an attitude of the mind. It is there and in your inner self that you must seek it. Purely pursuing money will not take you to happiness; rather it can become an obsession which prevents you from enjoying life. Conversely, living in poverty is no walk in the park either! The fact is that money is an excellent servant but a tyrannical master. What you need is a balanced and a planned approach to achieving first, wealth through happiness and second, happiness through your wealth. How to do it? There's a simple solution."

Again Josmas paused. The young man thought to himself how skillfully Josmas played him, teased him almost. Josmas, it seemed, knew just how to prime him with tantalising views on life and then leave him hanging on for the next gem, the follow up wisdom. So the young man waited. Josmas spoke again.

"The key to happiness is within everyone. With the key you will know without doubt if you are happy and if you are doing what it takes to make you happy."

Now Josmas paused and stopped walking. He turned to face the young man directly. Then he continued.

"Here is the key to knowing if you are happy. Once more it is a question. The question is – *Are you doing what you love doing?*"

Again he paused and took a deep breathe before continuing.

"If you are not doing what you love, then you are not happy. Do you spend your time dreaming about what you would like to be doing? Because, if you never actually do what you dream about, you are by definition not happy. When you never do what you really enjoy, you have given up on your dreams. Staying in work and life situations which you loathe, weighs you down, saps your spirit and does not lead to wealth."

"I'll go along with that for sure," agreed the young man, nodding his head sagely.

Josmas continued,

"Be brave and act. Do it now. Do not permit your fears to override your dreams of discovering those things which you really enjoy. Know where you are going and what you are looking for. Find the things you love. Happiness and wealth, in all their forms, will follow."

By now they had reached the château. Josmas shook the young man's hand (the first time he had done that) and they went their separate ways. The young man noticed that Josmas headed to the library, perhaps to partake of a nightcap or catch up on some late reading, he didn't know; but he did catch sight of Jocelyn slipping into the room behind him. She appeared to wear only a flowing negligèe as he had seen her grace the previous night. She carried a small silver tray.

Too Early For A Glass Of Wine?

In his room the young man found by his bedside a copy of Derren Brown's *Tricks Of The Mind'*. Accompanying it was a card which read, *"Best wishes, Martin. Remember – up, down, front, back or sideways."* The young man propped himself up on the bed and started to read. The text thoroughly absorbed him. It elaborated on much of what both Martin and Josmas had been speaking about that night.

As he read, he half expected, even hoped for, a knock on his door – but none came.

Joseph T.Riach

DOWN IN THE DOCKS

When Tommy returned to his home town it was not to the public adulation of *"Local Boy Becomes Football Star"* headlines which in his earlier years he had imagined. There was no fanfare, no ticker-tape parade and no-one waiting to greet him at the airport. The latter was no surprise. After all, no-one knew that he was coming. If they had known, what was there to celebrate? He was no hero, there was no great achievement. On the contrary, he felt himself to be a failure. His arrival back home felt more akin to a beaten dog slinking in the back door with tail between legs to sit chastened in a corner, unwanted, unloved. That at least is how Tommy saw it.

He went straight to his parents' home. That would not have been his first choice but he had nowhere else to go. Meeting them at least lifted his spirits a little. Not that they displayed any great enthusiasm in seeing him but, neither did they show any anger or disappointment. There was no crowing or, "Told you so." Their reaction was one of indifference and, "Yes, of course he could stay until he fixed up a place of his own."

With that decided, Tommy could at least lie low for a time and out of the public eye which he felt sure wanted to hunt him down and shame him for his failure to achieve the fame and glory he had promised; or at least which the press and media had promised when he first left home to become a 'famous footballer'. In the event he needn't have concerned himself. There was far less interest in his return home than there had been in his leaving of it. His football story, he soon came to realise, was yesterday's news.

With his brothers and sister long since departed to make their own ways in life and uncle Charlie sadly passed on, Tommy had, for the first time, a room of his own in the house. He didn't stay long.

With his bonus money from the football club Tommy was able, after a few days, to find himself a more than agreeable apartment in the centre of town. He moved in and soon got a job too. It was manual work at the docks. The money was good and the hours, early mornings and early finishes, suited Tommy too. Now he was just another working guy. In the rough and tumble world of the docks and the tough men who inhabited it, he could hide from public view and cultivate his newly acquired lack of self-esteem. From being a self-assured youth going somewhere in the sporting world he changed almost overnight into an easy to rile, wild hooligan living only for the day and drinking himself into oblivion most nights.

The latter, the drinking, was not difficult to do. Many dockworkers were habitual drinkers. Some wore their daily drunkeness as badges of honour. The drinkers were among the toughest and least forgiving of the dockworkers, often involved in disputes at work and brawls outside of it. Tommy found himself working with some of the country's most hardened of men and was invited, grudgingly at first, into their drinking fraternity at nights. Before that happened, he had to earn their respect.

This process started with his being allocated the dirtiest and most dangerous jobs in the docks, work that no-one would willingly do. For Tommy this most often entailed cleaning 'the tubes' of trawlers and freighters; narrow spaces deep in the bowels of ships, big enough only for a man to slide in on his back and lie as if in a coffin. Once inside, the only light came from the electric lamp powered from a cable which stretched back out of the 'hole'. Tommy was required to chip away at the rusted steel of the chamber walls with a small claw hammer although there was barely room to move his elbows. This was particularly terrifying for Tommy who hated confined spaces and it was made the more so by his workmates' pranks.

One of their pieces of foolery was to bang fiercely on the outer casing of the tube with a spanner, creating a mighty racket of steel on steel reverberations which were intolerable to the occupant inside. Another wheeze was to disconnect the power supply to Tommy's lamp so that he was left in total darkness. The third, most frightening trick of all though, was to close the door at the end of the tube and leave the unfortunate Tommy locked in there way beyond the prescribed thirty minute safety limit. In the meantime the rest of the crew went off for their tea break.

A typical scenario was for the foreman of the squad to come into the tea shop or bothy where the crew were enjoying their break and enquire, "Has anyone seen Tommy?" to be met by mock puzzled looks, raised shoulders and classic lines such as, "Tommy who?" followed by uproarious laughter.

Tommy only endured these times by employing his now well honed detach and dream strategy. He would lie back in the darkness and imagine himself not to be there in the oppressive claustrophobia of the tube but to be in one of his three favourite places on earth. He would remove himself to either a mountain top somewhere in his beloved highlands, to a football pitch and one of his great performances of youth or to the arms of one of his many girlfriends, enjoying the sensuality, kisses and caresses of a romantic encounter.

It was only through such mental gymnastics that he survived the ordeals – and confounded his tormentors. For, when they did return and release him from his hell, rather than emerge angry and threatening all and sundry as the other newcomers did, Tommy would slide himself out, raise himself upright, casually dust himself off and with a smile and an incongruent, "Boy, you should have seen the goal I just scored!" or "Wow, she was really something!" saunter off to his next task. His behaviour in this regard at first baffled the other men, then it made them laugh. Eventually it earned their respect.

It was through this respect that Tommy gradually became accepted by the crew as 'one of them'. With it came the privilege of being awarded 'better jobs' in the docks and the right to accompany the more seasoned dockers on their nights out and drinking binges. It was during one of these booze-ups in a dockside bar that Tommy met Andy Chav.

~

Andy was reputedly the toughest guy in town, a man to be feared. As far as Tommy could tell he certainly deserved the title. It was not because of his physique. He was a short five foot seven inches in height, although the battered New York Yankees baseball cap he habitually wore made him appear taller. He was of podgy rather than stocky build and bore a 'Glasgow smile' across his left cheek; that scar which is inflicted by a cut-throat razor (an old-fashioned long blade razor which folds out from the handle) and is caused by making a slash from the corner of a victim's mouth up to the ear, leaving a scar in the shape of a smile. This gave Andy a grotesque, evil countenance which reeked of the same viciousness that had caused the injury. Having learned his lesson the hard way, Andy reputedly carried a cut-throat with him at all times and was not averse to using it.

His prison record was 'impressive'. He boasted of having spent half of his thirty years 'inside' and the crimes for which he had been put away were all crimes of violence. In physical terms this was a man to be avoided, a man not to mess with. Yet, one Friday evening after picking up his wages from the docks and heading straight to a nearby bar to spend them with the rest of the crew, as was the custom, Tommy found himself seated at the same table opposite the notorious Andy Chav.

Andy proved to be an affable enough fellow, at least that was the case at first. He shared good-humouredly in the jokes and general banter and revealed in the course of it that his Chav title was actually a nickname derived from Charles and Avenue, the name of the street in which he had been born. This, rather than it being a reference to the derogatory slang word of the same, popular in referring to brash, young louts who engage in anti-social behaviour. Although, as Andy put it, 'he was quite happy to accept that definition as well'!

The revelation that Andy had been born and brought up in Charles Avenue which was in an upmarket part of town surprised Tommy. He had taken Andy to be a product of the 'wrong end' of town, the docks and the rough areas. But now he found himself in conversation with the most intellectually accomplished and well read thug that he had ever met. It quickly became apparent that Andy's literature of choice was predominantly mafia tales and stories of gangland violence. *No Mean City'* turned out to be his particular favourite. From these texts he took the inspiration for his real life savagery.

As the night progressed, the beers flowed freely and the talk became louder, more animated. All was fun ... until the dreaded subject of 'politics' reared its hideous head.

Tommy was instinctively to the right in his views, which he didn't consider to be political anyway. He simply believed that people should be individuals, act and take responsibility for their own lives and everything in them. Little did he suspect that his stand on these points was about to be seriously tested. Andy, on the other hand, was a die hard socialist. Soon he was lecturing Tommy about collective responsibility, state ownership and government involvement in every aspect of people's lives.

"That's not involvement!" shouted Tommy across the table, "That's interference. People can stand up for themselves," not for a moment suspecting that he had said anything untoward or offensive. He was, after all, only engaging in banter and stating an opinion. Suddenly the mood changed.

"We'll see about that!" screamed Andy totally without warning, and jumped from his seat. There were but three short steps for him to take in order for him to be in front of Tommy and confronting him. Tommy's mind raced into automatic overdrive.

"He's going to hit me!" was his only thought and, in those split seconds, he acted. As Andy arrived, fists clenched, in front of him, Tommy leapt upwards from his chair and threw himself at his would be assailant. The sudden thrust of his legs jack-knifing from a position below Andy's body and the full weight of Tommy's body thus brought to bear on his opponent, caught Andy completely off guard and off balance. He was thrown back across the room by the impact of Tommy's lunge. Tommy, with Andy's jacket lapels held firmly in either hand, lifted Andy off his feet and hurled him across the bar counter in what onlookers would later describe as 'classic western saloon punch-up' style. Andy crashed past two startled barmen into the bottles and optics behind the bar, slammed his head against the metal taps of a washup sink and slumped to the floor. Tommy flexed his fists at the customer side of the bar and waited for Andy to re-emerge and the inevitable onslaught of retaliation. None came. Andy was out cold.

Quickly afterwards, Tommy was grabbed by several bar staff and thrown out on to the street. He was joined there by some dockworker friends who had taken the opportunity afforded them by Tommy's brawl to throw some punches and 'settle a few scores' of their own. Tommy was none the worse for the wear, sporting only a bruise to his eye which would blacken overnight, but nothing more. His friends suggested that they should disappear to another pub and continue their boozing there. That's what they did. Unknown to any of them, news of Tommy's upstaging of Andy was already jungle drumming it's way around the docks.

The following day Tommy, being the couldn't-care-less character which he was, didn't give a thought to the events of the previous night. They were, as far as he was concerned, just things which had happened and they would be followed in due course by whatever other things might happen. Tommy felt neither enthralled nor frightened. In his characteristic way he was numbed out to it all. He carried on as if nothing had happened.

Yet, as the weekend and then the following week passed by, Tommy became aware of a change in his life. It started at work. More of the several hundred strong workforce around the docks, the majority of whom Tommy didn't know and the rest of whom he barely knew, started to greet him as he passed by. Maybe just a nod, a couple of "Hi Tommys", but Tommy definitely sensed a change in general attitude towards him. He was aware of no longer being an invisible kid. He was recognised and, dare he think it, he was being shown a degree of respect.

This manifested itself most glaringly in the dockside pubs. When Tommy entered, the general hubbub subsided just a bit, whispers were exchanged between the drinkers and Tommy was pointed out by some to others. Complete strangers approached and offered to buy him drinks. All this bemused Tommy, but he didn't dislike the attention. It was, after all, exactly as he had imagined that he would be treated had he become the famous football star that he had dreamed of becoming. Now here he was, without even kicking a ball or scoring a goal, receiving the same sort of adulation.

Tommy was smart enough however to realise that this wasn't the same as had he achieved fame on the football field. For a start it was only a small section of the community who held him in awe. They were mostly dockers, labourers, working men and the down-and-outs who frequented rough pubs in the industrial part of town. Hardly what would be called an extensive or sophisticated fan club.

And secondly, "What," reasoned Tommy as he knocked back another free pint one day, "Have I done to generate this dubious admiration? I simply got pissed, then got pissed off with someone else's opinion about something that didn't matter. Then I reacted in haste to an attack which was maybe never coming, got lucky and surprised my supposed attacker with a move of little skill and pure instinct. The entire incident was over in five seconds flat!"

He smiled to himself at that and downed his drink. He declined the offer of a further beer from an 'admirer' who sidled up to him to shake his hand as if he were some people's hero - "Or a politician," thought Tommy, "Heaven forbid!"

Had he accepted the offer it would have been his umpteenth free pint just that day; and he'd lost count of how many had come his way in the days since he had slam-dunked Andy. He declined the offer, shook the fellow's hand anyway, wiped the froth from his lips and left the pub. A few seconds later he was wishing that he had stayed inside and accepted the pint.

He had walked only a few yards along the road when he saw Andy, head bowed on the other side and walking towards him. At the same moment that Tommy saw him, the Chav looked up and saw Tommy. Tommy hesitated, but only fractionally, and carried on walking. Andy however, had broken his stride, and started to cross the road towards him.

"What to do?" thought Tommy. He was no coward and running was not an option. He stopped and turned to face his adversary.

As Andy came nearer Tommy locked his grip around the bunch of keys in his pocket, sliding several of the keys between his fingers so as to form an improvised knuckle duster. It was a trick he had been taught by some of the older dockers as a means of defending himself should he find himself in a spot of bother any time. He grasped the keys and waited for Andy to produce his cut-throat razor.

Andy came up to him full frontal, his hand flashed from his

pocket, Tommy twitched to defend himself and ... found Andy smiling broadly, empty hand outstretched in welcome and,

"Hi there big Tommy. Fancy a pint?"

At that moment Andy, even with his terrifying Glasgow smile, appeared benign and friendly to Tommy. And so he was. They returned to the pub from which Tommy had so recently departed and caused quite a stir among the drinkers and bar staff when they entered together. Over a couple of pints, supplied by a 'well-wisher', Andy confided to Tommy,

"I'm glad you did what you did, it lets me off the hook of bearing the tag of being the meanest dude in town. Now it's yours to carry." He laughed at that and raised his glass, "Cheers tough Tommy, you deserve it."

Tommy didn't find this revelation to be quite as amusing nor comforting as Andy obviously did. But he was put more at ease when Andy added,

"Don't worry. The reputation is the thing. Once you have that it does the work for you. When people believe you are the toughest guy in town then you become the toughest guy in town. It's self-fulfilling."

For the second time while with Andy (the first time had been the infamous night of the brawl) Tommy found himself rather liking the guy and appreciating his wisdom. Clearly there was a lot more to him than met the eye.

"Listen," continued Andy, " I admire the fact that you stood up to me, not many people do. Most are creeps. They fawn around me like adoring lapdogs and ply me with drinks to buy my favour, like this pathetic lot here." At that he indicated towards the drinkers scattered around them.

"Don't be like them Tommy, you can do better, much better. Don't concern yourself with me. I do my own thing, I'm my own worst enemy. But you, you can be something, be somebody. Now remember, you need any help, any time, I'm here for you. You can rely on me."

With that he held out his hand once more. The pair shook hands long and hard.

"Remember Tommy, anything at all," said Andy with real sincerity, then, "Let's get in another round."

So they did. It came free of course.

~

It soon became a common occurence around the docks for Tommy and Andy to be seen together. Frequently laughing, often deep in conversation and always scaring the shit out of any unfortunates who had, or who felt they had, crossed either of the hard men in some way. Andy was not the only career criminal often at Tommy's side. Brian Corder became another constant companion.

Brian was known to all and sundry as Fagin. As his nickname implied, the man was a thief. Not just any thief but a master thief; and he ran a gang of associate thieves. Fagin was not a thug like

Too Early For A Glass Of Wine?

Andy but he was tough enough to organise, control and discipline his gang. He was not a guy to be trifled with. But he had a sense of humour and was another literate and well read rogue. Because of those attributes he relished his Fagin title and reputation every bit as much as the original character of the name in Dickens' celebrated 'Oliver Twist' novel.

Tommy met Fagin for the first time in a dockside bar, where else? while he, Tommy, was negotiating to buy a leather trouser belt from a Norwegian seaman. Tommy had just agreed to pay the sailor by way of his own deer-bone handle sheath knife (knives were often necessary tools around the docks and of course with sailors) when Fagin, who had been standing nearby and overheard the conversation interrupted.

"I can get you a better belt than that and half the price. You can keep your knife. Exactly what kind of belt do you have in mind?"

Disengaging himself from his Norwegian 'friend', Tommy set about describing in detail the leather belt he would really like to own. The one he had in mind to buy if he could afford it was a rare designer brand available only in upmarket stores at considerable cost.

"If," he assured Fagin, "You could get a cheaper version of that, then that would be fine."

"I don't do cheaper versions," said Fagin acidly, "Same time here tomorrow all right?" and quoted a ridiculously low price for the item.

"Fine by me," said Tommy, fully expecting to see neither Fagin nor the belt on the following day. How wrong he was.

Just as promised, Fagin showed up at the bar at the designated time the next day.

"I don't have the belt," he solemnly pronounced.

"Just as I expected," thought Tommy but, before he could say it, Fagin added with a twinkle in his eye,

"But this young fellow does!"

With that a lad of only thirteen or fourteen years of age sprang from behind him brandishing the belt. Tommy took it and looked it over. Yes, it was the real McCoy. He paid Fagin the pre-agreed price of the purchase and shook hands on the deal. Then the pair sat down for a drink together.

Tommy immediately hit it off with the thief. Fagin was a quietly confident and quietly spoken young man. His whole character and demeanour put those who met him at immediate ease and, in contradiction of his chosen profession, he inspired a sense of confidence and trust in others.

"Did you pay the lad?" inquired Tommy, "I didn't see you give him any money."

"My team work on piece rate," replied Fagin, "We divvy up at the end of each week."

He then went on to describe the details of his operation. It very quickly became clear to Tommy that it was a serious enterprise and, rather than stealing at random, it worked more like an online mail order business.

Tommy had experienced having shady characters approach him in pubs, surreptitiously reveal an item hidden under their jacket and ask if he wanted to buy it. That was not Fagin's style. No, he and his team stole to order. The approach to punters in pubs was one of, "What can I get for you?"

If it was a shirt that you wanted then you would request it by label, size and colour. A price would be agreed and the garment would be delivered to you at a designated time and place as had happened with Tommy's belt.

Fagin's trade didn't stop at belts and shirts. He and his boys could steal anything. Fridges, freezers, washing machines and televisions – he supplied them all. Tommy heard it rumoured he acquired cars as well, but he never saw evidence of that.

What Tommy did see evidence of was the activity of 'grasses'; those snitches who would report illegal activities such as those of Fagin, and indeed Andy Chav, to the police in return for payment or to escape prosecution for their own crimes. Tommy detested such individuals every bit as much as the criminals loathed them. His disciplined upbringing had taught him many things, not all pleasant, but among his father's lessons, the one 'to never tell on your friends or colleagues' was engrained deep within him. He had many times taken childhood beatings, both parental and at school, on behalf of others he would not snitch on or who would not own up to their own misdeeds. His sister's vandalising of his mother's party dress when Tommy was only six being one such example.

Tommy was therefore first curious, then increasingly uneasy when, drinking in a regular dockside haunt one evening, he saw one of Fagin's lads deep in conversation with a man Tommy knew to be a police officer. Tommy also saw something change hands between the two under the table. The policeman and the lad then left the pub separately, first one then the other, five minutes apart. Within another five minutes Tommy had polished off his pint and was on his way to seek out Fagin.

~

Detective Sergeant Harry Milne was the man who Tommy had seen talking with Fagin's lad in the pub. Harry had been at school with Fagin, the man he called by his proper name of Brian Corder, and knew his adversary well. Both had been intelligent teenagers but, while Harry's family were devout presbyterians and strict disciplinarians, Brian's parents were lazy and disinterested in work, life generally and their son in particular. As a result Brian was left to his own devices, quit school at the earliest age possible, roamed the streets and took to the life of petty theft and then that of organised crime which he now followed. He sported a flamboyant 'teddy boy' hair style, wore drainpipe trousers and blue suede shoes.

Harry, by comparison, had an army style short back and sides haircut. He was kept on a strict parental leash, compelled to follow what his folks termed the 'straight and narrow' and taught that life was a simple black or white. There was the bad and there was the good, no in-betweens. He had to chose one path or the other. Not unsurprisingly, Harry chose the straight; donning the staid black and white uniform of the police force. His rise to the rank of sergeant, then detective sergeant had been rapid. He had no intention of it stopping there.

As he faced his hit team assembled for the night's raid, he sensed a rare opportunity to kill two birds with one stone. The target of the raid was to be his old friend and arch nemesis Brian Corder. Plus, when the operation went well, he anticipated the recognition of further promotion.

"Acting on intelligence passed to me," he began, "I have strong reason to believe that a large consignment of stolen cigarettes will be in a warehouse at the docks tonight. The gang responsible for their theft plan to move the load out in the morning. The gang leader is Brian Corder ... ", here he paused and looked around the room as if to impress on everyone the significance of the name he had just announced, then continued, "Who of course we all know as Fagin. He has evaded our grasp on many occasions, far too often in fact. This is your opportunity to put him away for a long time."

He then detailed his plan of attack which entailed approaching the warehouse in silence, blocking all entrances and potential escape routes and storming the premises to take the gang by surprise. His intention was that they be caught red handed with their illegal cargo.

"Any questions?" he asked when he had finished delivering his instructions.

Just one timid voice responded. "This Brian Corder, Fagin guy, he's an old school chum of yours ... is that right?"

Harry stared the officer in question down for a few seconds before replying,

"I'd hardly call him a chum, more a thorn in my flesh. He kept me out of the junior school rugby team for a couple of years so, yes, I'd like payback for that."

That brought a chuckle from the assembled group but then, turning more serious and reverting to the presbyterian righteousness of his upbringing, Harry continued,

"This man makes a mockery of the law, of you, of me, of every upstanding, law-abiding citizen. It is our duty to get him off the streets. Are you with me?"

"Yes!" went up a fragmented, not entirely convincing cry and the squad trooped from the briefing room and out to their waiting police vehicles. Harry brought up the rear smiling inwardly, "I've got you this time you bastard."

Harry was already picturing in his mind the moment of confronting Brian and uttering his favourite, 'You don't have to say anything but ... ' lines as he slapped on the handcuffs. More so he could envisage his promotion which would follow; the adulation he would receive, his elevation to the rank of inspector. Later he might even become chief of police ... he allowed himself to dream. In the event Harry would, in due course, realise all of those lofty ambitions. But it wasn't going to be tonight.

The convoy of police cars approached the warehouse with lights dimmed and no sirens sounding. Silently the police hit squad surrounded the building, each man taking up his designated position. Some remained outside to guard the exits and prevent any of the gang escaping. The rest readied themselves to storm inside on Harry's command, confront all those that they found there and sieze the load of stolen cigarettes. Harry gave the command.

A truck drove at, and smashed through the main entrance. Harry charged in at the head of his possé and shouted for everyone who was there to stand still and not resist arrest.

A gang of about twenty young men and lads were gathered around a number of vans, into which they were loading large cardboard cartons. Directing operations was Brian Corder – Fagin himself! All those in the warehouse did exactly as ordered. They ceased their work, almost too willingly, and waited for what would happen next. No-one did try to resist arrest. Nor did anyone flee. Everyone remained uncannily calm. Their demeanour was, in fact, positively flippant.

Harry could hardly contain himself. Strutting up to Corder he faced him, looked at the cases now scattered all around and said, "Well well Brian, what have we here?"

Very casually, and with remarkable restraint, Fagin said, "Cream buns." Then backed off nonchalantly as if to give Harry access to the nearest box, "It's cream buns for the poor kiddies mate ... oh, and fresh eggs too."

There followed a palpable silence. The whole warehouse went quiet. Police and villains alike stood still and waited. Harry hesitated. Then, with less confidence than before, said, "Pull the other one Brian," turned to one of his squad and commanded, "Break open that case!"

"Be careful," interjected Brian quickly, "They're very fragile."

Ignoring Fagin's warning Harry impatiently snatched the cutters with which his officer was about to open the first case and lunged into the task himself.

"Don't say I didn't warn you," cried Fagin.

As Harry smashed open the cardboard box, a trickle of creamy goo appeared. Then it was followed by a sticky stream of cream, bread crumbs and broken eggs. The more that Harry tore into the box, the more it first leaked, then sprayed it's creamy cargo. Harry hacked ever more frantically ... at the first box, then another, then another. All his efforts produced the same result. Every carton spilled out the same flood of yucky yokes and milky mess, a veritable cream buns and eggs galore moment.

All present started to giggle. Soon everyone, police officers and villains alike, were laughing uproariously. They had no option but to. They couldn't contain themselves. It was a scene of pure farce. The only one not laughing was Harry. He was beside himself with rage.

Eventually Fagin, who had been laughing his head off as much as anyone, stepped forward and put a restraining hand on Harry's arm. "Better leave off mate, you'll have to pay for these buns and eggs you know ... " and here he pointed round at the entire collection of cardboard boxes stacked high around them, some on the floor, some in the vans, " ... this load is due for delivery to children's homes around the town first thing in the morning. It's our donation to their children's week. Here is the purchase receipt from the bakers. All paid, above board. You only needed to ask."

He drew a slip of paper from his pocket and held it out to Harry, then stopped and waited for some response. None came. Harry's mind was racing, perplexed. He was, for perhaps the only time in his burgeoning police career, totally flummoxed. Fagin grabbed the moment and cut back in.

"I'll get the lads to clear up the mess your boys have made and get the vans loaded. I want the damaged goods replaced and you ... ", here Fagin turned more aggressive, pointing his finger firmly into Harry's chest, "You I want out of my premises – now!"

With that, he turned on his heel and went back to work loading the vans with his lads.

Harry stood red faced and simmering for several minutes then, composing himself with difficulty, he pulled back his shoulders, ordered his men from the warehouse and strode past them to lead them out. As he did so several of his officers started smirking, giggling and eventually laughing outright anew. They couldn't help themselves because of what they saw before them. As the story would soon circulate among police officers nationwide and in police stations around the country – Harry had egg on his face!

Later on in the day of Harry Milne's failed raid on Fagin's warehouse, Tommy received a small, brown paper bag delivered to him at his work in the docks. In it was a note which read, "Any help, any time, I'm here for you. Anything at all." The bag also contained a cream bun.

LOVE CAME IN DARKNESS

Josmas was seated on a wicker chair under a pergola awash with the brilliant translucence of bougainvillea flowers, the brightly coloured climbing plant which is widely cultivated in the tropics. The shrub seemed perfectly at home here too, as of course was Josmas. He wore the same shabby working clothes as he had done on the day of the young man's arrival at the château. He was drinking coffee. A fresh brew in a glass coffee plunger sat on the low table next to him.

"Join me," he cried to the young man who had just entered. "Chez Magicien was great fun, n'est-ce pas? You look like you need a good cup of coffee."

"I sure do," replied the young man, "That was quite a night." He meant what he said. He had found the whole of the previous two days, the events, the characters quite overwhelming. Of course he knew that he was in a different world from anything he had known before but, more than that, he felt different at his very core. It was as if a thousand bright new lights had been switched on inside his mind and more so, within his soul. He knew deep within himself that they would never be extinguished. He didn't want them to be. He poured himself a coffee and sat down on a bench under the shade. He cast his gaze around him

"Breathtaking, isn't it?" Josmas cut into the young man's thoughts, "All this." He held his hand out, palm upturned and indicated the vineyards stretching below them. Busy between the ranks, the pickers were filling the last baskets of the season's crop.

"Soon the harvest will be in," continued Josmas, "The grapes will be pressed and their precious juice prepared for fermentation. In due course the wine will be ready and eventually bottled. After appropriate storage the vintage will find its way all around the world. Just as you said is the case with books and will be the case with your writing, the wine will bring pleasure to thousands. What greater satisfaction could there be for any man than to know that an activity which gives me the greatest possible pleasure and satisfaction will likewise impact on the happiness of so many others. That, young man, is pure bliss!"

"Yes," replied the young man, "I can see that. I don't believe that I have ever seen 'pure bliss', as you put it, before. But yes, this must be it."

At that moment, he truly believed that he was indeed experiencing absolute bliss for the first time. He felt that he was no longer passing through life as a spectator or even voyeur; he was not the tourist viewing the sight from behind glass or through a camera lense or the holidaymaker proudly showing a postcard to jealous friends; he was no longer outside looking in. He felt that he was the character in the photo, the man featured on the postcard.

"It takes work of course," interjected Josmas, not entirely surprising the young man that he had anticipated exactly how he was feeling, "All this had to be created. Then again, when you are ambitious and imaginative you can create anything.

You know, 'Creative Solutions' is the name with which I christened that part of my business which undertook trouble shooting work for clients. I never considered what I did, the solutions I came up with, to be consistently brilliant. But I did realise that I tended to think of them while others didn't. So that was the essential difference.

In time I came to give thought to just what it was in my psychological make up which caused me to think in the way which I do. A bit like my creative solutions themselves, the answer I arrived at is not explosively revelationary, it is in fact remarkably simple –

I have never lost the curiosity of childhood."

Here he stopped, as he often did after making a particularly powerful point, to let the full impact of what he had said sink in. He was pleased to see that the young man was nodding in appreciation. Nonetheless, he repeated slowly and clearly,

"I have never lost the curiosity of childhood,"

Then, after another pause, and almost as an afterthought, "As a four year old, I sang 'I am a little teapot' at a holiday camp talent competition. I made up some words as I went along and actions to go with them. To this day I still make up silly rhymes and jingles and sing them out loud as I go around the château and estate. I generally convince all and sundry that I'm totally nuts! This causes some confusion.

Family and friends find it difficult to equate my nonsensical fun behaviour and my professional accomplishments as being from the same person. They fail to see that my professional and junior selves are actually one and the same, that they complement each other and exist because of each other; that it's the very fact that my inner child is alive and thriving which explains just where my creative inspiration comes from."

That last part hit home like a hammer blow with the young man. A bomb went off in his mind. He instantly knew that, rather than embracing his 'inner child' as Josmas had referred to it, or simply his childhood as the young man interpreted it, he had been pushing it away, rejecting it. He had felt it was unworthy, inappropriate to feel childishness. Yet here was Josmas admitting that being childish was the 'secret of his succes', or at least an essential element in living a happy and balanced life. Josmas had touched a nerve. The young man suddenly felt quite emotional. Josmas sensed his reaction to his words and carried on.

"As an adult you tend to think in ways conditioned by upbringing, education, peer pressure, society and the culture you live in. You forget how to dream – or at least you under value it. You fail to recognise how day dreaming can create endless streams of inspiration and ideas. On the other hand, when you relax and let your subconscious mind take over, and when you think as a child, then you are unhindered by those influences and restraints. You become spontaneous, imaginative and creative in your thinking.

When you invoke your childhood curiosity, allow yourself to wonder at things and detach yourself from reality, then everything becomes possible. Even those creative solutions to situations which most other people think are not!"

With that he slapped the table as if to emphasise his point or perhaps just to indicate to the young man that the particular lesson was concluded. Either way, he reached to pour both himself and the young man another cup of coffee. As he did so he briefly patted the young man's knee. It was a spontaneous action, a comforting, reassuring touch; a brief but sympathetic acknowledgement of the emotion which he knew he had kindled in the young man. The young man for his part appreciated the gesture. At that moment he felt like a son to Josmas.

So lost was he in his thoughts and in listening to Josmas's unending wisdom, the young man had not realised that lunch time had come around. He was reminded however by the arrival of Jocelyn, first with crockery and cutlery, and then assiette after assiette of fresh meats, cheeses and summer vegetables which she arranged with artistic care on the wicker coffee table.

When she brought in le plat de résistance both Josmas and the young man "Ooohhed" and applauded. It was a magnificent whole poached salmon topped with parsley and lemon. Served on a large, silver platter, Jocelyn placed it with appropriate ceremony as the centrepiece of the presentation..

Then she brought an ice-bucket to sit in its stand at the side of the table and introduced a bottle of wine for Josmas's inspection. He cast a glance at the label, nodded his approval and she flicked it open with Josmas's new *Crafty*. That made the young man smile. He caught Josmas's eye and he smiled back. The wine was a young Portuguese vinho verde, chilled and slightly sparkling. It accompanied the salmon as if the two were matched in heaven.

As they ate and talked on the terrace, the word 'bliss' drifted into the young man's mind once more. Yes, everything really was that good. Almost before they knew, it was late afternoon, the sun was dipping and the ever attentive Jocelyn was once more serving coffee.

~

With coffe cup in hand, Josmas stretched back contentedly in his chair and once more scanned the estate at work all around them.

"The activity you see here today is the physical embodiment of my creative thinking," he started. "As most people are capable of producing neither the original thought nor the subsequent implementation of it, there will always be demand for what I do. There will also always be those who will endeavour to steal one, the other or both. Part of your responsibility to yourself, your work and those reliant on you therefore is to guard against that."

"How do I do that," asked the young man, yet again instantly caught up in and intrigued by Josmas's words.

"Well," said Josmas, "I had a friend back in Scotland, McDougall was his name. His corner of paradise was that part in the glen where the river formed a still, dark pool below the waters cascading from the rocks high up on the mountainside. Here McDougall knew that the salmon lurked and he was adept at tempting them on to his hook with the flies which he tied himself from grouse feathers during the dark days of winter. He earned a modest income selling his flies to visitors and the salmon he hooked to local bars and restaurants. He asked for no more in life and was never happier than when casting his line on the waters in the long gloaming of summer evenings."

Josmas took a sip of coffee. The young man listened transfixed. It felt almost as if he were there, at the water's edge with McDougall and living every moment. Josmas knew that he had the young man hooked every bit as much as McDougall hooked his salmon. He went on.

"McDougall was not only the most enthusiastic of all the local fisherman, he was also the most prolific. While others would stand waist deep in the icy water for hours on end and with little to show for their efforts, he would land the silver darlings almost at will. His ghillie's bag was inevitably packed full as he headed homewards. He was generous with his success, always giving the others a fish to take back to their loved ones for a delicious supper and justification of their time spent by the river.

So McDougall was more than taken aback when, one day, he was approached by a 'committee' of local men complaining that he had cornered the market in catching salmon. They demanded that he share his catches more fully with all of them. Under threat of being marginalised in the community, and worse, McDougall reluctantly agreed. He reasoned he could still have enough left over from his regular catches to feed himself and earn an, albeit reduced, income from sales.

Soon however, the villagers demanded more, and then more. McDougall found himself supplying the entire village with salmon while having none left for himself. He still enjoyed the actual fishing, it was his passion; but he couldn't live, he had been taxed out of business. So he stopped fishing."

"That is scandalous," said the young man. Yet, even as he spoke he could think of many parallels of such behaviour which he had already encountered in his young life. He thought that he knew where Josmas was headed with this tale so he urged him to carry on.

"In little time, said Josmas, 'The 'committee' once more arrived at his door. They complained that the village had no fish and everyone was starving,

'That cannot be,' said McDougall, 'You do have fish. You have all the salmon in the river. You have all those that I used to catch and more. Now they are all yours.'

'No-one has the knowledge of the river and the skill that you have,' they retorted, 'You must help us!'

'Oh no I must not!' was McDougalls stern response. 'What you must do is take the time and learn, just as I did.'

'Who will teach us? How can we survive in the meantime?' they pleaded. McDougall allowed himself an ever so slightly smug, inward smile. 'Hook, line and sinker,' he thought.

A few weeks later life in the glen had returned to near normal. McDougall was once again contentedly ensconced most evenings by his favourite pool waiting for the salmon to bite. Except now around him was a group of men, locals and visitors, watching his every move and hooked on his every word. They were pupils of his newly founded salmon fly fishing school in which the villagers owned a forty-nine percent stake. The fish that McDougall caught he kept for himself and his restaurant customers as before; the fish the others caught went to the people of the glen. McDougall's sales of his hand tied flies increased so much that he opened a cottage industry which employed local people."

Here Josmas once again rested back in his chair, drained the last of his coffee and smiled the smile of a contented man, one fully in harmony with life and confident of the simple truth which he both lived and told of in his story. His conclusion followed.

"You see young man, for entrepreneurs like McDougall, there are no difficulties that cannot be overcome. Those like him recognise only opportunities and solutions. They know that success is not final and that failure is not the end. They understand that it is having the courage to continue which counts. No matter how dire the circumstances they refuse to give in. They rise above the difficulties. In fact, they make the difficulty work for them – think about that.

McDougall refused to be taxed out of business by those less worthy than himself. Instead he created an improved situation for both himself and his tormentors. He ensured that life would not only continue as before for him but that, from the waters cascading down the mountainside to the dark pools below and the salmon residing within, his corner of paradise would be preserved and enhanced for all to benefit from.

Do you possess such resilience, imagination and skill?"

"I don't know for sure," replied the young man, "I sure hope so."

"Hoping is not enough," barked Josmas, "You must take life by the horns and do it now. Come, let's take a walk before it's dark. I fancy a leg stretch and an early night."

~

They rose from the table and walked together out between the vines where the last of the picking had been completed for the day, and for the season. The pickers had made their way to the traditional celebration of the harvest. This included their bare foot dance in the huge vats of freshly picked grapes.

"We'll leave them to their fun, said Josmas, "We have more important things to attend to."

What those things might be, the young man couldn't even guess at but he walked in silence with Josmas, soaking in the cool night air and the scents of lemons and forest flowers. After a while the young man ventured,

"This is so lovely but ... ", and here he hesitated, then decided to continue, " ... You have created and enjoy an idyllic life here sir. Do you never become bored?" Instantly he regretted his question.

If looks could kill ... !

Josmas drew in his breath slowly. His response to the question came by way of narrowed eyes and a scathing stare. Eventually he replied.

"It is not that I haven't heard the asinine 'Don't you get bored?' query before, it is just that my disappointment with those who pose the question never lessens."

After several seconds of charged silence he raised his arm and made a slow, indicative sweep around himself.

"Can you smell the air?" he asked, "It's fresh and clean. Do you not feel the cool caress of the breeze? It carries the scent of wild flowers and the lavender where busy bees are buzzing about their business."

He pointed out the butterflies still fluttering by in the twilight, the dark silhouette of the mountains above and the sparkling emerald of the ocean below. Lastly he indicated to the château and the terrace where they had eaten. He reminded the young man of the superb salmon and accompanying spread of fresh local produce, cheeses, fruit, legumes and wine to delight any palate which they had enjoyed.

"In your question itself, therein lies the answer," he said. "You must look within your own existence in order to see with clarity why your question is senseless. Fortunately I do not see you as one of those hollow souls whose 'boredom' is relieved only by clattering cities, chattering technology, hectic greed and the frantic wastefulness of modern society. I believe that you are better than that, much better.

I have welcomed you in, so now I will reveal to you my simple way to sift out the noisy and unnecessary from life and to concentrate on just those basic things which really matter – fresh air, sunshine, nature, nourishment, laughter and love. First you, anyone, must possess the ambition to better your life in such a way. You must be open to ridding yourself of boredom fatigue. You must understand that the answers you seek are in the questions you ask. The choice you have to make is what I call 'to be or not to be simple'? Are you ready to make the choice?"

"Yes," said the young man, "I truly am. Please teach me."

He meant it too, from the bottom of his heart. He felt himself at that moment to be like a hitherto closed flower turning to the sun and asking for its warm rays to ease open its petals and let enlightenment shine in. He knew that from that point he would never go back. Josmas looked at the young man with his kindly, mirthful eyes. The young man knew that Josmas could read his emotions and he was grateful for it. Josmas nodded knowingly. He carried on.

"I am a great believer in simple. For me simple is best and simple works. Following on from that I assert that there is no need to have complexity in your life. In fact, the more complicated your life and those people and things in it, then the less likely you are to be successful in your pursuits and endeavours and the less likely you are to experience contentment and joy. It is necessary to expel the complex and the complicated from your life. This is what you must do.

When you get back to your room tonight, take a sheet of paper and draw a line down the middle of it. Now you will have two columns. At the head of the left hand column write the word 'Simple'. At the head of the right hand column write the word 'Complex'.

Next, list down in either column all those things in your life – activities, work, people, pursuits, hobbies, relationships, emotions, possessions, whatever – which you consider to be simple, as in easy to deal with, produce no stress or difficulty, are fun, light and enjoyable; and all those things you know to be complex – as in needless, confusing, consume too much time, cause you unhappiness, distress, loss of esteem etc. – in the respective columns. When you are finished you will most likely find that upwards of fifty percent of your items, often as high as ninety percent with many people, will be in the right hand, complex column. Yes, the majority of people fill their lives with complicated and therefore wasteful and unrewarding work, thoughts, pursuits and relationships. Whatever the result, the next bit is the important thing.

Score through the complex column with a heavy black line. Better still, rip it off and chuck it in the bin. Best of all, screw it up and burn it. Watch with joy as you see all those horrible and destructive complex matters go up in smoke. It will be like a huge release for you, a weight off your shoulders, a cleansing of the spirit.

From this day onwards, work only on doing and enjoying those things which remain in your intact left hand, simple column. These will henceforth form the mainstay of your existence. With all the complex stuff eliminated you will now have extra time and energy and the freedom to concentrate on your simple, and therefore more rewarding, aspects of life. That's it.

It may be that you are astounded by the sheer simplicity of what I am proposing. You shouldn't be. As I said at the outset – simple is best and simple works. To be or not to be simple is a simple no contest choice."

The young man nodded in agreement,

"Yes I appreciate that and yes, I can see that straightforward and uncomplicated must be a really enjoyable way to live. I'm actually looking forward to starting on it soon."

"Soon is no good young man," reprimanded Josmas severely, "Draw your list tonight. You will assume responsibility from tomorrow. Sleep well, or at least have a memorable night."

Josmas's words yet again puzzled the young man. Were they prophetic? What more did Josmas know about his future that he himself didn't know? What responsibility was he talking of? In what way could the night be memorable? ... or more memorable than was already the case?

The pair said their goodnights and parted in the hallway.

~

Arriving back in his room, the young man found once more that a book had been placed by his bedside. It was William Shakespeare's *Hamlet* and it lay open at the famous *'To be or not to be ... '* passage. He started to read.

"To be, or not to be," - there was no 'simple' he noted, and smiled at that - *"That is the question. Whether 'tis nobler in the mind to suffer the slings and arrows of outrageous fortune or to take arms against a sea of troubles and, by opposing, end them?"*

The young man took this to refer to his own life, becalmed in mediocrity as it undoubtedly was, versus Josmas's urging to be true to himself and stride out in pursuit of his passion. It reinforced in his mind that he should be brave and act, that he should do it now and not permit his fears to over-ride his dreams of discovering those things which he really enjoyed.

"Know where you are going and what you are looking for. Find the things you love. Happiness and wealth, in all their forms, will follow," so Josmas had said.

"He is a clever fellow," thought the young man, then added with a smile, "And that Shakespeare guy knew a thing or two as well."

After a couple of chapters, well engrossed in the murder, mayhem and madness of Hamlet's troubled life, he remembered the 'homework' set him by Josmas. He put the book to one side and took a notepad and a pen from the bedside table drawer. He scored a line down the middle of the first page as he had been instructed to. At the head of the left hand column created by the divide he wrote the word 'Simple' and at the head of the right hand column the word 'Complex'. He undressed, got into bed and started to write.

Once he had written down every conceivable element of his life, work, pastimes, relationships, ambitions and emotions that he could think of, he thought for a while … and then wrote some more. When he felt that there was at last nothing more that he could possibly add, he didn't score out or rip off the offending right hand column, but placed the pad on his bedside table beside Hamlet, rolled over and fell into a deep sleep.

~

The young man's dreams were of Denmark, *'alas poor Lady Chatterley I knew her well'*, confit de canard, fine wines disappearing up, down, or sideways and an erotic episode in which a nubile young lady lay naked on top of him and took his manhood inside her. Up and down, up and down, very slowly, very gently she rode him. He eased out of sleep and his wet dream to find that he was indeed wet … but in no way was he dreaming. The experience was real and happening now! In the pitch black of the shuttered room he could not see the face of his pleasurer but the scent was distinctly that of fresh honey and Jocelyn.

Too Early For A Glass Of Wine?

Whoever it was, she was lieing flat and full length on him, naked and sliding her body slowly, very slowly up the full length of his and then down again, over and over. It was such a languid, dreamlike motion that, as he slipped out of sleep, he truly was unsure as to whether he was still dreaming or not. But yes, sure enough, it was real, deliciously real. He was already erect and within Jocelyn, for it was surely she, was it not? The fragrance was certainly that of the previous encounter but the body seemed somehow more slender. How could he know in the inky blackness which served only to heighten his senses. Especially those of taste, touch and tongue.

As she slid upwards towards him, the woman's lips became level with his. Her tongue darted rapidly between his lips and her kisses sucked on them. At the same time, his penis drew almost completely out of her vagina. She reached a hand down to rub its tip around her hardened clitoris, pushing the clitoris into the crack of his cock. Then she took her fingers, soaked in their combined juices, and brought them up, first to his nipples, which she lubricated and caressed, then to his lips. He sucked eagerly.

Then, as she started the penis entry process again, she slid slowly downward. Her lips came level with his nipples and she lingered there to suck her own juice from them. His penis went deeper into her and, such was the fire that he was experiencing, he felt that it was many times larger than he'd ever known. Still she slid further down him and the penetration went deeper and deeper. Just when he felt that he must be tickling her tonsils with his huge beast, she stopped and slowly reversed the process. Now slowly, slowly sliding her body upwards once more over his with the resulting slow withdrawal of his cock from her vagina until the head once again was caressing the clitoris.

Then the whole process was repeated. Then again, again and again, and again …. She never increased the pace but maintained the slow tortuous intensity of pleasure which mounted to moments of near climax in each of them, then ebbed as she paused to kiss, lick, caress and prolong the sensations.

It seemed to the young man that his delicious 'ordeal' lasted all night, the rapture just went on and on. Eventually, as she slid down him once more causing his penis to thrust upwards to her very core, the young man felt a gathering sensation in his belly as the nerves started to pull. It was akin to the rumble of a volcano gathering pressure within and then starting to force the lava higher, ever higher. At last he could contain it no longer and his sperm shot from him like a bolt from a crossbow. No way could he rein back the wild horses pulling his buttocks upward and he almost threw the woman from him.

But she held on, clinging to him, her nails tearing the flesh of his back which was now arched shamelessly off the bed. After allowing a few seconds for his heaving to subside, she recommenced her careful upwards slide on his body once again, causing his penis to start its withdrawal from her vagina. She reached down, took the still erect head in her hand and massaged it around her clitoris as the sperm still seeped from it. Now there was urgency in her movement, the speed increased. The young man felt that her clitoris was itself like a miniature penis, hard and erect, as she masturbated herself to a frantic orgasm of her own. Her screams and shouts could have alerted the local fire brigade, such was their intensity.

The young man, in his state of exhaustion and barely recovered from his own hiatus, thought that others in the château must have been awakened at that point but, as she quietened and slumped into exhaustion like him, there was no evidence that the rest of the household was other than quiet and asleep.

"Jocelyn … ," the young man started to whisper, but the woman immediately lifted her finger to his lips in a silencing gesture. He sucked it lovingly, relishing the lingering sex scents. It was in that pose that he slipped back into sleep. When he awoke with the morning light streaming into the room, his seductress was gone.

Joseph T.Riach

DECEIT DOESN'T DIE

Tommy first met the twins, Jack and Jock Dildo, when they literally dropped in on him while he was working in a ship's hold. They swung down clinging to a container lowered from the overhead crane. Tommy had not come across them before as they had been working in another part of the port before being transferred to Tommy's area, but Tommy quickly established a good rapport with them. Tommy discovered that they were hard workers, well known around the docks and popular too. They were also gay.

They were not aggressively gay however, nor effeminate. They were in fact, remarkably ordinary, or at least as ordinary as any dock worker could be. The docks were a macho, high testosterone place to work and Jack and Jock pulled their weight at work like all the other guys and shared in all the usual banter and sexual innuendo. They appeared no different at all from the other dockers. They were strong, willing workers, laboured well and drank hard. That suited Tommy just fine. Very soon they were true workmates and spending a lot of time drinking together too.

On the odd occasions that the twins' sexuality became an issue, usually with some inebriated idiot in one of the dockside pubs or in the back streets around them, they handled the situation quietly and with ease. If they found themselves outnumbered Tommy was more than happy to step in to help. He had a natural lifelong affinity with the underdog anyway. With his reputation as the guy who flattened Andy Chav, his mere presence usually persuaded aggressors to back off. When that didn't work the three of them made for a fearsome fighting trio. If harmless mickey-taking turned to something more menacing, they left no-one in doubt as to their pugilistic ability and willingness to use it.

The Dildos had another ability. They were master computer hackers. Their skill came in handy not just to themselves but to many others around the docks. They had a constant stream of 'customers' requesting that they undertake all sorts of online and internet tasks for them This varied from harmless searches for information, to checks on suspected cheating partners, to more sinister requests and sometimes plain robbery. The Dildos in fact boasted that they could steal more money via the internet in ten minutes than Fagin and his lads could get their hands on in ten months. Fagin just laughed at that.

"Each to his own," he would say.

In reality though, the Dildos rarely used their talent in that direction, preferring instead to genuinely help people with personal difficulties in their lives. One day however, it was they who experienced the personal difficulty.

Too Early For A Glass Of Wine?

Just for a change of scenery, Tommy arranged to meet the boys in the bar of a motel situated on the edge of the city. The plan was to eat, down a few beers and then move on from there for a night on the town – or to 'paint the pool purple' as Tommy humourously expressed it! When Tommy arrived at the motel, he was concerned to find twenty or so Harleys and other bikes of a notoriously unpleasant chapter of the Hell's Angels parked outside. Tommy knew this particular group by reputation and even he didn't care to mix it with them.

He was concerned that the Dildo twins might have arrived before him and already encountered the gang. He went carefully to the door of the public bar, nudged it slightly ajar and peeked inside. Sure enough, his friends were there and already had attracted the attentions of the bikers. The hairy mob, many sporting bandanas and dark glasses, already surrounded his friends and were taunting them threateningly. Tommy reacted instinctively.

He backed out into the car park, then raced to the adjoining filling station. There he bought a jerry can and filled it with petrol at the pumps. In no time he was back at the bikes and splashing the fuel over them. Then, invoking the spirit of his inner childhood arsonist, he set the petrol alight. As the fuel and the bikes exploded into flames, he dived into the bar shouting, "Fire! Fire! Your bikes are on fire."

The reaction of the bikers was spontaneous. They rushed as one to the door. Tommy rushed in the opposite direction.

He reached the twins, who by then were pinned down on the bar counter and already receiving the beginnings of a beating, pulled them upright and dragged them to the back door. In seconds all three were running helter skelter down the grassy bank behind the motel, into nearby bushes and then on to safety.

Behind them they left the Hell's Angels desperately trying to extinguish the flames engulfing their precious bikes with jackets, other improvised beaters and hastily acquired fire extinguishers. Fire engines with klaxons blaring passed the three friends as they slowed their pace and made their way towards the safer, familiar territory of the docks. Once inside one of their favourite drinking holes they relaxed and drew breath. Beers were ordered and gulped down.

"What was all that about?" asked Tommy eventually, "Did they twig you were gay?"

The Dildos roared with laughter. Tommy looked puzzled. Eventually Jack spoke.

"When we arrived at the motel the bikers were already there. We thought about not going in but then realised that you might already be there and in need of our help."

Now Tommy laughed; it was a complete reversal of the situation he had envisaged when he had arrived there.

"So what happened?" he queried.

"Well," and this time it was Jock who spoke, "I recognised one of them as a fellow I did some computer hacking for a couple of years back. What I discovered from his live-in girl friend's emails at the time was that she was having an affair with another woman. When I told the guy what I had discovered he went absolutely mental. He flew off in a rage and refused to pay me."

Here Jock paused to take a swig of beer and mop his brow, still perspiring from their flight from the motel. It was Jack who carried on.

"When Jock saw the guy, he went straight for him. I think he kind of forgot that he was with about twenty of his mates." Here they laughed again. "He just said, 'Hey you, give me my fuckin' money', that was all. When the guy laughed back at him Jock repeated 'Give me my fuckin' money' – then added – 'Or I'll tell all your mates here that your girl friend is a fuckin' lesbian'!

At that point the whole group of bikers went quiet and looked kind of funny at their mate. One broke the silence with – 'So your girl is a lizzie'? That is when the first biker attacked his mate. Then all hell – hey you get it?, all hell … ," Jack and Jock both laughed again, "All hell broke loose and then you galloped into the rescue!" Jock slapped Tommy's back hard, not once but twice. Suddenly all three of them were very relaxed and ready to enjoy a thoroughly good night.

Later Tommy said, "So the punch up wasn't about you guys being gay … it was about the biker's girl being a lesbian!" Boy did they laugh but, just after that, Jack and Jock both turned serious.

"Joking apart Tommy," said Jack, "You saved us from a bad scene tonight. You're a real pal."

Jock cut in, "If there's anything, any time, anything at all that we can help you out with in any way, just ask. Okay?"

"Okay," replied Tommy with a modest shrug. He already had a particular favour in mind.

~

In the weeks and months which followed, Tommy spent more and more of his time with the Dildo twins, joined by Andy and Fagin too. The five of them together became known as 'the famous five' and a common sight around the bars and clubs of the bottom end of town where the docks and industrial areas were. After the motel incident with the bikers, they rarely ventured beyond the places where they were known and where they felt secure.

Although much of their behaviour was riotous, loud and lewd, they never caused difficulties in the bars they frequented. These bars, in turn, rarely experienced trouble. Anyone inclined to start a brawl soon became disinclined when they realised, or had pointed out to them, that 'the famous five' were there. No-one wanted to confront Jack, Jock, Andy, Fagin or Tommy, and certainly not all of them together.

Anyone who did transgress was usually singled out by other drinkers, rather than the five, and dealt with because they didn't want to cause offence to Tommy or his mates. On those occasions, after some toughs had sorted out one of their own kind, they would send over drinks to the five as an apology for the potential aggravation and a sign of 'loyalty'.

Too Early For A Glass Of Wine?

The lads in fact, rarely if ever paid for any drinks anywhere. Theirs was a hard drinking, wild and fun existence funded almost entirely from admirers, those scared of offending them and those terrified of their reputations as fearsome enemies. Far from not being welcome in many pubs because of who they were, many landlords welcomed them. They knew that while the five were on their premises that there would be no bother from anyone else. These pub owners too paid for all the five's drinks for just that reason – to keep them happy and in their pub and other rabble rousers away from it.

Tommy's life blurred into endless days of hard graft in the docks and even harder graft of a different kind most nights. His was a footloose and carefree existence, a string of girls came and went. Life was swinging along just great as he saw it. He cared for nothing and nobody – until he met Janice!

~

Janice McGills eighteenth birthday present from her parents was an impressively large jewelry box. It was hand carved in teak by her father, a carpenter to trade, and her name was embossed across the top. Inside it was a solitary eighteen carat gold bracelet, one carat to represent each of her tender eighteen years. The greetings card accompanying the box expressed her parents' hope that she would enjoy a prosperous life and that the box would, in due course, become home to much wealth. Janice took the message to heart and quickly set about acquiring said wealth.

Although a not unattractive girl, Janice's greatest social attributes were her bounce and vitality. It was her effervescent and fun personality which made her irresistable to males. She was well aware of this and used her flirtatious infectiousness to great effect. While other girls, less glamourous and more reserved, waited hopelessly for the attentions of members of the opposite sex which never came, Janice cultivated and enjoyed a constant stream of suitors and made it her mission to ensnare all of them in her carefully constructed web.

Because, while the lads intentions were entirely amorous and carnal, hers were anything but. She had only one aim – and that was to fill her jewelry box. Not just fill it, but stock it full of real and increasingly expensive gems. She had in fact made the accumulation of her treasure trove her sole purpose in life and she pursued her goal with ruthless efficiency.

Tommy was oblivious to this when he first set eyes on her. In no time at all after their first night club meeting, she was beguiling him with her fun and fantastic stories of future wealth and glittering success in her life. Tommy was told, as had all the other lads she was stringing along, that he was welcome to come along for the ride. However, he had to pay for the privilege. The price was the same for everyone – a piece of jewelry of value to put in her jewel box!

Of course she didn't ask outright for the 'payment' in so many words, she was more subtle than that. It was more a case of the, "If you really loved me you would … " type of line, accompanied by fluttering eyelashes and implied promises of sexual intimacy which, naturally, never materialised. Janice was far to clever to give of herself sexually. She knew that her power lay in the promise rather than the delivery - and she had no intention whatsoever of delivering.

Her trick was to get the payment, lock it in the box, make her excuses and move on to the next target. This she accomplished on an almost industrial scale and with such aplomb that her jewelry box quite soon housed a valuable collection of real gold, silver and precious stones.

Tommy, of course, knew nothing of this. He was head over heels madly in love with the first real love of his life. He rushed home from work each day in order to clean up, dress smartly and get out to be with her - blissfully unaware that a possé of other young men, some of whom Tommy knew, were doing exactly likewise. It was in fact one of those other guys who put Tommy straight about Janice. By then it was too late.

Within just a few weeks of his first encounter with Janice, she had sobbed to Tommy that, despite her great love of precious gems, she owned none. She felt that if Tommy truly loved her that he would show his feelings by providing the one thing in her life that she most longed for but felt that she would never possess. This 'one thing', rather handily for her, just happened to be in the window of the jewelry shop only a block away from Tommy's flat. It was a necklet consisting of a large heart-shaped amethyst on a thick twenty-four carat gold chain with several diamond inlays. The price to purchase it was equivalent to six months of Tommy's pay at the docks.

Despite that, Tommy duly purchased the gem. In his naive, love blinded optimism he believed the gift to be the key to Janice's heart - and other parts of her anatomy besides; it would guarantee her undying love and a life of blissful ecstasy together until the end of time. In the event, the end of their time together arrived rather more quickly.

Just twenty-four hours after gifting her the necklet and it being implied to him in vague expressions of double entendre that their relationship would be consummated on his next visit, he arrived at her home to be told by her parents that she had left and never wanted to see him again. On top of that, they warned Tommy that if he tried to see her and insisted on being a pest, they would have no alternative but to call the police.

It was that same night that Tommy, while drowning his completely confused sorrows in a local pub, confided to a sympathetic friend the reason for his drunken binge. The friend responded,

"What? Janice? Janice McGill? Oh she does that to everybody. I got taken for a couple of thousand just last year."

"What!" roared Tommy, a couple of thousand what? How?"

His friend said, "Pounds of course. A two thousand pound brooch. I gave it to her one night and she finished with me the next day. When I flipped my lid and threatened her, she set her three brothers on me and her dad called the police to say that I had attacked them! There were no charges against me but I spent a night in the cells and was ordered to stay away from her. That's what I did. He, her father, has connections high up in the police you know."

The fellow had barely finished his story than Tommy leaped to his feet and rushed to the door. In his blind fury he knocked over several drinkers' pints as he charged from the pub. It being Tommy, no-one complained. Shortly afterwards he was banging on the door of Janice's house, swearing loudly and demanding to see her. There was no response. He had just thrown a rock from the garden through the sitting room window when the police arrived.

The next morning Tommy appeared in court. He pleaded guilty to being drunk and disorderly, causing an affray and criminal damage. The proceedings reminded Tommy of the day his dad listed his catalogue of crimes to him following his drunken Barsac binge as a nine year old. This time there was no physical beating as punishment nor, thankfully for Tommy, any 'solitary confinement'. He was however fined the equivalent of three months of his wages at the docks. He was left in no doubt that anything other than a guilty plea on his part would result in a jail sentence.

He was also ordered to stay away from Janice, her family and her family home. He was warned that any attempt on his part to contact them in any way would result in the recall of his case and a custodial sentence being imposed. As being confined or losing his liberty to roam at will was the one thing that Tommy genuinely feared, he could never allow himself to be incarcerated. There was no way he would allow that to happen.

Tommy swallowed his pride and accepted his punishment. He had no intention however of either forgetting the incident nor of forgiving the perpetrator.

"This deceit doesn't die," he vowed to his friends, "I will fight another day."

–

For now though he had quite a different fight on his hands. The loss of the equivalent of nine months of income represented by the necklet purchase and the court fine hit him hard. As a consequence he could not afford to maintain his smart, city apartment. Once more he asked his parents if he could return to live with them. This presented no apparent difficulty for them. As before, there was neither great enthusiasm nor resistance to the proposal on their part. With no-one else in the house apart from themselves there was plenty available space and Tommy had more than one room to himself. He moved back into the family home; but life did not continue as before.

Perhaps because of the move or maybe just because he felt the need to live a more settled existence after his recent experiences, Tommy left his work at the docks and his friends there. He found work as an assistant accounts clerk in a local paper mill. There he settled into a mundane and predictable routine such as he had never known before.

The work was tedious and uninspiring. The excitement and daily action of his footballing days became but a distant memory. Even the more recent reckless adventure and camaraderie of his times as a dock worker felt to him as if they had happened somewhere else, to someone else. He kept up contact with the other members of 'the famous five' but their get-togethers and inevitable booze-ups became less and less frequent.

Tommy still went out most evenings but now visited quieter, more upmarket pubs. The kind of places with soft music and where married couples sat over just one cocktail all night and never exchanged a word. Tommy still enjoyed his drink but his beer consumption slowed and he took to drinking wine. At first his regular tipple was Piesporter white, a common choice among newcomers to wine drinking because of its light body and high alcohol content. Later he moved on to Paul Masson Californian red wine.

He also started to develop a greater appreciation of good food and particularly enjoyed visiting *La Bella Ragazza* (the beautiful girl) Italian restaurant near his home. There he learned the delights of eating fresh pastas, tomato ragu and spicey meat balls! The patron of the restaurant, a burly and jovial chef of Italian descent, insisted that Tommy try all the different dishes on the menu. Over the months that followed, Tommy did just that.

"It was hard," as he would happily tell allcomers, "But somebody had to do it!"

He also tried, and became extremely fond of, the Italian Valpolicella red wines with which he washed back the food in the traditional Italian way – huge mouthfuls and lots of them! He had never known such exuberant dining.

It was fun in a whole different way from the rough and tumble vulgarity of the dockside pubs which he had so revered. Now he was regularly in the company of girls, a different one most weeks, rather than the macho environment of the docks. The girls too enjoyed the wining and dining experiences which they shared enthusiastically as an integral part of their amorous liaisons.

In private though, Tommy remained disillusioned with his life. The weeks, months and years dragged by and he became more demotivated with each passing day. Although a supposedly independent young man in his early twenties, he was still living with his parents. A lot of his time 'at home' was spent secluded in his rooms.

There he comforted his restless soul with more and more reading. He still loved his books. He bought and read for the first time *'Asimov's Trilogy'.* When he finished the third book he went straight back to the first one and started reading it all over again. The series enthralled him.

While Asimov excited him, Thomas Hardy captivated him. One of Tommy's favourite novels of all time became Hardy's *'The Mayor Of Casterbridge'.* He found the twists and turns in the plot mirrored his perceptions of the ways people's lives, his own in particular, seemed to evolve in all eras. Then there was John Bradshaw's *'Homecoming'.* Both the title and the content stirred some emotion deep within Tommy. At the time he could not pinpoint quite what it

Too Early For A Glass Of Wine?

was. But he was soon to find out.

~

Returning to his parents' home in the early hours one morning after yet another night on the tiles and a skinful of Valpolicella, Tommy was surprised to find his dad sitting drinking a cup of tea in the kitchen. This was unheard of. It was three o'clock in the morning and Tommy had never, but never, encountered his dad up and about at that time. It got stranger still – his dad talked to him! Not just any talk but meaningful and intimate talk, talk such as Tommy thought his dad incapable of engaging in.

Yet here he was saying, "Amongst all those girls of yours, did you ever have an Italian girlfriend?"

"No, I don't think so ... no," replied Tommy, somewhat in shock at what was transpiring.

"You should," said his dad, "They are stunning. Most beautiful I ever saw."

He paused to draw breath, cleared his throat and coughed a little. Tommy assumed (rightly as it turned out) that his dad was referring to the war years during which he had served in Italy.

"Or at least they are beautiful until they are twenty," he added smiling, "Then they suddenly turn into demented, screaming banshees, quite frightening."

"But," he went on, now more thoughtful, reasoning, "It's the passion you know, the Latin passion, makes them like that. You take the beauty, you take the passion, that's the deal. You don't get one without the other. Does that make sense to you son?"

"Yes, I think it does," replied Tommy, reeling anew at the fact that his dad had just called him 'son'. That had never happened before either. It was an absolute first.

"You have passion," said his dad, "I've always known that. There is greatness in you, I can see it."

He paused to cough again. This time he held a paper tissue to his lips as he coughed. When he took it from his lips, there were flecks of red on it.

Seeing the immediate change in Tommy's demeanour at the sight of the blood, his dad intervened quickly,

"Yes it's blood but don't concern yourself with that, not just yet. Listen. Ever since the injury ended your football career and then that business with the Janice tramp," ...

... 'the Janice tramp'! ... Tommy had never heard his dad speak like this, never, but now he wanted to clap, cheer and slap him on the back. "How quickly one's perception of a person can change," thought Tommy.

"Ever since the Janice tramp," his dad went on, "Your light has gone out. You know what I mean. Well, do something for me, will you lad, will you do something just for me?"

"Anything dad," replied Tommy; and he meant it with all his heart and as he had never meant anything ever before in his life, "Anything at all dad," he repeated.

His dad looked slowly up at him, smiled warmly, then with grit in his voice barked - "Switch the bloody light on again!"

Tommy was speechless, he wanted to cry, but there was a more pressing matter to attend to. "The blood dad, you are coughing up blood."

"Yes son, I am. What do you think I should do?"

Tommy had no experience of this kind of situation but the stock answer was obvious,

"Better see a doctor," then added, "I'll take you down there first thing in the morning."

And that's what happened.

At nine o'clock sharp Tommy was by his dad's side at the doctor's clinic. By eleven o'clock his dad had been admitted as an emergency patient to the cancer ward at the local hospital. He was operated on at three o'clock in the afternoon, large parts of both his lungs were removed. Twelve hours later, twenty-fours almost to the minute after confiding in Tommy for the one and only time in his life, he died.

When Tommy heard the news, for the one and only time in his life, he cried. What his dad had tried hard and failed to bring about in Tommy's young life, he achieved effortlessly in death.

Joseph T.Riach

THE MASTER ROSE AT DAWN

The young man had already learned during his stay that Josmas was an early riser. He habitually got up at the crack of dawn and went out running for an hour. His routine was then to spend thirty minutes in meditation in his rose garden, inhaling its fresh morning scents, before preparing for the rest of the day. So, when the young man came down for breakfast, he was not surprised to find Josmas already alert, showered and seated in his usual position at the head of the table.

Josmas ate only light breakfasts, saving his serious meal of the day for either lunch or dinner, never both. Today his morning fayre was a simple tea, toast and scrambled eggs.

As he ate he was also reading, and apparently marking, what turned out to be the young man's simple/complex listing from the previous night. The young man had noted its disappearance from his room when he got up. He had wondered if his mystery partner in sex had taken it.

"I hope it's gold stars and 'well dones' and not a hideous black cross," thought the young man whimsically to himself as he seated himself beside his host; then was barely surprised when Josmas said,

"Gold stars it is young man. I'm impressed. You've learned a lot. You've still got some way to go to reach the complete serenity of a life such as mine but you are well on the way. For the sake of comparison would you like to see my simple list which I live my life by? There are no 'complexes', I eliminated all of those long ago."

With that he produced from a pocket a small scrap of paper. It was crumpled and world-weary. It had clearly seen many moons. Once again Josmas pre-empted the young man's thoughts.

"The list is everything to me. I drew it up when I was but a young man like you and determined to achieve a way of life most people only ever dream of. It goes everywhere with me. I read it often to reinforce my resolve. It's my declaration of intent, my talisman."

With that he handed the paper to the young man adding, "Be warned, my list is ultra simple. It encompasses all that I set out to achieve on a daily basis, no more no less."

The young man accepted and unfolded the note. It read -

* *Enjoy Nature – Exercise, Fresh Air, Sunshine, Flowers, Forests, Rivers, Mountains, Oceans, Wild Life*

* *Appreciate and Give Thanks Daily for – Health, Shelter, Happy Home, Good Food, Laughter and Love*

* *Be Kind, Helpful and Generous to Others – Spread Knowledge, Joyfulness and Fun*

Create Wealth – (a) Spiritual and (b) Financial and Material for (i) Others and (ii) Myself

"Simple, isn't it?" said Josmas, when he saw that the young man had completed the brief read.

Not for the first time that week, the young man found himself nodding in agreement. It was clear to him that he was becoming more in tune with the Josmas way of thinking, the mindset, with every passing moment. More than that he felt the urge to copy, to enact the style of life which Josmas radiated. After all, he really liked the list Josmas had shown him. Living like that truly appealed to him.

"Yes I do appreciate that and yes, I can see that straightforward and uncomplicated is the way to go," he paraphrased his own words from the previous evening. "But, how should I physically go about removing the complex from my life, the clutter?"

"As I said," replied Josmas, "You start like this!"

With that he picked up the young man's simple/complex list and dramatically ripped it in two. He screwed up into a ball the half which the young man rightly assumed to be his 'complex life list' and tossed it to the young man.

"Read it one last time then burn it," he instructed. The young man browsed quickly down the list of all those things which from this moment onward would be expelled from his life. He realised that there was not a single item on the list that he was going to miss, not one. In fact he felt quite euphoric as he placed the paper on one of the table burners which had been keeping the scrambled aggs warm, and watched it go up in flames.

"Well done!" shouted Josmas and reached out to shake the young man's hand as if the young man had just achieved some great success, won a world championship or something similar. In reality the young man had done just that, something far greater in fact. He had just determined to own his own future.

Now Josmas added,

"Ridding yourself of the existing clutter, as you rather nicely put it, is the harder part. It means removing certain things and people already in your life. However, you are young and resilient. It will be easier for you than would be the case with an older person possessing more of the negative baggage, people and situations in their lives and more set in their ways. Of course the bad stuff, the complex will always come knocking at your door, trying to force its way in. You must be constantly on guard and resistant to its overtures."

"How do I do that?" enquired the young man, now fully engaged in Josmas's every word.

"Surprisingly simply," was Josmas's reassuring response. "The baggage, the clutter, the complexities in life all come courtesy of people. The formula is to rid yourself of the people and you rid yourself of the difficulties they create. The people in question will inevitably be time wasters. Remember that time, and your integrity, are your most prized assets. Eliminate time wasters from your life, the people who carry the 'disease' and would devour your integrity, and you eradicate the complexity they transmit. It is simpler by far to identify and stop the 'carriers' at the gate, so to speak, than have to remove them once they have penetrated your defences."

Josmas was now in full flow, fired up and speaking quickly. The young man leaned in to absorb every word.

"Time is valuable. Especially yours. As you make your way in life and business you will find that many people will want to borrow a slice of your time; even more so once you become successful. Of course they rarely can, and rarely seek to, pay it back. When you give someone some of your time you are doing just that – giving it, not lending it. This being the case you need to be very careful how much time you give and to whom. To help me with this conundrum and to avoid my wasting precious time on dead-end interactions, I developed my ten minute test."

~

"Ten minute test?" the young man queried, "How does that work?"

Josmas drew in his breath. He looked earnestly at the young man.

"Let me repeat," he continued, "Time is valuable, it is your most treasured resource and it's all too easy to fritter it away. As it is never lent, only given, you can never have it back. Once it's gone, it's gone forever. Successful people don't waste their time and they didn't waste their time while they were becoming successful. In fact, their ability to focus on using their time only for productive purposes and with people deserving of their time is one of the main causes of their success. It follows therefore, once successful, they are certainly not going to alter that, or any aspect, of their life management success strategy.

The way to ensure that you spend time only on people who will add value to you, your life, your enterprise or your happiness is to weed out those who clearly will not add value at the very beginning, at the point of introduction. You need a quick way of accurately evaluating new introductions according to your desired criteria.

I for instance want to associate only with positive people who will add value to my life in the ways stated. My simple 'ten minute test' allows me to do just that. It works like this ...

The normal starting point to a 'relationship' is the 'name/age/origin/occupation'? questions format. People use it to give them a hook on which to hang the other guy's hat and afford them the opportunity to regale the other party with their own, preferably superior, version of such data. I have no time for that nonsense. I mean no 'time'."

Here he strongly emphasised the word *'time'*, drawing it out loud and slow, accompanied by a deep breath as if to further enforce his point. When he saw that the young man had taken in the full significance of his emphasis, he went on,

"I don't ask people where they are from or what they do for a living. I sometimes supply my name but I don't do age. Since I was fifteen I stopped responding to the age question. I've long held the belief that if you are good enough then you are old enough. My response to the age query is my simple – 'I don't do age!' That stops most people in their tracks. What I do is apply my ten minute test, I get stuck in straight away and ask my own questions. They knock most people off their stride. Here they are."

The young man leant in even more attentively than before so as not to miss a single strand of what Josmas was about to reveal.

" *'What is it that you are most passionate about in life? What is the one thing that you most love doing?'*

Assuming that they can answer that question with real conviction – the vast majority can't and are immediately eliminated from my reckoning – then I hit them with the follow up question –

'What are you doing about it?'

That's it.

Only those who answer both questions convincingly and show that their endeavours actively help others and do so in good humour, do I consider it worthwhile giving time to. These are the ones who display self-assurance, inner harmony and act as they say.

That's not to say that the ninety-five percent who 'fail' my test are bad people, mostly they're not. It's just that it's the confident, upbeat and focussed few who pass the test that I feel are worthy of my time. Do I sometimes throw the baby out with the bathwater in my quick vetting procedure? Inevitably yes … but so seldom as to be of no consequence. I have such confidence in my ten minute test you see that I know it works to great effect and quickly reveals the most dynamic and aware personalities to me almost all the time. And time remember is what it's all about.

It worked with you, didn't it?"

Here Josmas smiled and patted the young man on his shoulder in a possessive, fatherly-like way. His hand rested there as he concluded,

"So guard your time jealously young man, it is beyond value. Give it sparingly and only to those most deserving. My ten minute test will help ensure that you do just that."

~

"And now young man," he stood and stretched to his full height, "It is time for me to go. My work here is ended. I must move on to a new calling and carry on my work in another place far from here.

You, young man, have limitless potential to prosper and grow in any pursuit of your choosing. Take what I have taught you and use it wisely. I ask only that you pass on from time to time the gift of my knowledge to other young men or women who, like yourself, are open to receiving it. You will easily recognise those sent to you, there won't be many."

When Josmas had finished speaking, the young man asked hopefully,

"Can I stay on for one more day just to sort my stuff and prepare for my journey home. Perhaps Jocelyn can help me?"

"But oh young man, don't you understand?" replied Josmas, "You must remain here. You are staying here permanently. All of this is now yours. Don't worry about money, everything is taken care of."

The young man was completely taken aback by what he heard, flattened, dumbstruck. He was literally struck dumb. He could find no words. He stood mouth agape, completely unable to speak. He could not believe what he was hearing.

"Who would in this circumstance?" his inner voice eventually asked him, following up with, "There has to be a mistake. You must have misheard Josmas, you cannot possibly be staying here."

As usual though Josmas was ahead of the young man's thoughts. He continued for him,

"Believe me. You heard correctly. You will remain here. I have chosen you to carry on my work. I'm confident that you will do well.

Spend your time in the vineyards, there you will learn all that you need to know. Play some golf too, the game demands patience and builds character. And make the library your special place. There's nothing will be required of you in life that reading books won't better prepare you for ... perhaps you already have an inkling of that?" Here he paused and smiled.

"Let's share a final drink," he said at last. "Or do you consider it to be too early for a glass of wine?" His smile beamed out.

"Certainly not," replied the young man, regaining his composure and with it a new found conviction. "It is never too early." There was not a hint of hesitation and absolutely no doubt in his response.

Josmas filled two goblets from a bottle of Pauillac. He confirmed to the young man, 'just in case he was wondering', that the bottle had been opened the day previously. Both men laughed out loud at that. The clink of their cut crystal glasses as they toasted each other echoed through the château. It seemed to the young man to signal both the final chime of the day in their current relationship and the first chime of a new dawn in each of their lives. They looked at one another with profound and sincere affection. It was Josmas who spoke.

"Drink up young man. You can drink the wine today and pick the grapes tomorrow you know – or vice versa. You will flourish either way."

Then he proposed a final toast,

"To friends, authors, wines," cheered Josmas, "All three make the laughter of your life ring louder."

He cast what would prove to be his last, lingering gaze wistfully out of the window at the vineyards with their late summer golds and yellows glinting in the sun. Then he turned back quite abruptly, as if his final resolve had been made, and firmly confronted the young man,

"Jocelyn shall be coming with me. Her daughter will stay to assist you."

As he said that, Josmas swept out an arm to indicate that someone had entered the room behind the young man. He turned to see a radiant young woman of about his own age, almost the mirror image of Jocelyn.

"Her name is Erna," continued Josmas, "I believe you have already met."

The young man stared at Erna, she flashed her smile back and their eyes met.

"Yes," he knew with certainty, "We met last night."

But when he turned back to say just those words to Josmas, the great man was already gone.

Joseph T. Riach

FOUR VILLAINS AND A FUNERAL

It was the typically damp and depressingly grey kind of day which funeral directors seem to include as their default setting for kirkyard interments when taking the order and making the arrangements – or so Tommy imagined. He pictured the scene with the ingratiating undertaker which had been enacted with him just two days previously :

"Would sir prefer a coffin or a casket? Metal, wood, fibreglass or cardboard? Oak, mahogany, teak or walnut? Silk, satin or velvet interior? A standard hearse or perhaps the extra pomp of a horse drawn carriage? Flowers, what kind, how many? Professional mourners? – we have many choices, a clutch of weeping women through to a wailing throng? – Oh, and the weather. You could choose sunshine in some shape or form and a warm day too ... but dreich and dreary comes at no extra charge as part of our standard package. Most bereaved prefer the rain and mist, it is just so appropriate, don't you think?"

Tommy suspected that the 'dreich and dreary' choice was also a default in the choice of minister to conduct the ceremony.

The day after his dad's death, the Reverand Samuel Ballantyne from the local Church of Scotland, called at the house. A humourless, hounddog faced man, he solemnly introduced himself to Tommy's mum as 'being there to give her 'spiritual guidance'. He then imparted his standard message of - "Your husband is now in heaven and happy." This, she took entirely personally and retorted angrily,

"So before he was here and unhappy was he?"

The fact was that Tommy's mum and dad, although lifelong members of the church and therefore, as Ballantyne saw it, part of his flock, had not seen the inside of any church since the day of their marriage some forty years past. They were enthusiastic non-practicing presbyterians, openly hostile to so-called 'Holy Willies' - those pious hypocrites so aptly described in Robert Burns' *Holy Willie's Prayer*. Tommy's mum had almost to be physically restrained from kicking the religious zealot out of the house as soon he set foot in it.

Thereafter Ballantyne rambled through his set oration rather more quickly than was probably his norm. He was not offered the customary cup of tea and he scuttled off as soon as he finished.

Notwithstanding all that, it was accepted that Ballantyne would conduct the funeral service - in the church - and perform the burial ritual at the graveside afterwards.

So it was that Tommy, his mum, family and friends of his dad found themselves two days later, huddled together in the cold gloom of the cemetery.

Too Early For A Glass Of Wine?

"There is a time to be born and a time to die, a time to plant and a time to uproot, a time to kill and a time to heal, a time to tear down and a time to build, a time to weep and a time to laugh, a time to mourn and a time to dance ... "

At the same moment that Tommy stood head bowed at the graveside, enduring the very grim sermon of the very presbyterian Reverand Samuel Ballantyne, a cat burglar was scaling the wall surrounding the expensive detached property of a wealthy couple in London's affluent stockbroker belt. The intruder made his way stealthily across the manicured lawns to the rear of the house. Once there he easily found the access to the electronic alarm system and expertly disarmed it. From there he let himself into the property via a back door and immediately ascended the staircase to the study on the first floor.

He already knew the location of the safe to be behind a painting hung above the fireplace. In no time at all he had swung back the hinged frame of the portrait, twirled the combination lock, opened the safe and removed all of the contents. This included a very substantial sum of money, personal documents and high worth company share certificates.

"A most satisfying haul," smiled the burglar to himself and stuffed everything into the large holdall he carried with him for the purpose. He left the item he had really come for, the primary purpose of his visit, until last. It was the lady of the house's jewelry box. An impressive hand carved in teak affair with her name embossed across the top.

He removed it last from the safe and with particular care. He easily picked the insubstantial lock and peeked nervously inside. His eyes gleamed with delight at the sight within – almost as brightly as the assorted diamond, ruby, sapphire and gold collection which dazzled back at him. He permitted himself just a few seconds to revel in the ecstasy of his newly acquired wealth before running his fingers through the jewels in search of one particular piece. When he found the item that he sought he gave a satisfied grin, separated it from the rest of the treasure and put it in his pocket. All the others he swept into his swag bag.

His last act was to replace the empty jewel box in the safe as he had been instructed to do, close the safe and make good his escape. Before he departed, he looked around to see that he had left no trace of his visit.

"Job well done," he congratulated himself as he jumped down from the estate wall back on to the street, "And hugely profitable too!" All had gone according to plan.

As he casually sauntered from the scene of the crime, he playfully whistled *'You Got To Pick A Pocket Or Two'* to himself and fingered in his pocket the one item from the burglary which was not his to keep. It was an amethyst, gold and diamond necklet. Fagin was already looking forward to delivering it to its rightful owner.

~

In the churchyard Ballantyne droned on.

Too Early For A Glass Of Wine?

"Come to me, all you who are weary and burdened, and I will give you rest."

"Yes," thought Tommy, "We could all do with a rest. Was he the only one not chilled to the bone in the wintry blast and bored to tears with the reverand gentleman's meaningless monologue?"

He looked around him at the assembled mourners. It was an impressive turnout; his dad had been well liked. It was impossible to read the thoughts of the congregation. Tommy could only assume that they were as frozen as he and, like him, longing for the warmth of the reception awaiting them in a local hotel.

"I could certainly do with a slug of Beaujolais," mused Tommy, recalling the fresh fruity fullness of one of his favourite wines. At the same moment he thought suddenly of Sammy, "You'll be needing one too Sammy boy."

~

Sammy MacEvoy was indeed in need of a strong drink, and a good deal more besides.

He was at that very moment under sedation and being wheeled into an ambulance which, with blue light flashing and siren screaming, rushed him to the casualty department of the local hospital for emergency surgery. He had suffered a suspected fracture to his skull and severe compound fracturing in his left leg. The bone all around his knee was smashed to a pulp and shards of tibia, fibula and femur stuck grotesquely through his bloodied flesh.

Sammy was the victim of a vicious assault near to his home in

Manchester. He never knew what hit him. The assailant approached the footballer from behind in a quiet wooded area as he made his way to morning training. He caught his target entirely unawares, lost in thoughts about preparations for his next game. The thug sent Sammy sprawling forward on to the pathway with a single blow to the head then launched a savage and sustained attack on his left knee with a baseball bat. As Sammy curled semi-conscious on the ground, the attacker continued to rain blows on the same knee – and only there – until satisfied that the joint was wrecked. It was all over very quickly.

The aggressor resisted a strong urge to mark his victim with a 'Glasgow smile'. Instead he aimed a brutal kick at his head and shouted, "Goal!" as he did so. Then he straightened the battered New York Yankees baseball cap which he wore and departed the scene unhurriedly. No-one witnessed the attack.

~

Shortly afterwards, a young mother returning home with her infant son in a neighbourhood near to Sammy's home, found on her doorstep a bottle of wine tied with a bow and bearing a card. She turned to her child and said, "What have we here?"

She picked up the bottle and saw that the wine was a Chablis. The greetings card simply read, "Paid in full."

Pat sighed wistfully. She carelessly straightened strands of her son's mop of blond hair, looked lovingly at him, then took Tommy by the hand and went inside.

Too Early For A Glass Of Wine?

~

Within half an hour of both the Sammy and the Chablis incidents in Manchester, Andy Chav was on a train heading north out of the city. He was happy with both elements of his 'work'. Compassion, cruelty, each resided comfortably in his complex psyche. He already anticipated that the following morning's newspaper headline would read, *"Brutal Assault Ends Footballer's Career."* That thought pleased him – as did the prospect of informing a 'special friend' as to the success of his dual mission.

~

Sammy was not the only one experiencing a distinctly uncomfortable morning. The day was not going well for Hamish McIntosh either. As McIntosh left his downtown bedsit and passed a white transit van parked nearby, he was coshed from behind and bundled into the van by four men in painters' overalls. It happened so quickly that the few people in the vicinity never saw a thing.

McIntosh's abductors were members of an extreme sadomasochist organisation called *Whatever You Desire*. They operated via the darknet, that highly encrypted communication system often used for illegal activity and as a media exchange for paedophiles and terrorists. *Whatever You Desire*, as their name implied, specialised in providing bespoke experiences of any sexual perversion for paying customers.

In this instance their client, who they believed to be McIntosh, had ordered a week long ordeal of flagellation, torture, humiliation, rape and imprisonment. It was requested to start with a surprise capture of the 'victim' and, among the client's other stipulations, was one that he be gagged and chained throughout. The instruction was clear that, no matter how much the client screamed or pleaded, the week of terror had to continue to its conclusion.

McIntosh had, in fact, neither arranged nor payed for any of this. The payment for the event had indeed come from his bank account. This satisfied his tormentors that his was a genuine booking, and they set their plans accordingly. What they were ignorant of however was that it was Jack and Jock Dildo, using their skill as online hackers and robbers, who had booked the experience and paid the fee directly from McIntosh's account. When the perverts assaulted McIntosh in the street and hauled him off to face his week of hell in their sordid dungeon somewhere in the bowels of the city, they were acting in good faith; if such a thing as good faith could be said to exist in their vile world.

When McIntosh recovered consciousness following the initial assault in the street, he found himself manacled and chained face down over a hard, wooden table. He was naked except for a black leather helmet which had been put on his head. It had eye slits and a zip-up mouth. He was gagged with a black rubber ball. A studded leather collar with dog leash was tight around his throat.

He could hear some men talking behind him but could not see them. They were laughing loud and discussing among them which one would whip 'the bitch' and which one would 'fuck' him ... when and in what order.

All at once the leash was pulled sharply back, forcing his head upwards so that he saw in a corner of the hell hole the tiny barred cage that was to be his home for the next seven days. Beside it was a table laid out with an evil assortment of sexual torture devices. Also, in a large mirror placed in front of him, he saw the first lash coming, delivered by a leather-clad, brute of a man. It immediately ripped flesh from his buttocks. The first of the multiple rapes followed.

~

"For as much as it hath pleased almighty God of his great mercy to take unto himself the soul of our dear brother here departed, we therefore commit his body to the ground; earth to earth, ashes to ashes, dust to dust; in sure and certain hope of the resurrection to eternal life." - the Reverand Ballantyne eventually exhausted the dire script of his seemingly endless graveside homily.

~

Tommy was at last in the hotel and knocking back the first of several glasses of red wine. It wasn't the Beaujolais he had fantasised about while burying his dad but a fine Margaux generously donated by his dad's friend, Gordon Diack. Ballantyne had, thankfully, declined the invitation to attend the reception on account of his aversion to alcohol. He sent his daughter, a willowy, pretty girl, along in his place. She had none of her father's inhibitions. Her consumption of the demon drink more than compensated for her father's lack of it. She soon established herself as the life and soul of the dead man's party. Tommy appreciated her company.

The reverand's daughter apart, he found himself alone with just his mother – she had wanted to subject the mourners to her sweaty cabbage sludge until persuaded by family members that everyone had suffered enough and to leave the catering to the hotel – and some friends and acquaintances of his father, only a few of whom he knew.

Gordon Diack had worked with Tommy's dad for several years. The two families had holidayed together in the mountains many times when Tommy was a lad. Gordon had even taught Tommy to fish. An old photo of the two of them together, showing a seven year old Tommy proudly holding up the very first 'tiddler' he had caught with a piece of string, a bent pin and a worm, still existed somewhere among Tommy's childhood mementos. Tommy liked Gordon.

Now Gordon took Tommy aside.

"You know, in spite of his reticence to express himself and show his emotions, your dad cared for you a lot. He regretted the discipline dished out to you as a youngster but did believe that it would stand you in good stead. In part he was repeating the same regime that he experienced as a kid and in part he was relieving his own frustrations."

Gordon had Tommy's attention, and continued.

"Your dad was a superb engineer, talented and well qualified. He never received the professional recognition which his work merited. Other, less able people were promoted above him because they were political animals in nature and knew how to get on in business and profit at other people's expense. Your dad didn't want the same fate to befall you. He confided to me before he died that he was certain that you possessed the drive and determination to become influential in life which he lacked."

Tommy was all ears. He wanted so much to know about his dad, to know the dad that he never knew.

"Your dad," continued Gordon, "Often told the story that, while he and I as youths enjoyed getting a bit tipsy with a couple of beers on a Saturday night, you Tommy," and here Gordon gave Tommy a mock, soft punch on the shoulder, "You! You, you bugger got absolutely pissed every night!"

It surprised Tommy to hear that his dad had spoken in that way but it pleased him too. He wanted to know that his dad had been human and that he cared. Now he realised that that was true and Gordon confirmed it when he asked him the question directly,

"Did my dad really love me?"

"Yes Tommy, he did. More than you'll ever know. Your dad was a normal guy, great fun. His point about the beers was that, if you can do the drinking thing more full on than anyone else, then you can do anything else in life which you choose with the same level of success."

They laughed at that. Gordon carried on,

"Just as with your football you have it in you to be the best – barring injuries of course."

"Yes," agreed Tommy, "Barring injuries," and reflected with grim satisfaction on what he knew to be Sammy MacEvoy's present predicament in that respect. He also had in mind other current events in London and closer to home when he added,

"I know that I can take control of situations, make things happen. I've proved it." He paused, choked a little with emotion, "Thanks to you dad," … and here Tommy glanced heavenward … "My light is switched on again."

Gordon detected something cold, a certain steel, he didn't know quite what, in Tommy's tone but let it pass and said nothing,

"The thing is though, although I'm determined, I don't know how to get on in life from where I am. I feel stuck, I just don't know what to do," said Tommy.

"Perhaps," said Gordon, after a few moments of thought, "I can help there." With that he went into the inside jacket pocket of the dark suit he was wearing and withdrew from it a bulky envelope.

"On this envelope is written an address, no name. You must take this envelope and go to the address without delay. Under no circumstance must you open the envelope."

"Yes but … " stuttered Tommy, "What am I going there for, who am I going to see, I don't understand … "

Gordon cut him off abruptly. His mood had changed, his posture assertive.

"Don't ask questions. Take the envelope. Do as I say and go!"

With that he thrust the envelope into Tommy's hand. He placed his own hand firmly on Tommy's shoulder, held it there briefly, gave a reassuring squeeze, then turned and left.

Tommy stood there shocked, totally bewildered. He was unable to speak, to think. Eventually he looked at the envelope. On it was written an address ... in France!

Tommy had not the slightest idea where the place named on the envelope was located. He had neither the knowledge nor the means to get himself there. In spite of that, something stirred inside him; a curiosity, a crazy impulse, a desire to please his dad and make him proud of him.

"By god," he thought, "I'll do it!"

He resolved to get himself to the mysterious location – somehow.

He slept that night with Ballantyne's daughter. Very early the next morning he arose, packed a small holdall and set off for ... he knew not where? But he felt light of spirit. There was a spring in his step and hope in his heart.

Joseph T.Riach

Too Early For A Glass Of Wine?

BACK TO THE FUTURE

The same day that Josmas left Château d'Argentonesse, Erna commenced showing the young man around the great residence, the outbuildings and the entire estate. She introduced him to the workers and explained how everything functioned. She proved to be every bit as energetic, talented and industrious as her mother. She quite literally had her finger on the pulse of the whole operation. The young man not only loved her deeply but grew to respect her knowledge of, and dedication to, both himself and to all that Josmas had created. The two became inseparable.

The young man spent his days in the vineyards learning all about viticulture, terroir and the whole wine making process. He studied oenology. In due course he created and produced a fine new wine. He named it in honour of his mentor – Château d'Argentonesse Josmas. It was awarded Grand Cru status.

He also played golf regularly, developing both the patience and the character of a scratch player.

And he spent hours in his beloved library.

It truly was the treasure trove of learning and inspiration which Josmas had often referred to as his most valuable possession. The young man understood just why. He had barely to scratch the surface of the many great works of legendary authors such as Stevenson, Scott, Dumas, Doyle, Twain, Tolstoi, Hemmingway and Voltaire, to appreciate the wealth of wisdom which lay within their pages. From every sentence, every paragraph, the sagacity flowed. The young man drank from their texts with an unquenchable thirst for enlightenment. The greatest lesson he took from his studies was, just as Josmas insisted, the simplest – the more the young man read, the more he saw how little he knew.

Only when he achieved a level of understanding he felt to be worthy of it, did the young man assume the name Josmas for himself. It seemed like the right thing to do. The title sat easily with him.

~

One day, many years after the departure of Josmas, the young Josmas was working in his study on the writing of his great novel when Erna entered.

"A young man has called to see you," she announced, "He brought this."

She crossed quietly to his desk and on it placed a bulky envelope. Written on it was just the address of the château, nothing more. Josmas examined the seal. Although considerable skill had been employed to disguise the fact, the envelope had clearly been opened but then resealed.

Too Early For A Glass Of Wine?

He smiled to himself, took the envelope and made his way to the library. When he entered he found a young man perched nervously on the edge of a settee. He was browsing through a copy of Charles Dickens' *'Great Expectations'* taken from one of the shelves.

"Good morning Tommy," said the host to the visitor with no great ceremony, "I've been expecting you. Tell me, what is your great passion in life?"

Joseph T.Riach

Too Early For A Glass Of Wine?

EPILOGUE

... I finished my writing, put down my notepad and pen and turned to my darling Erna, still dosing on the lounger by the pool as she had been since finishing off the carpaccio. She wore only a brief bikini and her favourite heart-shaped amethyst, gold and diamond necklet. I pulled a rug around her. The air was still and warm, the sun had dipped behind the olive trees and it's final rays of the day glinted through the leaves. There was one last drop of rosé to drain before I retired inside for the night.

I stripped and took a cold shower, then retreated to the bedroom. I thought to read a few pages of Bradshaw, his 'Homecoming' had been my constant companion and source of comfort for a long time, but on this occasion decided against it. Soon I lay naked on the bed, part covered by just a single, linen sheet. A hint of a cool breeze wafted over my bare chest. In the semi-darkness I watched the vague outline of the roof fan rotate above me and was lulled by its slow, rhythmic beat. I didn't sleep, not yet.

Instead I whispered quietly the same words as I had done every night for many, many years past ...

"Hello Tommy, it's me. Are you there?"

There followed a pause of several seconds and then, from deep in the recesses of my mind, came the words I hoped to hear.

"Yes, I'm here. I'm always here."

"Are you well?" I asked.

"Yes I'm well. Better than that I feel safe, secure, loved; as I have done since you rediscovered me and took me back into your life."

"I know," I said, "Remember, it's the same for me too. Having found you and having you to care for has transformed my life entirely. Loving you and nurturing you has enhanced my whole being. It is impossible to imagine existence without you."

Here I paused and smiled softly to myself,

"I so, so regret the hurt and anguish you went through and which I denied for all those years. I am so sorry that I did not love myself, and therefore you, through all our dark days."

"That's okay," said Tommy, "Don't feel bad, don't blame yourself. I also hid myself and my feelings away from you. I did not want to admit that I needed your love and validation. I wanted to be tough."

"Aaahh," I drew out the word long and meaningfully, "Oh yes … tough, being tough. Boy, has acting the tough guy and denying our true emotions got a lot to answer for or hasn't it?" The question of course was rhetorical, satirical.

"But maybe you know, acting out that persona was a necessary phase to go through in order for us each to absorb our experiences, learn from them and bring us into the light of each other's love."

"Yes," replied Tommy in a knowledgeable, even profound tone, "I know now that you understand my hurt, have shared in my pain and that you will never leave me again. I love you."

"And I love you too Little Tommy. I am here to care for you now and will be forever. Good night, sleep well."

As I said the last words, I knew that Tommy was already fast asleep, as carefree and untroubled as he had ever been in his whole life. I knew him to be frolicking on a golden beach somewhere, swimming in the waves, splashing in the sunshine. I knew his dreams were of open air, mountains and places of freedom and joy. I knew that he was somewhere warm, friendly and fun – anywhere, in fact, that he wanted to be.

I turned on my side, satisfied, content, ready for sleep. The same sense of serenity engulfed me as it did every night at this time. I relished these precious moments of knowing that neither I, nor Tommy, were alone. Moments of the deepest bliss imaginable.

I smiled inwardly as my eyes slid shut. Their final sight of the day was of my lucky charm, my talisman, in its permanent place of honour beside me on my bedside table. *Smarty* watched over me.

End

Joseph T.Riach

Too Early For A Glass Of Wine?

THE LITERATURE AND THE WINES

A Tale Of Two Cities – *Charles Dickens*

Set in London and Paris, Dickens' historical classic unfolds against the conditions that led up to the French Revolution and the so-called 'reign of terror'. Among the many famous quotes that people remember are the opening – "It was the best of times, it was the worst of times … " and the closing – "It is a far, far better thing I do than I have ever done … "

Asimov's Trilogy – *Isaac Asimov*

Isaac Asimov was an American writer and professor of biochemistry at Boston University. He was known for his works of both science fiction and popular science. Set in a fictional universe, the three books – Foundation, Foundation And Empire and Second Foundation – won the one-time Hugo Award in 1966 for best all-time series. Asimov later added four more books to the series.

Great Expectations – *Charles Dickens*

Is Dickens' thirteenth novel. The story is set in Kent and in London and depicts the personal growth and development of an orphan nicknamed Pip. It is full of extreme imagery - poverty, prison ships and fights to the death. It boasts a typically colourful cast of characters such as the beautiful but cold Estella, reclusive Miss Havisham and Joe, the kindly blacksmith; all who have entered into popular culture.

Hamlet – *William Shakespeare*

The tragedy set in Denmark tells of Prince Hamlet and his revenge against his uncle Claudius for the murder of his father. It is Shakespeare's longest play and is considered among the most powerful and influential works of world literature, with a story capable of seemingly endless retelling and adaptation by others.

Holy Willie's Prayer – *Robert 'Rabbie' Burns*

Considered to be the national bard of Scotland's most crushing satirical poem and possibly the finest satire of all time, the work is a withering attack on the bigotry and hypocrisy of religion. Although written in the Scots dialect, the message of his words is clear to all. The popularity of the work ensures that there are versions available to all English speaking people; as well as there being translations of all of Burns' works available in almost every known language.

Homecoming – *John Bradshaw*

Bradshaw (June 29, 1933 – May 8, 2016) was a famous American educator, counselor, motivational speaker and author of several highly acclaimed books. *Homecoming* reached number one in the

New York Times best sellers list in 1990. The book takes you through the steps necessary in order to recognise and grow the inner you to match the person that you were born to be. During the '80s and '90s Bradshaw also hosted his own highly successful television shows based on his books.

Lady Chatterley's Lover – *D.H.Lawrence*

The infamous 1928 erotic novel tells the story of the affair between the Lady Chatterley of the title and her gamekeeper, Oliver. The class difference between the couple is a major motif of the novel; as is the psychological, as well as physical, experiences of the protagonists. The book gained notoriety for its explicit descriptions of sex and for its use of, then unprintable, four letter words. It was banned in many countries until a landmark case in 1960 Britain led to its general release and free availability.

Lochnagar (Lachin y Gair) – *Lord George Gordon Byron*

Lord Byron, the renowned writer of the romantic genre, authored his 'Lochnagar' poem in 1807. It discusses his childhood in north-east Scotland and his visits to, and love of, the mountain. It is one of his most Scottish works, both in theme and sentiment.

Moby Dick – *Herman Melville*

'Call me Ishmael' is the celebrated opening line of the novel which has been called the greatest book of the sea ever written. It tells the tale of Captain Ahab and his fanatical quest to hunt down the giant white sperm whale, Moby Dick, which bit off his leg below the knee on a previous whaling expedition.

Murder On The Links – *Agatha Christie*

Is the second Hercule Poirot murder mystery and one of Christie's earliest works. Published in 1923, it tells the story of Poirot being summoned to help a French acquaintance. On arrival at his client's home, local police greet Poirot with the news that he has been found dead that morning, stabbed in the back with a letter opener and left in a newly dug grave adjacent to a local golf course!

No Mean City – *H.Kingsley Long and Alexander McArthur*

The title of the book is taken from a biblical quotation of Paul the apostle but the story is an account of 1920s life in the run-down, inner city, slum districts of Glasgow and the tough guys and razor gangs who inhabited it. The book depicts working class life and gives real insight into both the private and public issues confronting ordinary people of that time and place.

Oliver Twist – *Charles Dickens*

This novel, also known as *The Parish Boy's Progress*, was Dickens's second to be published. It tells the story of an orphan born in a Victorian workhouse but who escapes to London and is befriended by a young member of a gang of juvenile pickpockets led by the criminal Fagin.

River God – *Wilbur Smith*

Wilbur Smith, the prolific author of best-selling novels, gives readers a rare glimpse of ancient Egypt, the Pharaohs who ruled it, their lives and conflicts. This engrossing story of power struggles and treachery also provides remarkable insight into this glorious civilisation of a bygone time. It is story telling at its brilliant best.

Soccer Coaching – *Walter Winterbottom*

Winterbottom was the manager of the English international football team from 1946 until 1962. But his real passion was for coaching and he had a vision of how it should develop. He created the first national coaching scheme and introduced residential summer coaching courses which attracted international participation and praise. He lectured all over the world and came to be regarded as one of the leading technical thinkers in football of his generation.

The Complete Works Of Winston Churchill – *Sir Winston Churchill*

As well as being a soldier, politician and painter, Winston Churchill was a prolific writer. He won the Nobel Prize in Literature in 1953 for his mastery of historical and biographical description as well as for brilliant oratory in defending exalted human values. His writings defines both the man and the times in which he lived. His most widely read work is the six volumes of The Second World War.

The Ghost Runner – *Bill Jones*

This astonishingly inspirational work tells the story of long distance runner John Tarrant who was banned for life from competing in post war athletics because he had unwittingly compromised his amateur status in a minor way as a teenager. With no friends in high places to support him, he took to gate-crashing races and became one of the greatest long distance runners the world has ever seen.

The Man Who Mistook His Wife For A Hat – *Oliver Sacks*

The world's best known neurologist recounts the stories of patients lost in a bizarre world of neurological disorder as strange as that of the most fantastic fiction. He demonstrates the awesome powers of the mind and shows just how delicately balanced one's sense of self identity can be.

The Mayor Of Casterbridge – *Thomas Hardy*

One of Hardy's Wessex novels, the book is rightly considered to be a masterpiece. It tells the story of a young hay trusser who marries but then, in a drunken stupor, sells at auction his wife along with their baby daughter. Full of remorse he gives up alcohol and many years later becomes a successful grain dealer - and the Mayor of Casterbridge.

The Thirty-Nine Steps – *John Buchan*

This classic spy thriller is Buchan's most famous work. It is set just prior to the first world war and features his Richard Hannay character for the first time. Buchan's writing style – crisp, clear and racey – has set the tone for just about every spy thriller since. The story has appeared in film several times.

The True Story Of The First Ascent Of Everest – *Sir Edmund Hilary*

With nimble words and a straightforward style, New Zealand mountaineering legend Hillary recollects the bravery and frustration, the agony and glory that marked his Everest odyssey. From the 1951 expedition that led to the discovery of the southern route, through the grueling Himalayan training of 1952, and on to the successful 1953 expedition. Educational and inspiring, this is a story of planning, preparation and achieving the supposedly impossible.

Tough Jews – *Rich Cohen*

Rich Cohen tells the story of people he knew as a kid from his father's generation and draws you right into the world of young thugs, shooting wars, perceived betrayals and labour rackets. This is both an exciting portrayal of real people and events as well as an extraordinarily well researched and accurate account of organised crime in the New York of the early twentieth century.

Tricks Of The Mind – *Derren Brown*

Alternately controversial, challenging and humourous, this journey into the structure and psychology of magic makes for irresistable reading. The author reveals a surprising amount about his art and the book is delightfully fascinating to anyone with even a passing interest in the things that people think and why they think them.

Twenty Thousand Leagues Under The Sea – *Jules Verne*

Verne's classic science fiction novel was highly acclaimed when it was released in 1871, and remains so to this day. It is regarded as one of the premiere adventure novels of all time and one of his greatest works. The description of Nemo's ship, the *Nautilus*, was considered ahead of its time, as it accurately describes features on modern submarines which, at the time, were very primitive vessels.

Who Dunnit – *Joseph T.Riach*

Although the author has, over the years, written many short humourous, topical, satirical, political and nonsense pieces, he has yet, at the time of writing, to put them together in a published work. *Who Dunnit*, written in 2006, did however appear in his *Self-Improvement Should Be Fun!* book as part of a fifteen strong collection of such work. It is a tribute to both Agatha Christie of crime fiction fame and to the legendary Scottish comedian, Chic Murray.

~

Aligote – Is a dry white Burgundy wine best drunk young and fresh. Less well known than other more popular wines grown on the same slopes it is an every day drinking wine and perfect for those looking to try something different and unique. If you're a wine geek it's definitely one to try.

Armagnac – Armagnac was one of the first areas in France to start distilling spirits. It is for the most part made and sold by small producers, hence its lesser popularity than the more widely known Cognac. It is distilled from wine made from a blend of grapes using column stills and is aged in oak barrels before release.

Bandol Rosé – Is a fresh, lively Provence wine, usually with gentle lemony aromas and a refreshing palate with flavours of peaches and pears. The Bandol wine region is located around the fishing village of Bandol near the coast, east of Marseille and Cassis. The Bandol appellation has a silicon and limestone soil ideally suited to the late ripening Mourvèdre grape which has to account for at least 50% of the blend.

Barsac – The town of Barsac, south of Bordeaux in south western France, gives its name to the renowned sweet white wines of the region. The wines tend towards honey, orange blossom and fresh, lively acidity, some of them being amongst the most expensive of wines and highly sought after. They pair brilliantly with tarte tartin or with blue and goats' cheeses.

Beaujolais – Takes its name from the wine producing regions in the Rhône and Rhône-Alpes north of Lyon. It is made from Gamay grapes with thin skins and low in tannins which accounts for the wine being light-bodied and easy drinking.

Chablis – The Chablis area is the northernmost district of the Burgundy wine producing region. The appellation d'origine contrôlée demands that only Chardonnay grapes are used in its production. It is a wine of greater acidity and with more fruity flavours than Chardonnay wines grown in warmer climates. The wines often have a flinty note described locally as goût de pierre à fusil (taste of flint).

Cheval Blanc – Is French for White Horse. It is produced in the Saint Émilion region of Bordeaux. As of 2012 the wine is only one of four Saint Émilions to receive the highest rank of premier grand cru classé (A) status. Saint Émilion wines generally are highly regarded, good quality and make for exhilarating drinking. The estate's second wine (sous-marque) is named Le Petit Cheval.

Haut-Brion, Lafite, Latour, Mouton – Are four of the five Bordeaux 'first growth' wines (the other is Margaux). The five were the first wines to be classified under Appellation d'Origine Contrôlée and as such all are top quality, highly sought after wines. The Haut-Brion estates lie just to the south of Bordeaux; the other three, and Margaux, are in the Medoc region to the north of the city.

Margaux – Is located on the north bank of the Garrone estuary in the Medoc region of France. The wine is one of the first five 'first growth' wines of Bordeaux, having been classified in 1855 along with Haut-Brion, Lafite, Latour and Mouton. It is therefore a very prestigious wine, much sought after and expensive. A bottle of Château Margaux 1787 holds the record as the most expensive bottle of wine ever broken; it was insured for two hundred and twenty-five thousand dollars. Margaux, and its less costly sous-marque Pavillon, is also rather nice to drink!

Pauillac – The wines of Pauillac are the archetype of Bordeaux and the blackcurrant taste of the cabernet sauvignon grape. Pauillacs are full bodied, concentrated and, at their peak, which may come twenty years or more after the vintage, they are rich, smooth and sophisticated. The top wines come from the individual château but generic Pauillac from a négociant offer tremendous value for money.

Paul Masson – These Californian wines are well known, in part because they have been sold in carafes rather than bottles. But the wines themselves are of good quality and make for pleasant drinking. Masson himself was an immigrant from the Burgundy region of France. He brought with him his experience and know-how and became an early pioneer of Californian viticulture in the late nineteenth century.

Pécharmant – Pécharmant wines are a super 'secret' of a wine produced to the north east of Bergerac in south-west France. They are typically tannic and full-bodied, ruby colored with fruity aromas often described as spicey. The name comes from pech (meaning hill) and charmant (meaning charming), thus means charming hill – an apt name for this beautiful region in the Perigord Noir.

Piesporter – Is made in and around the village of Piesport on the north bank of the Mosel wine region in Germany. The area has a long history of producing outstanding wine which is a white, light body wine that ranges from dry to off-dry. It can be made from Riesling, Muller Thurgau or Eibling grapes.

Petrus – The Château Pétrus is a small wine estate in the Pomerol appellation near to Saint-Emilion, Bordeaux. It produces a red wine entirely from Merlot grapes. Pomerol wines have never been classified but Petrus is widely regarded as the outstanding wine of the appellation and consistently ranks among the world's most expensive wines. The wine is a full bodied red but slightly lighter than the Medocs. Tasting of dark fruits, blackberries and plums, it is long and pleasant on the palate.

Valpolicella – Winemaking has existed in the Valpolicella region of the province of Verona, just east of Lake Garda, since Greek times and the economy of the region is heavily dependent on it. Among Italian wines, only in Chianti is more wine produced. Classic Valpolicella is a light, fragrant red wine made from three grape varieties and often drunk young in the style of the French Beaujolais.

Veuve Clicquot – La Grande Dame' is the crown jewel of the house of Veuve Clicquot champagnes; the ultimate fine champagne to drink on special occasions. But that is not to under-rate their other main offering - 'Yellow Label'. It is one of the most instantly recognisable labels in the world, thanks largely to its accessible pricing for a champagne of such rare and consistent quality.

Vinho Verde – From the Portuguese wine region of Minho in the north of the country. The name literally translates as 'green wine'. The term refers to the fact that it is a young wine which is released for consumption only three to six months after harvesting, rather than referring to its colour. The wine is drunk young and is slightly sparkling, giving it a distinctive and refreshing character.

Yquem – Château d'Yquem wines from the Sauternes region of Bordeaux are rare and very expensive. They are characterised by their complexity/sweetness balance and relatively high acidity. With proper care, a bottle will keep for a century or more! The fruity overtones will gradually fade and integrate with more complex secondary and tertiary flavours. Yquem commands higher prices over all other sweet white wines of its type.

~

Author's Amazon Pages – *Joseph T.Riach,*
https://www.amazon.com/-/e/B01MTQYSH3
https://www.amazon.co.uk/-/e/B01MTQYSH3

Author's Leisure And Learning Breaks In Portugal –
https://www.ibotoolbox.com/wakeup2wealth/pressrelease.aspx?prid=197923#

Author's Press Releases – *Joseph T.Riach,*
https://www.ibotoolbox.com/wakeup2wealth/pressrelease.aspx

Author's Web Site – *http://www.tomriach.com*

Joseph T.Riach

COPYRIGHT AND DISCLAIMER

Too Early For A Glass Of Wine?

Four Men - One Common Destiny. What Is The Secret That Binds Them?.

ISBN : 978-1698966922

© Joseph T.Riach 2019 all rights reserved

All proprietory rights and interest in this publication shall be vested in Joseph T.Riach and all other rights including, but without limitation, patent, registered design, copyright, trademark and service mark, connected with this publication shall also be vested in Joseph T.Riach.

No part of this publication may be reproduced, stored in a retrieval system, or transmitted in any form or by any means, electronic, mechanical, photocopying, recording or otherwise, without the prior written permission of the copyright owner, Joseph T.Riach.

The right of Joseph T.Riach to be identified as the author of this work has been asserted in accordance with the Copyright, Designs and Patents Act 1988.

Designations used by companies to distinguish their products are often claimed as trademarks. All brand names and product names used in this book are trade names, service marks, trademarks or registered trademarks of their respective owners. The publisher is not associated with any product or vendor mentioned in this book.

Limit of liability/disclaimer of warranty. While the publisher and author have used their best efforts in preparing this book, they make no representations or warranties with respect to the accuracy or completeness of the contents of this book and specifically disclaim any implied warranties of merchantability or fitness for a particular purpose. It is sold on the understanding that the publisher is not engaged in rendering professional services and neither the publisher nor the author shall be liable for damages arising herefrom. If professional advice or other expert assistance is required, the services of a competent professional should be sought. This manuscript relates only the personal experience of the author.

Too Early For A Glass Of Wine?

Too Early For A Glass Of Wine? is available direct from the Amazon book store (amazon.com or amazon.co.uk) in Paperback and Ebook formats, Barnes and Noble and other leading book suppliers.

"I hope you enjoyed the read!

Receive notifications of my new books and novels as they become available, free and reduced price book offers and entry to periodic promotions for signed or personalised copies of my books, by visiting me at tomriach.com, clicking 'Contact' and leaving a message.

Also, to help ensure that I can continue to create quality publications at affordable prices, I would really appreciate a review on Amazon. The number of reviews a book receives on a daily basis has a direct impact on how it sells, so just leaving a review, no matter how short, helps make it possible for me to continue writing books for you to enjoy. To see a selection of the many reviews sent directly to me, but not featured on Amazon, visit my website at tomriach.com and click 'Reviews'.

Thanking you for reading my work and for your ongoing support,"

Joseph Tom Riach

Printed in Great Britain
by Amazon